The Peace Between the Souls

by Nann Dunne

A Golden Keys Publishing Book

The Peace Between The Souls

Editor: Nann Dunne

Cover design: Nann Dunne

This book is published by Golden Keys Publishing, USA

www.goldenkeyspublishing.com

ISBN-10:   1-63304-106-9

ISBN-13:   978-1-63304-106-6

Imprint: Golden Keys Publishing

Printed in the United States of America.

Visit Nann's Website

http://www.GoldenKeysPublishing.com

Reviews for Nann's Books

Nann Dunne's series, Hearts-Minds-Souls, is exceptional. A unique glimpse into a tumultuous period in US history—the Civil War era—the story of Sarah-Bren and Faith allows us to see the harsh realities of the time. Their love is always strong and never wavers no matter what the world, fate, or history can throw at them. Readers will laugh, cry and love along with them as Dunne weaves the tale of their lives and touches our hearts.

~ Patty Schramm, author of Lesbian Romances with a difference;

Publisher of Flashpoint Publications

* * *

The War Between the Hearts [Book One in the Hearts, Minds, Souls Series]

This is the first book that I have read from Nann Dunne and I was not disappointed! I loved this book...and it really makes you think about how strong and courageous women are. The story is so believable and the characters are realistic. Sarah and Faith are amazing women. I was very touched by Ben, Faith's son and Lindsay, Sarah's sister-in-law. Lindsay is the support all of us want in our lives and Ben is the hope we want for our future. This book is so well written and it does a good job taking the reader back to the 1800's. I hope that there will be a sequel to this great book! This a timeless classic and a very easy read! I look forward to reading more from Nann Dunne.

~ C. Mahoney [from review on Amazon]

* * *

The Clash Between the Minds [Book Two in the Hearts, Minds, Souls Series]

After reading book one of the series by Nann Dunne, I went right into the second book, *The Clash Between The Minds* (Book Two in the Hearts, Minds, Soul Series) happy to say I was lost for about three hours, I had to Try and put it down to get things done. I LOVED the history in the first and second books. I wish more love stories were included along with history. Women played such important roles in the history of our country! I fell in love with Faith and Sara, Leah, Benjamin and other wonderful characters in this series, I cannot wait for book three! PLEASE HURRY WITH IT!

~ Frances Perez [from review on Amazon]

* * *

The Peace Between the Souls [Book Three in the Hearts, Minds, Souls Series]

The Peace Between the Souls is a well-crafted book, with exceptional dialogue and authentic setting by prolific author Nann Dunne. Sarah-Bren and Faith are confronted with challenges that test their strength, question their decisions, and cause them pause in their lives.

This is definitely a must-read book. Congratulations to Nann for sharing this wonderful story with us, her readers.

~ Phyllis Manfredi

Dedication

I dedicate this story to my family and friends who have been so supportive of my writing through the years. Your encouragement has kept me going on this solitary path.

Acknowledgments

I owe what I am as a writer to many, many friends and family members who have contributed to my education, some in small ways and some in big ways, but they all have had an impact. Of special note are my parents, my stepmother, and my children.

Friends who deserve to be mentioned are Lori L. Lake; Patty Schramm; Karen D. Badger and her wife, Barb (Bliss) Sawyer; Chris Paynter and her wife, Phyllis Manfredi; Lynne Pierce; and let me not forget Karen Surtees, who, years ago, pestered me into writing for publication and started me down this road.

I'm truly grateful to all of you and many others, too numerous to list. Thank you.

Nann Dunne's Other Books

The War Between the Hearts, Book One in the Hearts, Minds, Souls Series

The Clash Between the Minds, Book Two in the Hearts, Minds, Souls Series

Staying in the Game, a thrilling mystery with a softball background

Door Shaker and Other Short Stories, a compilation of Nann Dunne's short stories

Dunne With Editing, tips on self-editing for writers

True Colours, with co-author Karen Surtees

Many Roads to Travel, sequel to True Colours, with co-author Karen Surtees

Chapter 1

1881 Missouri

Faith's heart plummeted when the day's mail held a heavily embossed letter addressed to Sarah-Bren Coulter, the woman Faith loved and lived with. The letter came from Sarah's mother, and any missive from Cynthia Coulter caused an upheaval in Faith's and Sarah's lives. What would this one bring?

Faith thumbed through the rest of the mail—the *Bonneforte Tribune* weekly newspaper, a 100-page Montgomery Ward "Wish-Book" catalogue, and an advertising sheet from the local dry goods shop.

The *Tribune* diligently reported tidbits of local, national, and international news, and Faith and Sarah enjoyed reading it.

Faith tucked the offerings in her teaching workbag and left the Bonneforte, Missouri, Post Office. The late-afternoon April sun shone full on her face as she lifted a hand to shield her eyes. She nodded to a few of the townspeople whom she recognized and crossed the board-walk to her buggy. She pushed the bag under the buggy seat, unhooked Drummer's reins from the hitching rail, and climbed in.

The sun dropped lower in the sky during her short ride along a dirt road to the Coulter house. At home, she looped Drummer's reins over a post and pulled her school workbag from its spot under the seat. Lifting her long skirt at the knee, she ascended the back steps.

In the kitchen, Sarah met her with a quick kiss. "Hello, sweetheart. Fresh cookies on the table." She brushed past Faith and went out the door to take care of putting Drummer and the buggy into the barn.

Faith dumped her bag in the corner closet and put the mail on the table that was already set for dinner. Her stomach rumbled when a beef roast's enticing aroma emanated from the iron stove, underscored by a sugar cookie scent that wafted through the air.

She was tempted to plop down in one of the chairs; their kitchen exuded warmth and welcome. Pictures of the house and the schoolhouse, painted by Sarah, hung on the yellow walls and added to that feeling. But she would change out of her schoolmarm clothes first. Then she could thoroughly enjoy being home.

She snatched two sugar cookies on her way upstairs. Her teeth sank into the first bite, and she quickly caught a sprinkle of sugar on her fingers. As she entered the bedroom, she finished eating the first cookie and licked her fingers clean with a satisfied "ummm."

When Faith went back downstairs, Sarah was at the sink washing her hands. Faith noticed Sarah was dressed differently from this morning. Earlier, she had on brown pants and an orange shirt. Now she wore black pants and a yellow shirt. The bright color emphasized Sarah's long, chestnut-brown hair that hung down her back to her waist.

Before Faith could remark on the different clothing, Sarah spoke. "How was your day?" She dried her hands and picked up the mail from the table.

Faith blew out a long breath. "Busy." She undid the ribbon that held her red curls in check and tucked the shiny green silk into her apron pocket. Leaning back against the counter, she said, "I'm not sure making Friday a test day was such a good idea."

Sarah raised an eyebrow. "It gives you the weekend to correct all the papers. Wasn't that the purpose?"

"But I'm finding it makes Friday classes too intense, and it takes too much time out of the weekend. I'll be the first to admit my ideas aren't always perfect. But don't quote me in front of any of my students."

Sarah's wicked smile faded when Faith said, "You changed your clothes?"

"Not voluntarily. I finished writing a piece for the book and thought I'd get an early start on mucking out Redfire's stall. But my bad leg's been bothering me, and I slipped."

During the war, a Minie ball had broken the tibia in Sarah's leg. Rebroken before it healed, it subsequently fused badly and often troubled her.

"My leg twisted, and instead of mucking out the stall, I mucked into it." Sarah gave a wry grin. "It wasn't a pretty sight. Or a pretty smell."

"That must have hurt. How is your leg?"

"Eh." Sarah shrugged. "Could be worse." She set the mail on an empty chair. "Let's eat before we read the mail. I'm starving."

"Fine with me. Something smells delicious." Faith glanced at the counter behind her and saw a loaf of bread sitting on a plate. She sliced several pieces, set the plate on the table, and zigged around Sarah to get the butter from the icebox. Faith grinned when Sarah gently bumped a hip against hers as they passed each other.

Sarah lifted the roasting pan from the oven and dished up beef, potatoes, carrots, onions, and gravy into suitable dishes. She and Faith set the bowls on the table, sat down, and ate.

"This tastes so good, I can't help wanting more of it." Faith placed a second helping of everything on her plate.

Sarah paused in her attack on her food. "Glad you're enjoying it. Be careful, though. If you eat too much, I might not be able to pick you up."

Faith wrinkled her nose at her. "You can't pick me up, now." When Sarah pushed back her chair, Faith held up her hands. "No, no, that wasn't a challenge. I'm teasing you."

"All right, redhead, I'll let you go this time." Sarah scooted her chair back to the table and resumed eating.

After dinner had been finished and the table cleared, Sarah and Faith remained seated, drinking coffee.

Sarah retrieved the mail and slid the embossed letter from behind the weekly *Tribune*. "This letter's from Mother." She opened it and ran her gaze across it. "No special news, but she wants me to come visit next month."

"I don't suppose I'm included in that invitation." Faith sounded snippy, even to herself.

"Come here."

"What?"

Sarah pushed her chair away from the table and patted the thighs of her trouser-covered legs. "Come here."

Faith rose, ran the fingers of both hands through her curly hair to loosen it, and settled on Sarah's lap. She wound her arms around Sarah's neck, and Sarah eased her closer. "I'm sorry Mother neglects you."

They sat in an uncomfortable silence until Sarah said in a firm tone, "When I go to visit this time, I'm going to tell Mother and Father the truth about us."

Faith jerked away and gaped at Sarah. "Bren! Are you sure that's wise?"

"You called me Bren," Sarah said softly. "You rarely do that." She touched her knuckles to Faith's cheek. "That shows how much it upsets you that my parents think you and Benjamin are my boarders."

Faith forced her temper to ease. "Yes, it does upset me. But we've kept the secret this long, so why bring it up now?"

"When I pretend our relationship is that of owner and

boarder, I feel diminished. Our relationship feels diminished. I want to tell the truth about us. It's time."

"I'm not sure your mother can handle that revelation."

"What do you think she would do? Surely she wouldn't throw me out. She's my mother."

An odd expression flitted across Faith's face.

Sarah said, "What? What are you thinking?" She gazed into veiled green eyes, waiting for an answer that didn't come. Suddenly, she suspected what caused the strange look. She stood up so fast, Faith would have fallen to the floor if Sarah's arm hadn't tightened around her.

As soon as Faith gained her balance, Sarah moved her hands to Faith's shoulders and gave her a shake. "You're thinking about Jessie, aren't you?" she said in an accusing tone. "About my being her mother but giving her away."

Faith placed her hands on Sarah's chest. "I'm not being judgmental. We can talk about this later."

"You're thinking about it now, so we'll talk about it now."

"I can't help it. She popped into my head. You have to admit, it's a natural progression of thought." She lowered her arms, and Sarah released her.

"No, it's not." Sarah gritted her teeth. "That was an entirely different situation, and you know it. When I gave Jessie up, she was a baby. I hadn't spent years raising her. She was forced on me when I didn't have the slightest idea of what to do with a child. I didn't even want her. Besides, she's had a better life with Scott and Lindsay than I could have provided." Her voice pitched lower. "At that time, I was a single-minded, vengeance-driven woman who didn't have room in her life for a child. Jessie deserved more, and she got it."

"Be honest. You could have raised her, but you chose not to."

Sarah grabbed Faith's shoulder and shook her again. "You are so damned hardheaded when you want to be."

Faith rammed her hands into Sarah's chest and forced her away. "Stop shaking me! Leave me alone."

"I'll do that." Whirling away, Sarah stalked into the hall and up the steps to their bedroom. Staggering slightly, she tried to ignore the pain in her leg. She took a pistol and a holster from the bottom drawer of one of the bureaus.

Hurriedly belting on the holster, she tied it to her thigh and stuck the pistol in it. She put a box of shells in her pants pocket, which also held beef jerky—a habit left over from the war. You carried your food with you whenever you could. She'd put a fresh stash in after falling in the barn. The pocket also held a handkerchief folded over a hank of red hair.

Her peripheral vision caught movement in the mirror, and she turned to examine herself. Her flushed face made the scars that crinkled the skin around her left eye and across her left forehead stand out like white, tangled stripes. Thus reminded of her war injuries, she passed her fingers through the white blaze of hair that appeared to spring from the scars. With a growl and a quick spin away, she squelched the memories that only intensified her current anger.

She grabbed her hat, a light jacket, and a bedroll. She took the Spencer rifle from the corner of the closet, closed the closet door, and left the bedroom.

She wanted to stomp down the stairs but was wise enough not to put any more strain on her weakened leg. Faith stood in the kitchen, rubbing her shoulders.

Sarah strode past her, stuck on her hat, and slammed out the door. Paddy, a short-haired cross between an Irish retriever and a beagle, came running to her. "No, Paddy," she said without slowing down. "Stay." The red-coated dog immediately sat in place, his tail thumping against the ground. Sarah glanced back at him and felt bad for having spoken to him so meanly. She waved her hand at him. "Go," she said in a milder tone. "Go play." Paddy jumped up, hesitated for a second, and ran off toward the house.

When Sarah got to the barn, she went straight to Redfire. She set the bedroll and rifle on the floor, petted the horse for a few moments, and saddled him. Still seething, she hooked the bedroll behind the saddle. She attached a scabbard on the left side of the saddle rigging and slid the rifle into it.

She tossed her jacket and a box of rifle bullets into a saddlebag that she kept filled with extra clothes, blankets, and beef jerky, and hooked that to the saddle, too. From the box in her pocket, she thrust extra pistol shells into the loops on the belt that held her holster.

She led Redfire out of the barn, mounted, and spurred him toward the mountains.

* * *

Faith went to the window and watched until Sarah left the barn. She noticed the bedroll behind Redfire's saddle. Dejected, she let out a puff of air. "I'm sorry, Sarah. Me and my darned temper." She finished cleaning up the kitchen. Why couldn't she have kept her mouth shut? As she stood at the sink washing the dishes, she gazed out the window at the mountain range in the distance.

Sarah had developed the habit of occasionally spending a night or two alone in the forest. She claimed that being among the trees soothed and refreshed her. Faith had accompanied her a few times and enjoyed the respite from her routine. But she wasn't as enamored of the forest as Sarah was, nor was she attuned to roughing it, so Sarah often went alone.

But she had never taken off in anger like this time. Faith couldn't even guess how long she might stay away. If Sarah had her drawing and writing paraphernalia with her, she could stay away indefinitely. That thought placed an ache around Faith's heart like a fist compressing it. Her guilt at being the reason for Sarah's departure made the ache stronger. Please don't stay away long, she thought.

She heard hoofbeats near the front of the house and hurried down the hall to open the door. Sheriff Schmidt rode up the lane at a fast pace on Red Star, an offspring of Redfire. Schmidt matched Sarah's five-foot-nine-inch height but was a heavyset, bulky man, twice as wide as Sarah was, and then some. Over the years, he became a close friend.

He dismounted near the porch that ran across the entire front of the house and tied his horse to the hitching rail. Touching his hat, he said, "Good afternoon, Faith." In a friendly decision made some time ago, Schmidt called the women Miss Faith and Miss Sarah in public, but at their insistence, he called them Faith and Sarah in private. In turn, they called him Sheriff around town and Herman when they were alone.

"Hello, Herman. Come in and have some tea."

Paddy came running from the side of the porch, and Herman petted him and scratched his ears. Apparently satisfied with the attention, Paddy returned to his hunkering spot.

"I will, thank you." Herman's eyes searched the surroundings as they crossed the porch. "Is Sarah here?" He followed Faith through the hall into the kitchen and sat at the table.

"No, she's out on an overnight trip."

"Is your son home, by any chance?"

"No, Benjamin won't get a vacation from medical school for a while yet."

"So you're alone."

Herman's tone of voice piqued Faith's curiosity. "I am. What brings you here? Can I help?" She poured tea from the pot that always sat on the range, set out plates and forks and some sliced carrot cake she had made Wednesday evening in a burst of baking energy, and joined Herman at the table.

"The cake smells delicious." He speared a piece and set it on his plate. "I got word Doc Litchfield's been released from prison. Happened yesterday." He forked a bit of cake into his mouth.

Faith's hand flew to her face. "Oh, no." She reached blindly for her teacup and almost knocked it over. As it teetered on the edge of the saucer, Herman stopped it with the side of his hand and righted it.

"Sorry for the blunt notice. I came as soon as I got the news." He demolished the rest of his piece of cake and washed it down with the tea. In his meaty hand, the cup seemed like part of a child's play set.

Faith sat for a moment in silence, considering the implications of Joel Litchfield's release. Ten years ago, Dr. Joel Litchfield had tried hard to convince Faith to leave Sarah and be his wife. He insisted that the women's way of life endangered not only Faith but also her son, Benjamin. Tall, handsome, and full of self-confidence, Litchfield had been thunderstruck at her refusal and blamed it, rightly of course, on Sarah. When Faith's love for Sarah cemented itself into place, she'd rejected his reasoning and his advances, but not before Sarah had gone through hell worrying about what decision Faith would make.

For all his posturing, Litchfield had been exposed by Sarah and her friend Leah Showell as a thief and train robber, and they had been instrumental in sending him to prison. Now he was free.

Faith cringed. "Can you tell me anything more about Joel?"

Herman leaned back and stuck his thumbs behind his belt. "Not much, I'm afraid. I want you two to watch out for him. The good doctor struck me as the vengeful type." He lifted out a pocket watch and read it. "Sorry. I have to be getting back. Friday nights can be plenty active around the taverns." They stood and strolled onto the porch.

Paddy raised his head from his resting place on the porch and wagged his tail.

"Thank you for bringing me the news." Faith gazed toward the mountains. "I sure wish Sarah were here." She folded her arms around her body and shivered.

"Thank you for the refreshments." Herman gestured with his hat as he put it back on. "I wish Sarah was here, too. I'd feel a lot better than leaving you out here by yourself. Maybe you can visit with some friends while she's gone."

Faith sauntered down the steps with him. "No, I'll be all right. She might even come back tonight, and she'd be the one here alone."

"But she can shoot better than most of us," Herman said with a laugh.

"Indeed she can. In case of trouble, she keeps a loaded rifle hanging over the fireplace and she taught me how to use it." Faith grimaced. "Though I hope I never have to."

"Me, too. I remember that rifle. Sarah scared the bejeezus out of the idiots who tried to burn a cross in your yard. Her shot nailed it right at the crossbar." He mounted Red Star. "I'll keep an eye and ear out in town, see if I can learn anything. You be careful, you hear?"

Faith gave the horse a pat on his neck and got a tickling nibble on her shoulder in return. "I'll do that. And thanks again."

Herman touched his hat and left.

Faith folded her arms around her body once again and climbed the porch steps. She surveyed the area, and her safe, serene home seemed dark and full of menacing shadows. Stop that, she told herself. But she called Paddy into the house earlier than usual. When she closed the front door, she locked it and hurried through the house to secure the kitchen door, something they hadn't done in years. The house had two other outer doors, seldom used and always kept locked.

Paddy followed her around and finally lay down on his bed in the kitchen. Faith went to him and rubbed his shoulder. "You be my protector tonight, okay?"

He barked once, as if answering her.

"Good boy."

She sat at the table, and thoughts from the past tumbled through her mind again. Was Herman right? Would Joel want revenge? He had vowed to get vengeance back then. Would he feel the same after all these years?

* * *

Sarah slowed Redfire once they entered the forest. She welcomed the separate world the forest afforded with its   sun-dappled earth, shadowed bushes, and ground cover. This evening, at dusk, it was cool and damp, thanks to a downpour earlier in the week.

She let the horse meander for close to five hours and

absorbed the peace and tranquility she often found among the trees. As a child, she had ridden all over the Virginia mountains—parts of which became West Virginia during the war—and she had fallen in love with them. Most forests had the same effect on her.

She asked herself why she felt so strongly about the forest, why she considered it a living friend. Part of the answer might have been that she looked upon the trees as silent sentinels whose branches spread protectively over her or brushed gently against her cheeks. To Sarah, the trees were anything but silent when they were in full leaf and their limbs dashed to and fro as they withstood strong winds or lashing rains. They whispered in light breezes, too, their susurration as calming as the steady swoosh of ocean waves against a beach.

Years of fallen leaves served as padding and gave Redfire's hooves a different, but recognizable, sound as they disturbed the surface of the matted vegetation and set free the pungent aroma imprisoned in the rich, black soil beneath. Inhaling, Sarah could almost taste the earth in the back of her throat.

She heard birdsong, faint skitterings, and the flapping of wings as she rode along. Although most forest dwellers hid from humans, the area was alive with living beings from the tiniest insect to snakes and lizards, squirrels and rabbits, wolves, bobcats, deer, black bears... And think of all the birds! Their number and variety were immeasurable.

She even gave due credit to the piled up brush she came upon, and the sometimes-thorny bushes or new growth that forced her to go around them. Such impediments taught her patience.

Patience. She hadn't shown much of that with Faith. Grimacing, she reined in Redfire next to Respite Lake, the body of water on their holdings that Faith had named. She dismounted, stretched, and swung the saddlebag off Redfire's back. She yanked out her jacket and donned it. Rifling through the saddlebag, her hand closed on the sack of beef jerky. She extricated several pieces and reclosed the sack. She added a few chunks to those already in her pants pocket and put one in her mouth. Gnawing on the jerky, she stood there next to Redfire and thought about Faith.

Faith wasn't as strong a lover of the outdoors as Sarah, but she admitted to enjoying occasional overnight trips to the lake during the school year as a breather from her responsibilities. The thought increased Sarah's guilt.

Faith said she'd had a busy day, and she rarely said anything negative about her time spent at school. So, today's activities must have been wearing on her. And instead of giving her the understanding and solace she meant to give, Sarah had made the situation worse by losing her temper about Jessie. That Faith was right about Jessie made Sarah feel worse.

She bowed her head. After a moment, she lifted her chin, straightened up, and climbed back into the saddle. Faith deserved an apology, and Sarah would give her one. Feeling infinitely better for having made this decision, she turned Redfire toward home.

* * *

Faith woke with a start. Her heart thudded as she heard a surreptitious stirring at the front door. Oh my God, she thought, Joel's here already! She threw the covers back and leaped from the bed. In her nightgown, she rushed down the steps into the sitting room and lifted the Spencer repeating rifle from above the fireplace. Paddy came from his bed in the kitchen and joined her in the living room. He lifted his head but didn't bark or make a sound. The oddity of that didn't register with her. The front doorknob rattled a bit. Thank goodness she had locked it. Someone was trying to sneak into the house.

Nearly scared out of her wits, Faith trembled as she levered the trigger guard to load a cartridge the way Bren...Sarah...had shown her.

Everything happened at once. The door flew open, Faith cocked the hammer, and the intruder stepped into the house. Faith found the trigger and fired. The person's body hit the floor with a crash, and the table next to it fell, also.

Faith stood for a moment, breathing heavily. The figure didn't move even when Paddy pawed at it and pushed his head into it, whining. Faith levered another cartridge into the chamber. She set the rifle against the wall and lit the oil lamp near the entrance. She picked the rifle back up, and her hands shook as she approached the form and nudged it with her foot. No reaction. She grabbed one shoulder and turned the person over.

She dropped the rifle and fell to her knees. "Sarah-Bren! Oh my God, Sarah!" She had blood on her mouth and throat and on her forehead. Paddy licked the side of her face.

"Stay back, Paddy." Faith eased the dog away and searched frantically for other wounds. Her hands slowed when she heard Sarah groan and say, "Why the hell did you shoot at me?"

"Stay still. Let me check you for wounds."

Sarah paid no attention. She sat up and hauled at Faith's shoulder until Faith helped her stagger to her feet and led her to a seat on the sofa. Fear made Faith's voice into a shriek. "Did I shoot you in the head? Do you have any other wounds?"

Sarah put her elbows on her knees. "No, you didn't shoot me." She leaned her head into her hands. "I heard the snick of the hammer cocking, and I dove out of the way."

Tears welled in Faith's eyes. "But you have blood all over your face."

"I fell into the marble table, and then I hit the floor." Sarah fingered her nose. "I think I broke my damn nose." Her hand moved to her forehead. "And I'll probably have a goose egg under this gash tomorrow."

"I'm so sorry. Thank God I didn't hit you. Let me get you cleaned up."

Faith hurried into the kitchen. She came back with a basin of water and two towels and wiped the blood from Sarah's face with hands that still shook. She put medicine and a bandage on the head wound. She made sure Sarah's nose was straight and the bleeding had stopped. "I think your nose will be all right, but it's already swelling and sure to be pretty sore. I'll put some ice together for you."

When she returned everything to the kitchen, Faith brought back chopped ice wrapped in a dish towel and sat next to Sarah. Sarah held the ice to her head and nose and closed her free hand over Faith's. "Would you tell me now why you shot at me? And why the door was locked?"

"Herman Schmidt was here today. Or yesterday, I guess. Soon after you left. He told me Joel Litchfield was released from prison on Thursday and to keep an eye out for him."

Sarah hissed as she sucked in a breath past her teeth. Her words hurtled out of her. "That son of a bitch! That charlatan should have stayed in jail forever. I doubt he'll ever change."

Faith wiped at the tears falling from her eyes, and Sarah helped brush them away. "As soon as Herman left," Faith said, "I locked all the doors and windows. I had trouble sleeping. I tossed and turned and finally drifted off. Then a noise at the door woke me. I jumped up, believing it was Joel. I was sure he was out to hurt me. So I came down and got the rifle. I should have known it wasn't him when Paddy didn't bark, but I was too frightened to make that connection." She spread her hands out in supplication. "Please forgive me."

Sarah set down the cold towel, reached for Faith, and drew her close. "Forgive you? I need to have you forgive me. You told the truth about Jessie. I was the one who lost my temper and left." She kissed the top of Faith's head then drew back to speak. "When

I calmed down and was thinking straight, I realized I was wrong—and rude—to walk out on you. So I came home to apologize." She gave Faith a grin. "Although I didn't expect to get shot at for my transgressions."

Faith grabbed a hank of Sarah's chestnut-brown hair and tugged it. "How can you laugh about it? I could have killed you. Joel Litchfield would have loved that."

"No doubt." Sarah's expression turned serious. "But we will have to stay alert. I'm hoping he has the good sense to let us be, but I don't have much confidence he'll make that choice. I think he'll want revenge."

But the next few weeks were quiet, and Sarah and Faith decided they couldn't stay on watch forever. The one concession they did make was to ask Leah Showell and her husband, Phillip, if Faith could stay with them when Sarah went to visit her parents.

Chapter 2

Joel Litchfield emerged from prison penniless, bitter, and with a monstrous headache. Burt Dembroke, one of his former prison mates, met him at the gate with an extra horse. "Hi, Doc," he said. "Ready to celebrate?"

Litchfield mounted the horse and sat for a moment. He frowned at Dembroke. "I won't celebrate until I get even with that bitch."

Dembroke gave a short laugh. "And which bitch is that?"

Litchfield rubbed his head and mentally cursed the inmate who had attacked him shortly after his arrival at the prison. When the inmate knocked him down, Litchfield hit his head on a corner of the cement-block wall. He'd sat there, stupefied, with blood running down his face and the side of his head. Dembroke intervened in the fight and took Litchfield to the infirmary. They'd been close ever since.

When they got to know each other better, Dembroke suggested they get together after they got out of prison. "We should be able to figger out ways to make new lives for ourselves. I trust you, and it's hard to find a partner you can say that about."

"I feel good about you, too," Litchfield said. "You probably saved my life when I first got here."

Dembroke stuck out his hand, and Litchfield shook it. "One thing I think we should do," Dembroke said, "is get a ranch to live on, maybe for the rest of our lives. We could do that together."

"That sounds like a good idea."

Over time, Litchfield had told Dembroke the story behind his incarceration, how Sarah Coulter had been his nemesis. "That woman stole my life from me. And I want to pay her back for that."

Dembroke promised to help him get revenge when he got out of prison.

Litchfield's headache never went away, and sometimes it confused his thinking. But he knew the answer to this question. So did Dembroke in spite of his acting stupid. "Sarah Coulter, who thinks she's got the balls of a man. She stole the woman I love, and

I'm going to take her back."

Dembroke sounded tentative. "I know you're fixed on getting this here Faith, but are you sure she'll come with you?"

"I might have to force her at first, but once she has a taste of what I can offer, I'm sure she'll return to me."

"Thought you said she was married afore."

"She was, and I bet she's learned that a woman can't give her the satisfaction a man can. When I have her to myself, I'll remind her of that and bring her to her senses."

Dembroke gave a little shrug. "I ain't sure you're right about her, but I said I'd help you and I ain't going back on my word."

The area closest to the prison had been cleared of trees, and the bright sunlight made Litchfield squint. The road entered the forest farther up ahead. "Let's get moving." He spurred his horse into a trot, and Dembroke rode alongside him. Litchfield's wavy, light-brown hair stirred in the slight breeze made by their movement.

"Listen," Dembroke shouted, "I know you want to get even, but afore I help you do that, you promised to help me set up someplace to call home. A place where we can stay for the rest of our days."

"Plenty of time to do that after my plans are finished."

"But you'll need a place to take your girlfriend to, and you'll want to show off how rich you are."

Litchfield rubbed his head and groaned. "All right, all right, that makes sense, but it's going to take a lot of money. And a lot of time. You got anything set up?"

"Not yet, but I got some ideas. Fastest way to get a stake is to rob a bank."

Litchfield gestured with his thumb back toward the prison they were riding away from. "That's how I got there in the first place—robbing trains."

A hawk flew overhead and squawked. Litchfield stared at it. "It feels good to be as free as that bird. I don't want to lose this."

"Yeah, you got caught the last time. So did I. Next time, we'll be more careful. Hit a bank and lay low for a couple of months. Hit another one in another state and lay low again. We'll keep doing that. If we jump around from state to state, they'll never catch us. Maybe Jesse James will get blamed." He snickered. "Maybe we can even rob the bank in the town your girlfriend lives in."

"That would have to be the last one in our plan, but it

sounds good to me." Litchfield blinked his eyes several times as they finally moved out of the sunshine into the trees. Both men reined their horses to a canter.

"Why the last?"

"Because I'm going to get Faith back and get rid of that bitch, and I'll have to lay low afterward. I might as well figure on permanently retiring after that."

"Sounds like we got a lot of bank robbing to do afore that happens."

"Could be. Right now, I want a steak dinner. Have you got the money for that?"

"Naw, but keep thinking about all the things you want. We'll get them sooner or later. Ain't no hurry. Those women ain't going nowhere."

Yes, Litchfield thought. It would be better to wait. If they suspected he might come after them, they'd be watching for him now. Wait a while and they'd let their guard down. In the meantime, he'd work at getting enough money to make Faith Pruitt happy to stay with him.

He grew pensive. They could have had a good life together. He would have given Faith anything she wanted—a beautiful house, jewelry—and children, something that Coulter whore couldn't give her. He would never understand why Faith had chosen that woman instead of him.

He grew angry again, and his head pounded. No woman could cross Doc Litchfield and not pay for it. He'd show Faith what a man could do. And he'd make that Coulter bitch watch. He'd do the same with her and make Faith watch. After that, he'd kill them both.

He twisted his head every which way, trying to get rid of the agonizing pain. No, no, he thought. That wasn't the plan. He didn't want to hurt Faith, he wanted to win her back and take her with him. He had to remember that. He would remember it. It was the Coulter whore he wanted to kill.

An evil smile made its way across his face. He didn't care how long it took—weeks, months—his thirst for revenge would keep him going until the time was right. You wait, you bitch. You'll get what's coming to you.

Aroused by his thoughts of Faith, he fingered his aching crotch. Dembroke gave him a puzzled glance when he laughed out loud. And I'll get what's coming to me, too.

Chapter 3

"Fiddlesticks!" Getting dressed up in womanly attire and adorning herself with jewelry was definitely not Sarah-Bren's forte. She unhooked the carnelian-and-white cameo brooch from the throat of her copper-colored silk suit. In three tries, she hadn't gotten it hooked straight. She picked up a dark-brown, veiled hat from the bureau, turned it over, and dropped the brooch into it. After adding matching gloves and a handful of hairpins, she headed downstairs, hat in hand.

She trailed her other hand along the banister to be on the safe side. She had no desire to trip over the unfamiliar skirt and go tail over teakettle down the staircase.

Breakfast aromas of French toast and coffee clung to the air, and she heard the clink of cutlery as Faith finished cleaning up the kitchen. Normally, that was one of Sarah's morning chores, but not today. She had to be at the train station by 7:30 a.m. She tilted her head down and lifted her lapel watch with her fingers: 6:45. Still plenty of time.

As she reached the bottom of the stairs, Faith came bustling out of the kitchen and barely stopped short of running Sarah down. "Glory be, that was close. I didn't hear you."

Sarah chuckled. "At least you didn't drop a platter on my leg this time. Though I have to admit that was a fortuitous platter-dropping. It helped bring us back together."

"I won't argue with that." Faith gave her a quick one-armed hug. "Why are you carrying your hat?"

"I need some help." Sarah set the hat on the table in the foyer and lifted out the brooch. "I can't get this fandangled thing to sit straight."

"Give it here." Faith peered at it. "This was your grandmother's, wasn't it?"

"Yes. Mother gave it to me when Grandmother died. Though I was too young to remember that. I don't recall any of my grandparents at all."

Sarah lifted her chin while Faith attempted to attach the brooch to the throat of her suit. "Stay still, Sarah-Bren," Faith said in her best schoolmarm voice, "or one of us is going to get stuck with the pin."

"It better not be me, if you know what's good for you."

Faith snickered. "Careful there, woman. I'm the one holding the sharp object." The pin snapped into the C-hook and locked against it. "There, it's fastened. We both survived."

Faith stepped back and swept her gaze over Sarah, head to foot. "I so seldom see you in a dress. I'd forgotten how good you look. You fill it out beautifully."

With some prodding from Faith, Sarah had chosen the two-piece suit for her trip. Faith said the color enhanced the copper highlights in her chestnut-brown hair and sharpened the bursts of gold in her amber eyes.

"Flattery will not make me feel any better about this." Sarah smoothed a hand against her skirt.

"I'm sure your parents will be happier to see you in that rather than the trousers and shirt you usually wear."

"Heh. You can place a winning wager on that statement." Sarah picked up the hat and hairpins from the foyer table. She examined herself in the mirror on the wall above the table and touched the brooch to settle it more comfortably against her neck. She'd already plaited her waist-long hair, and she twisted it chignon-style against the back of her head and pinned it in place.

"I'd like to be brave enough to wear my trousers. I want to be honest with them about you and me. It's been close to fifteen years now, and we're still pretending. I'm God-awful tired of dissembling."

Faith put her arms around Sarah's waist from behind and leaned her head on Sarah's shoulder. "I am, too. But maybe we should be happy that most of the town tolerates us and forget about anyone else."

"I can't forget my parents." Sarah turned around within Faith's embrace and put her hands on either side of Faith's face. Loose strands of Faith's curly red hair tickled the backs of her fingers. "I wish you could come with me. Maybe if they could get to know you—"

"This is the third time you've answered their invitation to visit, and it's always been during the school year. You know I can't take a week off from teaching for anything less than an emergency." Faith stopped talking for a minute and looked thoughtful. "Could they be doing that on purpose? Maybe they have some suspicions about us."

"You think so? After this visit, their suspicions will be confirmed."

"Sarah, please." Faith stroked the side of Sarah's face with her fingertips. "Don't upset them on my account. We've steered away from this issue all these years. There's no need to broach it now."

"After all this time, I feel an increasing need to be honest. I want my parents to love me for who I am and not have to keep acting as if I fit into their restrictive mold. The older I get, the more I want that."

She brushed a kiss onto Faith's lips and gathered her into a hug. "Too many days away from you," she murmured into Faith's ear. "I'm going to miss you so much."

In a husky voice, Faith said, "I'll miss you, too."

Sarah nipped her earlobe. "I wish I weren't leaving so early."

"Ummm. Hold onto that thought until you return."

"I definitely will." Sarah released Faith, gazed in the mirror, and settled the hat on her hair. She gave the veil a tug. "At least these female hats have something I can hide my scars with." She angled the filmy material to cover the scars. With the hat hiding much of the white blaze in her hair, she appeared unmarked.

"I think you're beautiful. With or without the hat."

"Bless you, oh biased one."

Faith always seemed to sense when Sarah was nervous. The sweet words helped to calm her. She heard Paddy's excited barking outside and glanced toward the window. "Phillip must be here with the buggy."

When Faith opened the door, Phillip was bent down petting Paddy. While she let Phillip in, Sarah donned her brown kidskin gloves and fastened the single pearl button at the heel of each one.

She approached the door as Faith finished giving Phillip a hug. When he saw Sarah, he yanked off his hat and stood there, staring.

"Cat got your tongue?" Sarah said.

"Faith," Phillip said, "please introduce me to your beautiful visitor."

Sarah walked toward him and punched him in the arm. Phillip Showell, married to Sarah's best friend, Leah, had grown up with Sarah and her twin brother, Scott. Sarah's inch-and-a-half boot heels raised her height close to five-foot-eleven, but at six-foot-two, Phillip was one of the few people taller than she was.

"Stop giving me that awestruck look," Sarah said, "or I'll tell Leah on you."

"I'm pretty sure Leah would be giving you the same look.

What a difference from your usual trousers. It certainly brings back memories of you dressed in skirts."

"All right, all right." Sarah pointed to two trunks sitting by the door. "Would you please load those and get me on my way?"

"Happy to, madam." Laughing, Phillip jerked out of the way of Sarah's swipe at him and carted the first trunk out the door.

Sarah embraced Faith and they kissed.

Sarah murmured the mantra that had carried her through many tight spots. "I can do this. I can do this."

"Please be certain of what it is you're doing," Faith said as they parted.

"I will. Wish me luck."

Faith tapped her on the nose. "Your parents might be the ones who need luck."

Sarah gave a wolfish grin. "That could very well be."

* * *

At the train station, Sarah purchased her ticket and Phillip made arrangements to have her trunks loaded onto the train when it arrived. He handed her the claim ticket and stood by silently.

Sarah examined the other people waiting for the train. She didn't notice anyone she knew until she saw Sheriff Herman Schmidt coming their way. He nodded to Phillip and doffed his hat to Sarah. "I don't believe I've met your companion, Phillip."

Sarah gave a full smile and said in a low tone, "We've met, Sheriff, but you're used to seeing me in different attire."

Schmidt hesitated a moment, gave a belly laugh, and settled his hat back on his head. "Your 'attire' had me fooled, Sarah, but you can't disguise that voice or that smile. Why the clothing change?"

Sheriff Schmidt was a good friend who always had been supportive of Sarah and Faith's right to live by their own standards, so Sarah felt comfortable confiding in him. "I'm on my way to visit my parents in Virginia, and they wouldn't approve of my usual garb. Or of my life with Faith. They don't know me as well as they think they do. I'm planning to tell them of our relationship, but I don't want to hit them in the face with it as soon as they see me."

"I hope that turns out well," he said, "but, as my mother used to tell me, 'No sense in borrowing trouble.'"

"Ha!" Phillip said. "Don't all women say that? I've heard it more than once from Leah."

Sarah tapped his arm with her purse. "Yes, wives say it, too. Probably because it's such good advice." She felt a pang in her heart as she spoke. Wouldn't it be wonderful if her parents accepted her life with Faith? Maybe one needed to be brave about the possibility of borrowing trouble once in a while. She tucked that thought away as the sheriff spoke.

"Speaking of good advice, I'm glad Faith's going to stay with Phillip and Leah while you're gone. I'll be nervous about Litchfield until I know for sure where he is."

You're right," Phillip said to the sheriff. "He's snake enough to try to hurt Faith or Sarah. I'll be taking Faith back and forth to school each day and bringing her to our house."

"Don't forget," Sarah said, "Leah played a part in getting him convicted. He might want to harm her, too."

Phillip nodded. "That's right. We'll all keep an eye out for him."

Sarah raised her voice to be heard over the noise the train made as it entered the station. "Please remind Leah about it so she'll be careful."

The three of them ambled toward a coach. Pieces of soot rained down on them, and Sarah brushed it off her face and clothes. She wrinkled her nose at the smells the train brought with it—soot, burning wood, hot grease from the wheels. Those smells would be with her during her ride. And so would the sounds of the chugging train, the grinding wheels, and the clackety-clack of the track. Not to mention the ear-splitting whistle. Whistles sounded good at a distance, though sometimes plaintive. But up close, they endangered your eardrums.

Remind me again, Sarah thought, why I didn't ride Redfire to my parents' house. Oh, yes, the time difference. The train would save a couple of days. And Redfire couldn't carry all the clothes I'll need.

She bit off a sigh and offered her hand to the sheriff. "I'll let you know when I return, and you can fill me in on what you've learned about him, if anything."

Schmidt shook her hand and touched the edge of his hat. "I'll do that, Sarah. Enjoy your vacation."

"Heh. I'll try." She kissed Phillip's cheek, thanked him for his help, and climbed aboard. The train chuffed away, and as she waved goodbye, she mused on two problems to address. First, she was determined at long last to disclose her relationship with Faith to her parents. She felt guilty for carrying on the pretense—essentially lying to them—for so many years. She would play that by ear.

Second, Joel Litchfield concerned her. He was a vindictive man, and more than once during his trial, he had fixed Sarah with venomous stares. She fully expected him to try to get even with her. After all, Faith had chosen her over Litchfield. He might even plan to use Faith to hurt Sarah. Or somehow force Faith to his side by threatening Sarah—or Leah. But she couldn't do anything about Litchfield until he showed up in their lives again, if ever.

Two problems, but she could tackle only the first one at the moment. Would she be brave enough to follow through on that?

Chapter 4

On the evening of the third day, after one change of trains, Sarah was nearing her destination. She'd be happy to get off the train. The constant trail of smoke seeped through the closed windows and irritated her eyes and nose. The lingering taste of it interfered with her enjoyment of the food in the dining car. And no matter how diligently the porters tried to keep everything wiped off, the constant spewing of new soot from the engine's smokestack sabotaged their efforts.

She reminded herself that the one saving grace of putting up with those aggravations, and with the boring clack, clack, clack of the wheels and the chug, chug, chug of the engine, was the speed of the trip. Time-wise, it sure outdid making the journey on horseback. In all other ways by far, she'd rather be on Redfire.

The train slowed as it reached the station and eased to a stop. Sarah debarked, handed her claim ticket to the baggage handler, and waited for her trunks to be off-loaded. Almost exactly at the moment her trunks were set beside her, the Coulters' butler, Matthias, with a younger man beside him, rode up to the lantern-lit train platform in a buggy. Matthias, now gray-haired and slightly stooped, had been born a slave at Red Oak Manor when Sarah's mother, Cynthia's, family owned it when Cynthia was a girl. In 1845, when Cynthia inherited Red Oak Manor, she and Sarah's father, Prescott, had agreed to sell off the slaves and most of the two thousand acres of land.

Matthias and the other slaves who had been kept on were freed by Prescott Coulter even before the war began, and they were given the chance to leave or stay on as paid workers. Matthias, his wife, Pearl, and two of their five children had been among those who chose to stay. Sarah considered them to be good and faithful friends, and the care they took of her mother and father touched her heart and pleased her immensely.

Brushing off her clothes, she strode toward the men as they clambered down and removed their hats. She shook Matthias's hand. "How good to see you, my friend. Your arthritis hasn't slowed you much."

"Thank you, Miss Sarah. I wish that could be true." He gestured toward the muscular young man next to him. "My son Amos do most of what I used to. You 'member him, don't you?"

Amos made a slight bow.

Sarah shook his hand. "I surely do. When we played Hide and Seek, Amos could get into the tiniest places I ever did see. How are you, Amos?"

"Growed a little bigger now, ma'am."

Sarah laughed. "Much bigger. You wouldn't fit in those nooks and crannies now. If you'll be kind enough to load my trunks, we can get on our way."

While Amos gathered the trunks and stashed them, Matthias produced a stool and gave Sarah a hand up into the passenger seat of the buggy.

"Matthias, how are Mother and Father, honestly?"

He put the stool in the buggy. "They's doing pretty good, Miss Sarah. Getting older and creakier, like me and Pearl. But keeping up as best they can."

"I miss seeing them. And you and Pearl, too. Is Pearl still doing the housekeeping?"

"Last week, for the first time, she let some of it go to Amos's wife, Sadie. But Pearl makes sure Sadie do everything perfect. Drives the poor gal crazy."

"I'll bet. I'm eager to see them all." Sarah sat back and tried to relax. Amos and Matthias climbed into the front seat, and they started along the darkened streets to Red Oak Manor. The only light came from the lanterns that swung from each front side of the buggy.

Sarah took a deep breath of the fresh air. Yes, she was eager to see her parents, but she was dreading it, too.

* * *

As they approached the house, Sarah noticed lanterns hung along the veranda as they used to be before the war. A young, colored boy jumped out of a chair and disappeared inside. Several moments later, Sarah's parents came forth. Matthias set the stool beside the buggy and gave Sarah a hand down. She hurried up the steps toward her parents and embraced her mother then her father.

Prescott, a tall man with dark hair and amber eyes to match Sarah's, gave her shoulders a squeeze before he stepped back. Sarah noted shocks of gray at his temples and a few silvery threads in his full head of hair.

Cynthia gazed at her with the familiar appraising stare that always made Sarah feel like squirming. She refused to allow herself to do that, but she did hold her breath a second or two longer. One never knew what her mother might say.

"You look well, Sarah. A little heavier, perhaps, but you should be able to control that by watching what you eat." A petite woman, with graying, brown hair and blue eyes, Cynthia always managed to make Sarah feel somewhat gawky.

"You look well, too, Mother." Damn, Sarah thought as she cringed inside, I guess that means every bite I take will be scrutinized. Welcome home. She shook off the uncharitable thought and entered the house behind her parents. Amos followed with her trunks. He took them straight up the ornate staircase that opened in the foyer.

"Come into the parlor, dear," her mother said. "We'll have some tea, and afterwards, you can freshen up."

Sarah would have preferred to freshen up first; she felt grimy from her travels. But she hesitated to thwart her mother's wishes right away. That could make for an uncomfortable visit. Better to fit into the routine. "Very well. I would welcome some tea."

She sat in a stuffed chair near the coffee table. Cynthia pulled a bell cord, and her parents settled on the sofa catercorner to her.

That preparations had been made for Sarah's visit became apparent when a young colored woman carried in a tea tray and set it on the table. A moment later, she brought in a plate of cookies and sandwiches cut into quarters. As she turned to go, Sarah said, "Excuse me, I don't believe we've met."

After a slight pause, Cynthia said rather firmly, "This is Eula, the eldest of Pearl's granddaughters."

Sarah extended her hand and waited until Eula grasped it. "I'm pleased to meet you, Eula." The girl had a dazzling smile, marred only by a missing eyetooth. They let their hands drop.

"Thank you, ma'am." Eula made an abbreviated curtsy and left the room.

Cynthia poured the tea and said, "Matthias and Pearl haven't been able to keep up with all their responsibilities, so we've added some of the younger generation to the household staff. It's worked out well for us...and for them."

"Yes," Prescott said, "Amos has been the perfect stand-in for Matthias. Lifting, carrying, hitching the horses. He's helped a lot. Didn't your mother write you about the changes in our staff?"

Sarah swallowed a bite of sandwich. "Some of it, yes, and I was pleased to hear about it." That her mother was repeating what she had already said in her letters disturbed Sarah. Was that sharp mind of hers finally slipping?

Sarah finished the sandwich half, lifted her cup and saucer from the table, and held them in her lap. "We...I've been concerned that Matthias and Pearl might need help as they grow older." Uh-oh, did Mother catch that slip?

Sarah nearly blew her tea through her nose when her mother said, "We?"

"Uh, yes. I usually read your letters to Faith. She has taken an interest in my family."

Cynthia's lips pursed. "I'm not certain I approve of that. I consider my letters to be part of a personal conversation. Reading them to someone else, especially someone outside the family, is like encouraging that person to eavesdrop."

Sarah drank the rest of her tea and glanced at her father. He gave her a wink that brought a quick answering smile from her. He said, "Perhaps Sarah would like to freshen up, now, Cynthia. The train trip had to be tiring."

"And dirty." Sarah set her cup and saucer on the table as the others did the same.

"Of course, my dear," her mother said. "Where are my manners. You go right on up and take care of your ablutions. And rest for the balance of the evening. Take some cookies with you, and we'll see you at breakfast tomorrow."

Sarah caught the look that went from her mother to her father. It unnerved her a bit. Was something going on? She was too tired to dwell on it. Tomorrow would be soon enough to find out.

* * *

The next day, they had no sooner finished their breakfast than Prescott invited them into his study while Eula cleaned up after the meal. The study was thirty-foot long and airy, with four windows in the outside wall that let in the morning sun. A dark brown desk and three overstuffed chairs sat at one end, surrounded by walls barely tinged a lighter brown and hung with paintings of hunting scenes.

After Sarah and Cynthia took their seats, Prescott bustled around behind the desk and sat down. He picked up one of the papers sitting there and unfolded it until it nearly covered the desktop.

He tapped the paper with a pencil, and Sarah leaned forward for a better view. "This is a copy of the plat of Red Oak Manor, Sarah, showing the property boundaries and geography. I've penciled in our house and the outbuildings as well as the houses that Matthias and his family live in."

Sarah got up from the seat next to Cynthia and sauntered around to stand near her father's chair. "I never gave a lot of thought to the size of Red Oak. How many acres are there?"

"Down to a hundred and fifty now. We've gradually done away with the cotton fields and kept a few to grow tobacco. I say 'we,' but Amos pretty much runs the plantation, paperwork and all."

Prescott raised his head and seemed to be studying Sarah's face. "I suppose you're wondering why I'm telling you this."

"The question had crossed my mind."

"Your mother and I are getting up in years, and frankly, I'm slowing down to the point where I don't want to have to worry about making decisions on the thousand miniscule things that come up in the business of running Red Oak Manor."

"I can understand that. Believe it or not, my little writing business presents the need for myriad decisions, too."

Cynthia's voice had a bite to it. "You even speak like a writer."

Sarah stood up straight. "Do you consider that a problem?"

"No." Cynthia's tone softened. "Actually, I admire it."

The corners of Sarah's lips turned up. "Thank you. I value the compliment."

Prescott cleared his throat. "Your mother and I have discussed an agreement about the property that I want you to know about before we come to a final conclusion."

Sarah returned to her seat. Cynthia's eyes suddenly stared toward the floor. Sarah glanced at her and back to her father. She wondered if the "agreement" might be a little one-sided.

"And what's that, Father?"

"We've already spoken to Scott about this, but it's only fair that you should know, too. We're considering signing the property over to Matthias and his family with the understanding that we live here until our deaths."

Sarah sat still for a moment, shocked speechless. "But..." She stopped. And why not? she thought. The property belongs to Mother and Father. It's theirs to do with as they wish.

She nodded. "I think that's a marvelous idea. And so very generous of both of you."

"But," Cynthia said, "don't you think you and Scott should inherit it?"

Sarah turned fully toward her mother and briefly touched her arm. "Mother, Scott and I haven't done anything at Red Oak Manor to deserve it or know how to run it. Matthias and his family have worked this property and kept it in good order since he was a young man. It seems fitting to me that they should inherit it."

Cynthia sniffed. "That's what your father says. But I thought you and Scott might feel differently."

"I can't speak for Scott, but I like that Red Oak will go into the hands of the people who worked it and kept it productive after the war."

"Scott says that, too." Cynthia fingered a handkerchief that was tucked into her sleeve at her wrist. "You'd be turning away a good income."

Prescott held up a hand before Sarah could speak. "I believe Coulter Foundry provides you and Scott with sufficient income, even with the changes in supervision that have been made there. Am I right?"

"Yes, Father, it does. Scott doesn't seem to want for anything—except better health—and I haven't even had to touch my part of the income. I plan for that to go to Jessie at a time yet to be decided. Add what I earn as a writer and illustrator to what Faith earns as a schoolteacher, and we get along fine."

Oh, no. Again, Sarah realized her slip as soon as she said the words. But they couldn't be taken back. Perhaps her subconscious was reinforcing that the time had come to open up about her relationship with Faith.

Cynthia jerked ramrod straight. "'What Faith earns as a schoolteacher'? '*We* get along fine'?"

Sarah studied her mother's expression. She already knew. "Mother. Father. Faith and I have been sharing our home, our lives, and our son, Benjamin, for the past ten years. We love each other, in the same way you two do."

Cynthia jumped up from her chair and turned toward Prescott, who also rose. "I knew it!" her mother said. "I knew it." She stamped her foot. "I've been telling you for years they were in an unnatural relationship. But you wouldn't listen." She pointed to Sarah but didn't look at her. "Tell her to get out of this house. I won't have her under my roof for one more minute. We'll have her trunks sent."

Sarah stood, too, and gazed at her father.

"Cynthia." Prescott raised his hands in supplication. "You

can't mean that. Sarah's our daughter."

"I do mean it. I'm glad she's not inheriting Red Oak Manor. My parents would be mortified. She's no daughter of mine. She's Satan's daughter. Claiming she's in love with that...that...woman who corrupted her." She glared at Prescott. "And you corrupted her, too. Allowing her to ride all over the countryside like a boy in spite of my wishes. This is what your lack of guidance has resulted in. A woman who thinks she's a man—an abomination. Tell her to leave this house, or I'll leave. And I won't come back."

Prescott dropped his hands. His voice sounded tight. "I'm sorry, Sarah, but I have to ask you to leave. If you'll get your things together, I'll have Matthias bring the buggy around and take you to the train station." He squinched his eyes closed and reopened them. "I'm sorry."

"Sorry?" Cynthia yelled. "Don't apologize to that...that ...deceiver. She's lied to us all these years while she was living in sin with that whore. Get her out of here. Now!" Cynthia flounced out of the room.

Prescott's shoulders slumped and his hands shook as he gestured toward Sarah. "Sarah, please understand. I don't condemn you for choosing your own path, but I can't go against your mother's wishes."

"I don't fault you, Father. I kept quiet all these years because I didn't have the courage to stand up for myself...and Faith. I can't very well criticize you for not standing up for us. I won't take long to pack. I didn't unpack much yet." She moved slowly toward the door.

"I love you, Sarah. Please remember that. Your mother loves you, too. She's upset by your revelation."

Sarah turned and gave him a wry smile. "I love both of you, too. This whole situation would be easier if I didn't." She opened the door and left.

Chapter 5

Sarah wired Faith and Phillip that she was coming home early, but she didn't explain why. She wanted to tell Faith personally, although she suspected Faith already had a good idea of what the problem was.

Phillip met her at the station, gathered her trunks for her, and put them in the buggy.

Sarah rubbed Drummer's nose as she paused by the stallion. "Hi there, boy. Glad to see me?" Drummer whuffled and flicked his ears back and forth.

"I'm glad to see you, too, Sarah." Phillip offered a hand to help her climb into the buggy, which she accepted without argument. As he hauled himself into the driver's seat, he said, "I have to confess, though, I'm surprised to see you back so soon. I did let Herman know you're back."

"Thank you. I ran into some problems. I'll tell you all about it, later. I want to talk to Faith first."

"Of course." Phillip glanced at Sarah. "I guess I assumed you would stop to visit Scott and Lindsay while you were traveling. You passed so near their home."

Sarah barely shook her head, and Phillip stopped his remarks.

Sarah knew he would forgive her lack of conversation. As an old friend, he was aware she could be moody on occasion. During the train ride home, she had mulled over her mother's reaction and had come to terms with it, or hoped she had. But she still felt out of sorts, and the heavy feeling in her stomach persisted no matter what excuses she tried to make for her mother's behavior.

She was anxious to hear Faith's thoughts. And she couldn't wait to get out of the damn dress.

Faith stood on the porch. Sarah picked up one of the trunks and shushed Phillip when he objected. Shrugging, he picked up the other trunk, and they carried them into the house while Faith held the door open.

"Do you want these upstairs?" Phillip asked.

"You may leave them here," Faith said. "We'll take care of

them later."

They set them on the kitchen floor, and Phillip said, "Well, ladies, I have to be getting back to work."

Faith tugged his sleeve. "I made a fresh pot of coffee. Won't you stay and have some and perhaps a bite to eat?"

"Thank you, it's tempting, but Mr. Van Zandt is waiting for me to finish his new porch."

Sarah said, "Thank you for picking me up. I'm sorry I was such miserable company."

"That's all right," he said with a grin. "I'll get even with you one of these days."

The women gave him a hug and he left.

Sarah turned to Faith and opened her arms. They embraced and kissed. Sarah continued to hold on to Faith. She clasped her even closer and shut her eyes. The tension in her body lessened with each passing moment.

"Are you all right?" Faith rubbed her hand in a circle against Sarah's back. "What happened?"

"Let me get changed first, and I'll tell you all about it." Sarah released her and stepped away. "I refuse to wear this dress one more second." She raised a finger. "I'll be right back. Don't go anywhere."

"Don't worry. I'll be here." She gave a laugh as Sarah lifted her skirt high and sprinted up the steps.

After removing her clothes and washing the soot off her body, Sarah changed into brown pants and a burnt-yellow cotton shirt that buttoned down the front. She rolled up her shirtsleeves partway as she went downstairs into the kitchen. Faith was pouring her a cup of coffee. A sliced pork and tomato sandwich waited on a plate at Sarah's place. She sat, added butter, salt, and pepper to the sandwich, and took a bite from it. "Um, exactly what I needed. I was starving. Thank you."

Faith sat next to Sarah and waited until she finished the sandwich. "Do you feel like talking now?"

Sarah nudged the plate aside, moved her chair away from the table, and rose. She opened her mouth to speak and shut it again. Her throat had closed, and she began to breathe heavily. *Damn.* She gripped the back of her chair and struggled to get the words out. "My...my...mother..." She sucked in a breath and glanced at Faith, who looked stricken.

Faith put a hand on Sarah's forearm and rubbed her thumb along Sarah's skin. "Take it easy, sweetheart," she said in a soothing tone.

Tears welled in Sarah's eyes, and she slashed at them with her free hand. "She threw me out of the house."

"Oh, Sarah, I'm so sorry." Faith half-stood, wiped a tear from Sarah's cheek, and slumped back into her chair.

"I told her about us, that I loved you the same way she loved Father, and she screamed at me." Sarah's voice was raspy, but it came easier now. "She called me abominable and said I was Satan's daughter, not hers. She said you were a whore who corrupted me. And that Father corrupted me when I was younger by letting me ride all over Virginia dressed like a boy." Sarah swallowed. "I've never seen her so angry. Or so mean."

Faith got up and grabbed a dishtowel. She came around the table and sat on Sarah's lap. Lifting the towel to Sarah's face, Faith patted her tears away. Her voice sounded tentative. "Do you think I corrupted you? I kissed you first, and I did come after you. Maybe—"

"Hush." Sarah took the towel from her and tossed it on the table. She tilted her head at an angle to see Faith better. "I bless the day you kissed me. I bless the day you came after me." She touched her lips briefly to Faith's. When they parted, she said, "If we hadn't gotten together, I'd have become a bitter woman who never found her way in life, who never found love. Instead, you made me whole. Don't ever doubt that."

They embraced for several moments before Sarah said, "I don't understand."

Faith leaned away and peered into her face. "You don't understand what?"

"How she could hate me so much. She even said she was glad I wasn't inheriting Red Oak Manor—"

"What? Not inheriting Red Oak Manor? But—but why?"

"I'll explain later. That's a whole different story." Sarah sniffled, but she refused to cry anymore. "I figured Mother would be upset about us. But you know something? She said she told Father years ago that we were in an 'unnatural relationship.' I was still the same person all that time, but she never did anything mean about it until now."

"I suppose as long as you didn't admit it, she could convince herself it wasn't so. Hide her head in the sand, as they say."

"Sounds kind of hypocritical, doesn't it?"

"Of course it does, but your mother isn't the only hypocrite in the world."

Sarah tilted her head and felt a tiny grin coming on. Faith had soothed her mood once more. "Are you serious?"

Faith tapped the end of Sarah's nose with her forefinger. "Yes. We've got our share of them here in Bonneforte."

"That's no lie."

They sat quietly for several moments. Then Faith got up. "You got a letter while you were gone." She fetched the letter from a cupboard and handed it to Sarah.

Sarah turned it over. "It's from Rusty." About 10 years back, when Faith had briefly questioned her relationship with Sarah, Sarah had traveled in search of a new home. In Wyoming, she had stayed with Ruth "Rusty" Gunther and her brother, Mel. That had been a wrenching time for her, but Rusty and Mel had alleviated her torment by opening their home and their hearts to her. She and Rusty had kept in touch ever since.

She opened the envelope, and her shoulders slumped as she read it. "She and her partner broke up. Several months ago. She says she didn't tell me before because she wanted time to at least partially heal from the wound it left." Sarah finished reading the letter in silence.

Faith stood behind her and rubbed her shoulders. Sarah reached up and patted her hand. "I feel bad about this news. Rusty's a good person. She deserves to find someone she can have a permanent relationship with. Like we have."

"Not everyone's that fortunate. And we almost lost each other a couple of times." She lifted Sarah's chestnut-brown hair and kissed the back of her neck. "But that won't ever happen again."

"Mmm, especially if you keep kissing me like that." She tugged Faith onto her lap and wound her arms around her. "I have an idea about Rusty, if it's all right with you."

"What's that?"

"I'd like to ask her to come visit us." Sarah felt Faith stiffen a little, and she hid a smile. Faith always did have a small jealous streak. Sarah kind of liked that, as long as it didn't get out of hand. "Would you mind?"

"Should I?" Faith nudged Sarah's arm with her elbow. "Forget I said that. Of course I don't mind. I'd like to meet her."

"She'll talk your ears off, but you'll like her, I think, and she'll like you. I want her to see that it's possible to find a woman you can love forever. Besides, she's asked me a thousand questions about you over the years."

"And what did you answer?"

"I told her she'd have to come visit us and find those answers herself."

Faith laughed. "No one ever accused you of being slow on the uptake."

It was Sarah's turn to laugh. "Not when I have you around to test my wits every day."

* * *

Later, Sarah wrote to Rusty and her invitation was accepted. An autumn date was suggested because Rusty said she was taking music classes and wouldn't be free until then. Music classes? Rusty hadn't mentioned them in previous letters. What was she up to now?

Days and weeks went by, and life settled into its normal routine. Sarah tried to push any regrets about her mother's reaction into the dark part of her mind that she reserved for situations she couldn't change, but she wished she'd been able to. Once in a while, she visited that dark part and rehashed the memories, but she recognized that any chance for a change was futile in most respects. Still, she continued to harbor the hope that her mother's lack of acceptance might someday soften.

Chapter 6

Sarah went into town to mail her latest edits to her publisher. Her tenth book in as many years was about to be published, most of them based in the war years. Her royalties had gradually increased, a pleasant addition to her income. While at the post office, she picked up her family's mail and shuffled through it. Newspaper, flyers, catalogues. Nothing memorable.

As she emerged onto the boardwalk, a young woman plowed into her and the mail scattered hither and yon.

The woman gasped. "I'm terribly sorry. Let me help you." She joined Sarah in picking up the pieces. Sarah's hair flowed around her shoulders as she bent to the task. They finished and stood up, and the woman searched Sarah's face. "Are you Sarah Coulter?"

"Yes, I am."

The woman glanced around in a surreptitious manner. "My name's Della Kumber. Could I please speak with you privately? Maybe in the alley behind the dry goods store in about fifteen minutes?"

Sarah angled her head back as she wondered at the odd request. The woman appeared to be at least ten years younger and was half a head shorter than Sarah. Her long black hair, tilted brown eyes, and tan skin gave her an attractive appearance, enhanced by her beige dress and brown bonnet.

"Please," Miss Kumber said. "It's important to me."

Sarah couldn't think of a reason not to do as she asked. Besides, she was curious. "All right."

"Thank you so much." Miss Kumber dashed away across the street. Sarah's gaze followed her. The woman met an older man who barked something at her and pointed in Sarah's direction. Sarah became even more curious and hoped the next fifteen minutes would pass quickly.

Uh-oh. The man came across the street and strode up to her. He jabbed Sarah's chest with his pointed index finger. In a loud voice, he said, "You stay away from my daughter."

His daughter? He was tall and fair-skinned, and the girl

didn't resemble him at all. But something about him did seem vaguely familiar. Sarah let that thought pass and shoved his hand away. "I don't even know who you are. Or who your daughter is."

Half a dozen people gathered around them, attracted by the commotion Kumber made. Sarah saw Sheriff Schmidt come up the boardwalk and stop some distance behind Kumber.

The man's body shook so much, it was a wonder he wasn't spouting fire. "I'm Elias Kumber, and you were speaking to my daughter, Della. This town doesn't need people like you."

Sarah hooked a thumb in her gun belt. "I've been living in this town for around ten years, and I would guess you recently got here. Who are you to say whether the town needs me?"

He flapped his hand toward her. "You're unbelievable. Pretending to be a man. You're an abomination, like the Lord says you are."

Sarah's lip curled. "If you're going to use the Bible to rationalize your behavior, you could at least get it right. The Lord didn't say anything against people like me, and neither did God's Ten Commandments." She could see her argument went right over his head. In her experience, true bigots didn't have open minds, and he was no exception.

His voice grew derisive. "What you say doesn't mean anything. I've heard about you. You're Sarah Coulter, a fount of perversion, and I'm ordering you to stay away from my daughter."

A fount of perversion? That turn of phrase led Sarah to assume Kumber was an educated man. Educated but not enlightened.

"I am Sarah Coulter, but you're speaking to the wrong person. Order your daughter around if you want to, but don't try to order me around. You have no authority over me."

Without warning, Kumber lunged at Sarah and punched her in the face. She slammed into the person behind her. Before she could react, Sheriff Schmidt put a gun to Kumber's back. "I'm the sheriff, Kumber, and what I say does mean something. You're under arrest for assaulting a citizen."

"No, Sheriff," Sarah said. She turned slightly and thanked the man who had kept her from falling. She put a hand to the blood oozing from her nose and wiped her hand on Kumber's shirt and jacket while he glared at her. "He's new in town, and for some reason, he thinks he runs it. How about you let him go this time? I guarantee I won't wind up with a bloody nose next time. He caught me unawares, but that won't happen again."

Schmidt holstered his gun and jerked Kumber around to

face him. "Count yourself lucky that Miss Sarah wants me to let you go. You should be spending the night in jail. Now, get out of here."

Kumber turned on his heel and shouldered his way through the gathered bystanders.

Schmidt said, "The rest of you might as well go about your business. No more spectacle here." He took Sarah's arm and steered her toward his office. "Come with me, Miss Sarah, and we'll get you cleaned up."

"Who is he? Do you know anything about him?" She cupped a hand in front of her nose to keep the blood from spilling on her shirt.

"Let's get the bleeding stopped first." He pressed a handkerchief into her hands.

When they got to the jailhouse, Sarah entered the water closet. Recently, the town had installed running water and most of the establishments, including the sheriff's office, were connected to it. Sarah was pleased with the convenience of the tiny sink. Much better than cleaning up in the horse trough. In the next few years, homes outside the town would probably be connected, too.

Sarah wrung out the handkerchief one last time and checked to make sure the blood had stopped dripping. She washed her face and hands and returned to the office.

"Your nose all right?" Herman peered at her.

"Yeah, but your hankie has seen better days." She held it out.

"Keep it. Your eye's swollen a bit. Maybe your face, too."

Sarah felt gently around her eye. "My nose is okay. My cheek took most of the hit. And I think you're right about the swelling. Wait until Faith sees me. She'll chastise me for fighting."

Herman barked a laugh. "You send her to me. I'll vouch for you. Not your fault at all. The man's a maniac."

"He's dressed well and sounds educated. What do you know about him and his daughter?"

"Only that the two of them showed up one day last week and are staying at the hotel. Came in by train, though he's been renting a horse from the livery stable." He sat at his desk and waved Sarah to a chair. "Have a seat."

"No, thanks. I'm supposed to be meeting the daughter behind the dry goods store."

"You're what? Why?"

"I have no idea what she wants. Before this confrontation with her father, she literally ran into me as I came out of the post office. That's when he saw us 'together.'" Sarah rolled her eyes. "While she helped me pick up the mail I dropped, she asked me to meet her. Said it was important."

"We can be pretty damned sure the man's a hothead if that's all that happened. And you're going to meet her even after he slugged you?" Herman's raised eyebrows furrowed his forehead.

"I agreed to meet her then because I was curious. Now I'm doubly curious." Sarah turned toward the door. Herman still had a surprised expression on his face when she left.

* * *

Sarah strode down an alley to the back of the jailhouse. The path met a wider alley that ran between the buildings that faced Main Street and those that faced First Avenue. Sarah moved up several buildings to the appointed spot. Dust swirled around her boots with each step. Although the buildings blocked some of the sunlight, their proximity to each other captured the heat and intensified it. She wondered whether Miss Kumber would still meet her.

The thought no sooner passed through her mind than Miss Kumber arrived, breathing hard as though she had been running. "Oh, I'm so glad you waited. Thank you."

Sarah checked to make sure no one had followed the woman, then she spoke. "Did you see what happened between your father and me?"

"I did." She seemed suddenly shy. "And I apologize, as he should. But he won't. I'm sorry for the way he acted, and I'm sorry he hurt you."

"Apology accepted." Sarah removed her hat, wiped the damp band with a finger, and settled the hat back on her head. "You said you wanted to talk to me, Miss Kumber?"

"Please call me Della." She twisted her hands together. "I'm new in town. My papa and I recently moved here. I have to confess I knew who you were when I bumped into you."

"Oh?"

"You're the only woman in town who wears long pants." She blushed. "At least as far as anyone knows."

Sarah smiled at that and winced at the pain it caused in her swollen cheek. "I've wondered about that myself."

"Maybe you're the only one bold enough to show her true self."

Sarah touched her sore face. "When I run into people as prejudiced as your father, I wonder whether boldness is wise."

"Oh, Miss Coulter, I'm thrilled that you're so bold. I, too, am like you. I love women. I thought I was the only woman who did." Her expression turned sad. "But my father believes I can change. He beats me when he thinks I've looked at someone the wrong way."

"Beats you?" Sarah's jaw hardened.

Della gazed at the ground. "With his belt. Sometimes the buckle end."

"Why…" Sarah swallowed hard. "Why do you stay with him?"

Della raised her head and stuck her hands out from her sides, palms up. "I would leave in a minute, but where would I go? What could I do to make a living? I couldn't be a tavern woman." She gave Sarah a questioning look. "How do you provide for yourself?"

"I write and illustrate books, and my wife is a schoolteacher."

Della clasped her hands together. "Your wife? Are you married, truly?"

"Not by man's laws, but we consider ourselves married under God's laws."

"How marvelous! And you're a writer! You're so fortunate. I wish I had some skills."

Sarah sucked her bottom lip between her teeth and bit down on it. She shook her head slowly before she spoke. "I wish I could help you, but I don't know how I can."

"You've helped me by being who you are," Della said. "Now I know I'm not alone. Other women like me exist."

She threw her arms around Sarah and kissed her unmarked cheek. "Thank you. I have to go now." She hurried off.

Sarah stood still for a moment. She rubbed her neck and mused about what Della had said. As she left the alley, she grimaced over what Della was suffering at the hands of her own father. Beatings with a belt? He'd better not touch her whenever Sarah was around.

* * *

When Faith got in from school that afternoon, Sarah was standing at the kitchen sink. Faith grimaced at Sarah's obvious injuries and said, "I heard what happened in town. But I suspect I didn't get the whole story." She set her school bag in the corner closet and they kissed. "Let's sit down and you can tell me about it."

They sat next to each other at the table, and Sarah explained the encounter with Della Kumber and her father.

Faith's expression went from surprise to anger to sympathy. "That poor woman. Can we do anything for her?"

"I had to bite my lip to keep from offering to let her stay here." Sarah gave a little laugh. "Then I came to my senses. Her father would probably do something rash, and one of us might get hurt."

"I suppose you're right. He sounds nasty."

Sarah pointed to her swollen cheek and the eye with a darkening semicircle beneath it. "He is. Too bad he had to mess up the good side of my face."

"Stop that. All sides of your face are good." Faith squeezed Sarah's forearm.

"You know, this kind of puts my mother's reactions in perspective. She might disapprove of who I am, but she has never beat me for it." Sarah paused and gave that some thought. "But she's still being abusive. Emotionally abusive."

"Give her time, Sarah, and hope for the best."

"I guess that's all I can do."

Faith sighed. "That's probably all we can do for Della, too."

* * *

That evening, Sarah sat at the kitchen table reading the *Bonneforte Tribune* by light from an oil lamp. Faith relaxed near her, prepared to discuss whatever news the paper provided.

Sarah placed her finger on the top front section. "Here's a really interesting article. You remember Clara Barton from the war?"

"I do indeed. She went onto battlefields and gave aid and comfort to the wounded and sometimes cooked for them."

"Yes, the troops called her the 'Angel of the Battlefield' and rightly so. It took tremendous courage to do what she did."

"Did you ever meet her?"

"No, I didn't have that privilege. Anyway..." Sarah continued reading. "She went to Europe after the war." She read the next part word for word, "In Geneva, Switzerland, she came across an organization named the Red Cross, which called for international agreements to protect the sick and wounded during wartime and for the formation of national societies to give aid voluntarily on a neutral basis."

"What a marvelous idea," Faith said.

"Yes, and Miss Barton liked it so well she founded the American Red Cross, and she's the president of it."

"But we're not at war right now."

"Part of their mission is to give aid wherever it's needed—at natural and man-made disasters, for instance."

"I'm sure it will find many uses. I hope we never need it, though."

"Me, too." Sarah leaned back in her chair and grinned. "I guess for our small needs, we have to be our own Red Cross—or maybe you do."

Faith flicked her on the arm with the back of her hand. "Thou hast said it."

Sarah rubbed her arm and grimaced. "You must admit you're the Clara Barton in this pair, even though you hit me."

Faith kissed two fingers and touched them to Sarah's arm. "That little tap wasn't a hit, but I'll kiss it for you anyway."

Sarah raised her eyebrows and lowered her tone of voice. "Maybe you can hit me on the lips."

Thus ended the reading of the newspaper for the night.

Chapter 7

On a warm day in May, Sarah-Bren sat on the porch with her art supplies spread out on a table and worked at her drawing. Hoofbeats galloping in her direction interrupted her concentration. Paddy jumped up from his spot near her feet and ran off the porch toward the newcomer.

From the shade surrounding her, Sarah squinted through her spectacles and recognized the postmaster's sixteen-year-old son, Eric Grunder. The youngster reined in his horse as Faith came through the kitchen door and joined Sarah. Faith wore a pastel green dress, one of Sarah's favorites, and held a glass of lemonade in one hand. With her other hand, she brushed long, red curls back over her shoulder.

Eric tipped his hat. "Mrs. Pruitt, Miss Sarah."

Sarah said, "Hello, Eric."

He dismounted, dropped the reins to the ground, and scrubbed his fingers on the dog's head. "Hi, Paddy." The dog jumped around and gave a friendly bark. Eric climbed up the porch stairs, and Paddy resumed his place at Sarah's feet. Eric removed his hat. His shaggy black hair glistened damply along the indentation it left. He tugged against the bright red bandanna he wore around his neck.

"Miss Sarah." He lifted a telegram from his denim shirt pocket. "This arrived, and my papa said I should bring it out to you straightaway."

Sarah took the telegram. "It's from Lindsay."

Faith offered the glass of lemonade to Eric and placed her hand on Sarah's shoulder.

"Thank you, ma'am," Eric said. "You must have read my mind. I sure appreciate this." He gulped at the drink.

"You're welcome," Faith said. "That ride was a hot and dry one. I was at the kitchen window and saw your dust even before you turned up the lane."

Sarah opened the telegram and read it aloud. "Scott is suddenly very weak. Please come." Sarah looked up at Faith. "Can you come, too?"

"I'll say my brother-in-law has a medical emergency. I think I can get Mrs. Wharton to substitute for me at the school. I'll write to Benjamin and fill him in on everything so he knows where we are."

Sarah placed her hand on the one resting on her shoulder and gave it a squeeze. She squirmed sideways and reached into her pants pocket for some coins. "Eric, can you get your papa to send an answer for me?"

"Yes, I can, Miss Sarah. He already has the address recorded."

"Good." She handed Eric the coins. "I want him to say, 'Faith and I are coming at once.' Have him sign my name, 'Sarah.' Keep the extra money for yourself."

"Thank you, ma'am." His dark brown eyes crinkled in a smile. "That's kind of you." He finished his lemonade and gave the glass to Faith, who set it on the round table. "I'll get right to it." He put on his hat and hurried off.

Faith tugged out a chair and sat next to Sarah. "It sounds like Scott's taken a turn for the worse."

Tears stung Sarah's amber eyes. "We haven't seen Scott and his family for a while. I should have stopped there on my way back from Mother's, but I was too rattled. I wanted to get home as soon as possible." She touched Faith's arm. "To you."

Sarah leaned an elbow on the table and put her head in her hand. Her straight, dark hair, tied at the nape of her neck with a rawhide string, flowed down her back, almost touching the belt of her trousers.

She lifted her head. "Scott's been fighting those lung problems off and on for the past ten years. I wish he'd brought his family here to live with us like I wanted him to."

Faith patted Sarah's back. "You pestered him with enough invitations. It's not your fault he didn't come. Maybe this time, he'll see the good sense of coming here and living in the country."

"If it's not too late." Sarah shook that awful thought away. "We better get ready to go."

She packed her art supplies in their case. "I'll ride over to ask Phillip to take care of Paddy and the horses and keep an eye on the place. If we're still away when Benjamin's classes end, he can take over when he gets home." She rose. "Maybe Phillip can give us a ride to the train. That way, I won't have to board Redfire at the livery stable."

Sarah rubbed the back of her neck. "I felt edgy this past week and wondered why. Maybe, because Scott and I are twins, I was picking up on the worsening of his illness." She stuck her current drawing into her art portfolio. "I hope..." She couldn't finish the sentence.

Faith got up and wrapped her arms around her. "Don't let go of that hoping, sweetheart."

Sarah clung to her, trying to absorb some of Faith's strength. She was glad it was Saturday and Faith had been home when the telegram came. She let go of her and said, "I'll hitch Drummer to the buggy so you can go see whether Mrs. Wharton can take your classes. Meantime, I'll ride Redfire to Phillip and Leah's. I'll meet you back here to pack."

"Take Paddy with you. You know Leah will want to keep him at her place."

"Good idea."

* * *

Leah reached up and twined her arms around Sarah's neck to give her a hug. "Haven't seen you for a month, Sarah-Bren Coulter, and that's far too long between visits."

Sarah embraced her and kissed the top of her blonde curls. Leah always smelled sweet, like her nature. Sarah bent and kissed her cheek. "You're right, and I apologize. I had a book deadline to meet, and I barely made it."

"All right, I'll forgive you. Of course, I didn't come to visit you either." Leah's dimples showed as she smiled. "Phillip," she called as she released her friend, "Sarah's here." She leaned down and ruffled Paddy's hair around his ears. "And how are you doing, boy? I bet you want to go into the backyard with Brendan."

Sarah followed as Leah led Paddy to the kitchen and let him out the door. They heard Brendan's squeals greet him, intermingled with Paddy's barks.

"He does love that dog," Leah said. "Have a seat, Sarah. Care for some coffee and cake?"

"I'd be a fool to turn down your cake." Sarah was about to sit when Phillip came into the kitchen.

"Make that two pieces of cake," he said. He grabbed Sarah into a bear hug, swung her around, and set her back on the floor. Tears welled in Sarah's eyes, and her voice broke. "Scott...Scott used to do that."

"Hey, what's wrong?" he asked. Sarah sat down, and he sat next to her. "Is Scott all right?"

Emotion choked her attempt to speak, so Sarah took the

telegram from her pocket and handed it to him. Leah put the cake plates on the table and stood to read over Phillip's shoulder. She put her hand to her mouth. "Oh no. That sounds bad."

Sarah nodded and used some time to compose herself. "Lindsay isn't easily alarmed so it must be. Faith and I are leaving as soon as possible. I came to ask if you'll tend to Paddy and the horses and perhaps give us a ride to the 5 o'clock train."

"No," Phillip said. Sarah and Leah stared at him. He stood up with a grim expression on his face. "If it's all right with Leah, I'm going with you. You and Scott have been my best friends since we were children together. If he's in trouble, I want to be there." He looked at Leah.

"Of course, darlin'. Amy and Franklin can help with the business and the horses. Go." Leah's daughter, Amy, had married Franklin Schmidt, the sheriff's son. Franklin worked as a foreman in Phillip's construction business.

Sarah said, "Yes, please come. I'd appreciate having you with us."

Phillip checked his pocket watch. "That's settled then. We can pick up you and Faith in about two hours."

Sarah stood and hugged them both. "I couldn't ask for better friends."

"And, Sarah," Leah said, "don't even try to take Paddy home with you. He's staying right here."

Sarah wiped tears from her cheeks. "Faith told me you would say that."

Leah grinned impishly. "That's one time she's been right about me." She tugged Sarah back into a seat. "You have time to eat this cake, don't you? You can use the nourishment."

Sarah picked up her fork. "I wouldn't miss it." She noticed that Phillip limped slightly as he went back to his chair. "Is your leg sore?"

"I banged my knee on a trunk yesterday while I was working on a house. No real damage, but the damn thing hurts like hell."

"Watch your language, dear," Leah said.

"What? In front of Sarah? Who do you think I learned it from?"

Sarah punched his arm and laughed, glad to have their friendly banter cheer her up.

Phillip waved his fork at Leah and spoke to Sarah. "The woman gives me no sympathy. When I told her I hurt my knee, she said maybe it should be made of wood like the rest of the leg. Does that sound like a loving wife?"

Sarah tapped his arm, this time with her fist. "If Leah said it, I know it came from a loving wife."

"Come to think of it," Phillip said, "I got this wooden leg from you." His face turned serious. "If I hadn't, I'd have been a goner. Leah and I both are thankful to you for saving my life."

"Most of the time," Leah said with her customary sauciness, and they all laughed.

* * *

The three travelers boarded the train in Bonneforte, Missouri, and disembarked in Wheeling, West Virginia. They switched to a local train that took them to Fairmont, West Virginia, where Scott's relatives still lived and where Sarah and Phillip had grown up.

When they arrived in Fairmont, they rented a buggy and loaded their baggage on it. Phillip guided the horse and buggy to the livery stable in the residential area near Scott's home and paid the owner of the stable to take care of it. Phillip carried two bags, and Sarah and Faith each carried one while they hustled along the block to Scott's.

Lindsay opened the door to Sarah's knock and practically fell into her arms. Sarah barely had time to drop the bag she was carrying and grab hold of her. "Thank God, you're here," Lindsay said.

While she hugged Faith and Phillip, Sarah said, "Phillip insisted on coming, too."

"I'm delighted that you came, Phillip, and you as well, Faith. I know Scott will be pleased to see you."

Sarah picked up the bag she had dropped and followed Lindsay into the kitchen. "Leave your things here, and I'll get you settled later. We've turned the living room into a place for Scott to sleep so he doesn't have to climb the stairs."

"Is he well enough to receive us?" Faith asked.

"He's weak and coughing a lot," Lindsay said, "but he has almost miraculously recovered from that last bout that caused me to send the telegram. Thank God. That scared me."

"Scared us, too," Sarah said.

Lindsay touched Sarah's arm. "I'm sorry. It was…"

Sarah patted her hand. "No, no. You did the right thing. Never hesitate to get in touch when you feel the need."

"Thank you. It's good to know that. He's expecting you and Faith, and he insisted on getting dressed and sitting on the sofa.

Why don't you two come on in and see him, and we'll save Phillip for a surprise." Phillip nodded his agreement, and Lindsay led Sarah and Faith into the room.

Sarah glanced quickly around. A bed filled one corner of the room. Next to it stood an eighteen-inch-square table with medications, bowls, glasses, and spoons on it. Scott sat on a sofa in the other corner. "Scott..." Sarah strode over, sat next to him, and gave him a careful hug. He felt so frail, she hesitated to squeeze him and did it gently. Lindsay sat on Scott's other side.

"Sarah." Scott seemed loath to let her go, but he eventually did and turned his gaze toward Faith. "Hello, Mrs. Pruitt," he said in a formal tone. "Please have a seat." Faith sat in one of the stuffed chairs.

Sarah scrutinized her brother and decided he could stand what she had to say. She gave his shirtsleeve a strong tug. "I'm getting tired of this, Scott, so let's get it straight right away. Faith is as much my spouse as Lindsay is yours. You call her 'Faith,' or we leave."

Scott pressed his lips together and shook his head, but he said, "Faith it is."

Faith dipped her head in acknowledgment as Phillip came through the door.

Scott's face lit up. "Phillip! How good to see you." Phillip shook Scott's hand and bent down and hugged him.

"What are you doing," Phillip said, "scaring all of us? How are you feeling?" He sat in another of the stuffed chairs.

"Better than I did for the past week." Scott stopped and had a fit of coughing. "Sorry. Can't seem to get over this."

"Last week," Lindsay said, "it was never ending. Scott couldn't get out of bed."

She got up and went to the table filled with medications. She picked one up, poured some of it into a spoon, and fed it to Scott. He lifted a handkerchief and wiped his mouth. "Thank you, dear." Lindsay put the implements down and reseated herself.

"You're using laudanum?" Faith asked.

"Yes," Lindsay said. "We're trying to use as little as possible, but sometimes Scott is so wracked with coughs, it seems as though he might burst apart. When that happens, I give him enough to quiet the coughing."

"Scott," Sarah said in a firm tone, "you need fresh air. It's bad enough that you've spent so many years breathing that foul air at the foundry. But this is an industrial area, and most of what you breathe is tainted. Your weak lungs can't stand up to that. You and your family need to come live with us."

Scott's jaw set. "I keep telling you no, and I mean it. We're not going to move."

"Lindsay," Sarah said, "how do you feel about it?"

Lindsay touched Scott's arm and gave him a guilty look. "I have come to believe Sarah's right. You need better air, and you're not going to get it here. The longer we stay here, the worse you get. I think we should go with her."

Scott's face got beet red and he squirmed. "I don't want to live in a household where two women pretend to be married to each other. They're living in sin and flaunting it."

Sarah was surprised at Scott's reaction. Early on, he had appeared to accept Sarah's relationship with Faith. Apparently, over the years, he changed his mind.

"Mother would be appalled," he said.

Aha, Sarah thought. There's the reason for the change of attitude. That saddened her. Why couldn't Scott think for himself?

"Then live at my house," Phillip said.

"No!" Sarah's tone was vehement. "He's my brother." She turned to Scott. "And you're going to live in my house whether you like it or not. And whether Mother likes it or not. You have a family to think of. Are you going to let your prejudice make you stay here and die and leave them to struggle without you?"

Scott coughed and wiped his mouth. "They have plenty of money. They won't want for anything."

"Money's good," Sarah said, "but it isn't the most important consideration in a family. Lindsay needs a husband, and the children need a father. I'm sure they'd trade all the money in the world to make sure you stay with them."

"Of course we would," Lindsay said with passion. She took Scott's hand. "We want you to get over this sickness. We want the old Scott back. As soon as Mother and Father Coulter's visit is over, we'll leave to join Sarah."

"Are Mother and Father here?" Sarah asked before Scott could continue his protests.

"They should be here tomorrow." Lindsay shook Scott's arm. "We're going with Sarah, dearest. I have to seize what could be the last chance to keep you with us, in spite of how you feel about Sarah and Faith."

"Give us a chance, Scott," Faith said. "You might actually learn to respect our right to our views in our own home, even though you don't agree with them."

Scott glared at her and turned to Sarah. "I'll agree to go

with you on one condition. You'll accept fair payment for our living expenses. We won't accept charity, nor do we need to. Coulter Foundry provides enough for all of us."

"All right," Sarah said. "Although I don't consider helping family members to be charity."

Scott opened his mouth to speak but was interrupted by someone bursting through the back door.

There were a couple of thumps, and a young man and woman entered the living room. "Aunt Sarah!" Prescott stopped in front of her, and Sarah stood and hugged him. Jessie hung back.

"Pres," Sarah said as she released him, "how you've grown. You're a shade taller than I am. And I hear you're in college."

"Yes, ma'am, I board at the University of Missouri in Columbia. But with Papa so sick…" He paused and gritted his teeth. "Mama called me back home."

With chestnut-brown hair and the Coulter amber eyes, Pres was the image of his father, and as a result, resembled Sarah. But he had Lindsay's sweet disposition.

Jessie had features similar to Scott and Sarah, but she had black hair and blue eyes, which most people would assume were inherited from Lindsay. Jessie's eyes, though, were an unusual and striking silver-blue. Sarah knew where those blue eyes came from, and seeing them always brought back harsh memories. But she mentally pushed that knowledge away.

Faith greeted Pres with a hug. "We hope you're back for a false alarm."

Sarah opened her arms to Jessie, and the young woman moved closer to Sarah to awkwardly return the hug.

"You're sixteen, now, aren't you?" Sarah asked. "And in your third year of high school? Or did you skip any more grades?" Of course, Sarah knew how old Jessie was, but the Coulter twins didn't make a fuss over family birthdays, so Sarah pretended not to be certain of Jessie's age.

"No, I only skipped seventh." Jessie took a step back. "I turned sixteen, and I'll be a senior next school year."

Faith turned toward Lindsay. "Jessie skipped a grade?"

"Yes. Seventh and eighth grades were both in the same room. Jessie came in first in the midyear exams for seventh grade, so the teacher gave her the eighth grade exam and she came in first again. They immediately moved her into eighth grade, and since then, she's always been the youngest in her class. She does very well in school. So does Pres." Lindsay's voice conveyed her obvious pride.

Faith gave Jessie a hug and said, "Well done, Jessie. As a teacher, I'm always happy to hear when a student excels. Maybe your family could come live with us, and we could talk together about your school studies. Would you like that?"

Jessie examined Faith as though measuring her. "I suppose so."

Pres glanced toward his mother and frowned. "Are we going to live with them?"

"We might," Lindsay said. "But you'll still board at college."

He gave a shrug. "Guess I won't be around much anyway."

Jessie bounced on her toes. "Papa says I'm a lot like you, Aunt Sarah."

Sarah was surprised. "When does he say that?"

"Whenever I'm bad."

Sarah bit her lip to keep from laughing. "What do you do that's bad?"

"She pushes me," Pres said, "when I won't do what she wants me to."

"Does that hurt you?" Sarah said.

Pres stuck out his lip. "No, but I don't like it, and she knows I won't hit her. She's always trying to order me around. And she won't do anything I want to unless I listen to her ideas first."

Phillip slapped his own leg. "Your papa's right. Jessie is very much like her Aunt Sarah. Ornery."

Sarah glared at him, but he laughed. "I have to say that ornery streak never showed up in Scott, but yours was enough for you both. Isn't that right, Scott?"

"More than right," Scott said. "It's a good thing you and I kept her under control, Phillip." Scott's laugh turned into a coughing spell. He stifled it with his handkerchief.

Lindsay patted his back until he stopped. She stood. "All right, everyone, get your hands washed. It's time for dinner."

* * *

The next day, Phillip said, "I'll get the buggy from the livery stable and pick up Mr. and Mrs. Coulter at the train station."

Sarah rose and moved toward the door. "I'll go with you."

Lindsay put a hand on her arm to slow her. "I got your letter about your last visit to your parents, but do Mother and Father Coulter know you never wear dresses anymore?"

"No, I wore a dress there, and we didn't discuss my choice

of clothing. But I'm tired of the pretense. It's time they understood who I am."

"But," Lindsay said, "having them learn that for the first time in a public place might not be a good idea."

Sarah raised an eyebrow, but Lindsay continued to hold onto her arm, gave a sweet smile, and looked her in the eye. Sarah always did have a soft spot in her heart for Lindsay. "You're probably right. I'll wait here."

Lindsay patted the arm she held and let go of it. "Thank you."

A short time later, Phillip delivered the elder Coulters, set their suitcases in the foyer, and went back out. Sarah and Faith stayed in the kitchen while Sarah's parents greeted Lindsay and Scott and their grandchildren. Sarah strode ahead of Faith into the living room and heard her father say, "Has Sarah-Bren arrived yet?" She stopped inside the doorway, and Faith stood at her side.

"Yes, Father, I'm here." Sarah moved forward and embraced him. When she stepped away, he seemed puzzled and Sarah's mother had a sour-lemon expression on her face. She turned away when Sarah approached her for a hug.

Ignoring the rebuff, Sarah motioned Faith forward and put an arm around her waist. "This is Faith Pruitt, the woman I share my life with."

"How do you do, Mrs. Pruitt?" Prescott shook the hand Faith offered. Cynthia didn't acknowledge her.

"I'm well, thank you," Faith said. "It's a pleasure to meet both of you at last."

"Please," Lindsay said, "everyone be seated."

Sarah and Faith remained in the doorway while the others settled down.

"Sarah-Bren…" Cynthia's lip curled, and she said in a disparaging tone, "why are you wearing trousers?"

"I always wear them now, Mother. You know I was never happy in a dress."

"No decent woman wears trousers."

Here we go, Sarah thought. "I happen to disagree. I consider myself a decent woman, and I believe what I wear is my own choice."

At that moment, Phillip came in and Lindsay said, "Any problem at the livery stable?"

"Not a one," Phillip said. "Should I take the suitcases upstairs?"

"Wait!" Cynthia fairly shouted. "I won't stay overnight in

the same house with Sarah-Bren and that...that...woman."

"Mother," Lindsay said in a calm voice, "Sarah and Faith are our guests, and I told you to expect them. I asked them to come here, and I won't make them leave."

Cynthia stood. Shaking with anger, she pointed a finger at Sarah. "I insist you leave." She jabbed the finger at Faith. "And take that...that...evil person with you." She made "person" sound like a dirty word. "You are a disgrace to this family."

Sarah opened her mouth but closed it when Faith squeezed her arm. She whirled on her heel and hurried into the kitchen. Faith followed and Sarah turned to meet her. Tears trickled down her cheeks, and she buried her face against Faith's hair.

Faith embraced her. "Oh, Sarah, please don't cry."

"She's my mother. What she's saying hurts me."

Faith stroked Sarah's shoulder. "Perhaps I should go home."

"No!" Sarah tangled her fingers in the back of Faith's dress and drew her closer. Her voice was choked with emotion. "I need you here. I need your support. More than ever."

Faith tipped her head up and brushed Sarah's lips with a kiss. "Then I'll stay as long as you want me to."

Sarah heard footsteps and felt a pat on her back. "Sarah," her father said, "your mother and I love you. But we don't understand your choices."

Sarah raised her head and met his gaze with tears still wetting her cheeks. "Mother won't even try to understand. Faith and I love each other. Is that so terrible?" She lifted an arm and wiped her face against the cloth sleeve of her suit jacket.

"That's not for me to judge," Prescott said. A moment of quiet followed before he continued. "Phillip suggested we stay overnight at his brother Theo's house, and your mother and I accepted. We'll see you again in the morning." He gave a small bow of his head toward Faith. "I apologize for my wife's rudeness to both of you."

"Thank you," Faith said. He nodded and left the room.

Sarah buried her face once more in Faith's hair and absorbed her soothing warmth.

A few minutes later, Faith took Sarah's hand, led her into the backyard, and they sat on the lawn swing. Faith smoothed her fingers over the back of Sarah's hand again and again. "Do you want to talk about it?"

Sarah took a handkerchief from her pants pocket and wiped her cheeks. She saw a monogram on it and realized the handkerchief was one of Faith's with FPC embroidered in the corner. FPC for Faith Pruitt Coulter. It warmed her heart. "I think I've talked as much as I can about it. I had hoped that after Mother fretted for a while, she would accept you. But she won't. So be it. I'm certainly not leaving you and Benjamin."

"Parents," Faith said, "have predetermined ideas of what their children should do and how they should act. When a child doesn't fit into that mold, it can be traumatic for the parent. And if the parent won't try to understand the child's true self, it can be traumatic for the child. Maybe your mother needs more time. Maybe someday she'll be less judgmental."

Sarah gazed around the yard. She could smell the cut grass and some of the sweet scents that emanated from the flowerbeds neatly bordering the back of the house. A late-spring assortment of blooms displayed a variety of colors. The swing set Scott had asked Phillip to build for the children when they were small had weathered over the years, and one seat hung lopsided from its chains. She lifted her gaze above the treetops to a brilliant sky laced with frothy clouds.

She believed in a Supreme Being. She felt that everything in existence contained a spark of energy from that eternal source and that the whole world was interconnected. She didn't believe that God condemned any of his creations, including women who loved women. God didn't turn his back on his creatures—even though some turned their backs on him. People were the ones who compartmentalized everyone and judged that some weren't as good or as worthy as others. Sarah thought maybe those people needed someone to disparage so they could convince themselves they were more superior. She had hoped her mother wouldn't be like that.

"Maybe my mother will be less judgmental, someday, as you suggest," Sarah said aloud. "Or maybe I should quit caring about what she says." Sarah knew that was unlikely to happen, but oh, how she wished it didn't hurt so much.

* * *

Sarah managed to get through the next day by staying out of her mother's sight. As she came out into the hallway, Lindsay reached the top of the stairs with two large, empty carpetbags.

"Good morning," Lindsay said. "If we're going back with you, I figured we need to get a quick start on packing." She handed Sarah the bags. "Faith's going to help me. How about you give Jessie a hand to pack up her room?"

Sarah took the carpetbags. "Um...Jessie? How about I help Pres?"

"Oh, no. I'll take care of Pres. I feel safer pairing you with Jessie. Pres will want to take everything, and he shouldn't. Jessie's more efficient at making those decisions."

Sarah feigned an innocent expression. "Are you insinuating I would let Pres take whatever he wants?"

"I'm not insinuating anything. I *know* you'd let him take whatever he wants." Lindsay gave her a playful nudge toward Jessie's bedroom door. "Jessie's up. She's already sorting things. Go on in and help her."

Sarah tapped her boot against the bottom of Jessie's door. "Two empty carpetbags coming in."

Jessie opened the door and made way for her to enter. "Set them by the bed, Aunt Sarah." She pointed to a spot.

"What can I do to help?" Sarah rubbed her hands together.

"Whatever I put on the bed gets packed, okay?"

"Fine with me."

Sarah folded the clothes already on the bed and set them in the carpetbag. She glanced up at the wall over Jessie's desk and halted her actions, feeling like her heart stopped for a split-second. Pictures covered the wall, some pen and ink, some in crayon, all finely detailed. "Did you draw those?"

Jessie glanced past her closet door. "Yes. I love to draw."

Sarah leaned in closer to them and touched some of them. "These are amazing. I didn't know you drew so well."

Jessie blushed. "Mama said I take after Papa's side of the family. She said you're an artist in both drawing and writing."

"These are uncommonly good, Jessie."

"A teacher at school showed me how to do some of the shading, but I need help with that and with perspective. She was going to show me next semester." Jessie's face fell. "Now I won't be here for that."

"I can teach you how to do that." The words spilled out of Sarah's mouth, and she couldn't believe her own ears. The last thing she wanted was to spend too much time alone with her cast-off daughter. Perhaps Jessie intuited Sarah's reluctance. She often seemed as uncomfortable as Sarah did, and Sarah thought it safer to keep it that way.

"Wonderful!" Jessie shocked Sarah. She rushed over and hugged her before she could move out of the way. Sarah stood like a stick, and Jessie quickly released her. "I...I'm sorry," Jessie gazed at the floor. "I'm so happy you'll help me." She looked up.

"You still will, won't you?"

Sarah groaned inside but said the only thing she could think to say. "I always keep my word."

The next day, Cynthia and Prescott left for home at noon, and the packing escalated. Sarah grabbed Phillip to help Scott pack, and by evening's end, everything that could be carried was ready to go. Lindsay had arranged for a mover to pack some of their furniture to send by rail, and she left other pieces there to be taken care of later.

Bright and early the next day, they boarded the train, with Scott in a wheelchair, to travel to Sarah's home.

Sarah gazed at them as they took their seats. Guess her family was growing. She was surprised that she liked the idea.

Chapter 8

Three weeks passed before everything was unpacked and situated and everyone was settled. Pres had returned to his university. Phillip helped prepare a room for Scott with the hospital bed and furniture, but he had to work each day and wasn't available much of the time. Leah lent a hand on several of the days while Faith had to teach at school. Faith reported to Scott and Lindsay about the high school and some of the teachers that she knew. Bonneforte had grown enough to support its own high school—the same one Benjamin had attended—and it had a good reputation. Jessie would go there as a senior when the new school year started.

Benjamin wrote to say he'd accepted an opportunity to be a physician's helper in Iowa during the summer. He promised to try to squeeze in a visit home if he could.

Instead of working on her profession during the day, Sarah managed to shift her writing and drawing time to the evenings by gaslight. During daylight hours, she and Lindsay and Faith—when she was available—did the bulk of the unpacking and arranging of the three bedrooms and sitting room in the north wing where Scott, Lindsay, and Jessie would live. Since Pres boarded at his college during the school year, he was given the smallest bedroom, which he said was fine with him. The whole family ate together in the kitchen.

On every clear day, Sarah and Lindsay helped Scott hobble outside to sit in a rocking chair on the porch for several hours, and Lindsay spent some time with him.

* * *

Finally school closed for the summer, Pres returned home, and in her usual friendly way, Faith procured library books for Scott to read to help his idle hours hold more interest. Lindsay or Jessie occasionally read aloud to him on days when he felt too weak to hold the books.

One afternoon, Sarah finished cleaning up after dinner and went out onto the porch. Faith stood at the rail, gazing out toward the woods. She didn't seem to hear Sarah. Sarah sneaked up behind her, snaked an arm around her waist, nudged her hair aside, and kissed her on the neck. After a moment of nearly jumping out of her skin, Faith eased back against Sarah.

Scott also was on the front porch, in his usual chair. Sarah's peripheral vision caught him with a sour expression on his face. She ignored it. "Take a walk with me?" she murmured in Faith's ear.

"Of course," Faith answered with enthusiasm.

Sarah took her hand and led her along a path in the woods. After some time had passed, Faith said, "Are we walking all the way to the lake?"

"No, but certainly far enough to be out of earshot of the house."

"Oooh. That sounds promising."

"I intend to make wild love to you, and I know how you like to scream."

Faith poked her elbow into Sarah's side. "I'm not the only one. You like to scream, too. Having other people in the house has silenced both of us."

They stopped at a flat area covered in sweet-smelling grass. "This looks good, doesn't it?" Sarah reached under her shirt. "And I came prepared." She pulled out a folded sheet that she had stuck in the top of her trousers.

"You think of everything." Faith helped her unfold the sheet and lay it on the grass.

Sarah pulled Faith up against her. They kissed and gradually wound up lying together on the sheet.

Sarah continued to kiss Faith while unbuttoning the front of her dress. She lifted Faith's breasts in turn from the material supporting them and lavished kisses and suckling on each.

Faith said, breathless, "Take your shirt off." Sarah stopped long enough to grab the back of her shirt at the neck and yank it off. Faith's hands immediately closed on Sarah's breasts, and she used her thumbs to flick at Sarah's nipples.

Sarah moaned. "I've been thinking about this all day. I wanted to hold you, to see you, to feel you, to taste you." She accompanied her words with kisses on Faith's face and lips and breasts. Faith writhed with pleasure. Sarah put a hand under her skirt and slid it slowly up Faith's leg until she felt the source of her wetness. "And to enter you." Faith pumped her hips against Sarah's hand in an increasing tempo. Sarah plunged her fingers in and out at the same pace.

Suddenly Faith stopped and tensed. She moved slowly against Sarah's fingers twice. When Sarah felt Faith's muscles clench inside, she curled her fingers, pushed them against bone, and Faith screamed. And screamed. Sarah opened and curled her fingers over and over until Faith stopped screaming. When Faith's muscles quieted down, Sarah withdrew her hand. They clung to each other and kissed each other on the mouth.

"Oh, Bren, Sarah-Bren," Faith whispered. "I love you so much."

"I love you, too, sweetheart."

Faith brushed her hand across Sarah's cheek and then reached for her belt. "It's my turn to give you pleasure."

Faith had been right. Sarah screamed, too.

Chapter 9

After a leisurely Saturday morning breakfast, Faith and Lindsay cleaned the kitchen while the others went their separate ways. A knock came at the back door. Faith dried her hands on a towel and answered the summons. "It's Phillip," she said to Lindsay, having seen him through the windowpane. She opened the door.

"Hello, Phillip. Please, come in."

"Good morning, Faith." Phillip entered, hung his hat on the rack by the door, and nodded to Lindsay. "Lindsay."

Lindsay nodded in return. "Good morning." She put the last of the cleaned dishes in the cupboard.

"Is Sarah here?"

Faith said, "She is. Have a seat, and I'll fetch her." She found Sarah in her writing room, as she expected. "Sarah, Phillip's here and he's asking for you."

Sarah placed her glasses on her drawing board and raised an eyebrow as she prepared to follow Faith. "It's unusual for him to stop so early on a Saturday. Did he say why?"

"No. He asked for you, and I came to get you."

Sarah followed her to the kitchen. "Hello, Phillip." When Phillip began to stand, Sarah waved him back to his seat. "What brings you here this morning?" Sarah and Faith joined Phillip at the table. Lindsay made her excuses and left.

"I was in town this morning when some startling news arrived by telegraph. I thought you should be told. A man shot and wounded President Garfield."

Faith's hand flew to her mouth. "Oh, no."

Sarah said, "How badly? Is he in danger of dying?"

"I don't think anyone knows that for sure yet."

Sarah frowned. "Did they catch the one who did this?"

Phillip shrugged. "Yes, but I don't know any more about it. Instead of telling about it over and over, Hans is going to print a special edition of the *Tribune* with all the news he received. Eric will deliver it around the area."

Hans Grunder, the postmaster, also owned a print shop that

operated in the rear of the postal building and produced the *Bonneforte Tribune*. His son, Eric, doubled as his chief assistant in both areas.

"Good," Sarah said. "I'm sure everyone's interested in hearing all the details. I hope the president gets through this."

Faith clasped her hands together. "I pray that he does. He's a good man."

"And a veteran," Sarah added. They sat in silence for a moment.

Faith touched Phillip's arm and broke the mood. "Would you like a cup of coffee?"

"No, thanks. I have to get moving. Sam Bernard wants an estimate on a toolshed." Phillip stood and Sarah accompanied him to the door.

"Thanks for bringing us the news," she said.

"I figured you'd want to hear it right away." Phillip lifted his hat from the rack and settled it on his head. "Eric will be coming by this afternoon with the print news, I'm guessing. Goodbye, Faith."

"Goodbye, Phillip."

He and Sarah walked outside, and Phillip mounted his horse.

Sarah patted the horse on the nose. "I didn't hear you ride in. I must have been too engrossed in my drawing. Tell Leah I said hello."

Phillip touched the brim of his hat. "I'll do that. Goodbye."

"Goodbye."

He rode off and Sarah returned to the kitchen. She sat at the table, and Faith rose to get them both a cup of coffee. After she set the cups down, Sarah grabbed her hand and kissed the knuckles. Faith raised her eyebrows.

"Just to show my appreciation, Red. I don't think I do that often enough."

Faith leaned down, and what began as a peck on the lips became a full-blown expression of passion. "I appreciate you, too," she said. Sarah pulled her onto her lap and hugged her.

Faith caught her breath and whispered, "Hearing bad news about someone like the president makes us more aware of our own loved ones."

Sarah touched her forehead to Faith's. "You're right about that."

After a moment of silence, Faith said, "I'll go tell Lindsay and Scott."

"Yes, and suggest they join us when Eric comes."

* * *

Eric brought the extra newspaper issue as expected and left to continue his other deliveries. Lindsay and Scott heard him arrive, and they all assembled on the porch.

They sat at the table, and Sarah read the news aloud: "'On Saturday, July 2, President James A. Garfield was shot in the back by Charles Guiteau, a lawyer, in the Baltimore and Potomac Railroad Station in Washington, D.C. When President Garfield entered the station, Guiteau stepped up behind him and shot him twice. One bullet grazed the president's arm, but the other hit him in the back, and he fell to the ground. As police arrested Guiteau and dragged him away, he shouted, 'I am a Stalwart and Arthur is now president.'

"'Conscious but in pain, Garfield was taken back to the White House where he is being attended by a bevy of doctors.'

"'This newspaper will keep the public informed of further information as we receive it.'"

Sarah laid the paper on the table.

Scott said, "Sad news, indeed. But at least he's still alive." He put a handkerchief to his mouth in a futile attempt to stifle a cough.

Lindsay patted his back.

Sarah looked toward them. "Yes, he's alive, but a bullet in the back can cause a lot of damage. We can't know what the future will bring him."

Faith touched Sarah's arm. "We can pray for him and hope that helps."

Sarah grimaced. "Hope. That's all we can do right now."

* * *

By the middle of August, Scott was looking better, although he was still weak and shaky and the cough had barely improved. Step-by-step, Sarah told herself. Be patient. The local weather was so much better for him than what he had been used to. She counted on the healing power of fresh air and sunshine.

Her mind turned to the president. The constant reports on his health had been ambivalent. One would sound promising, and the next wouldn't. The entire country seemed to be hanging on tenterhooks, rightly so, as to whether or not he would recover. Sort of like Scott's situation.

As if they all didn't have enough to worry about, tragedy struck. Sarah and Faith and Lindsay and Scott were sitting on the front porch on a balmy September evening when young Eric Grunder showed up with another telegram, this one addressed to Scott. It was from his mother. He tore it open and read it aloud. "'Red Oak Manor damaged in fire last night. Your father's heart failed. He is in hospital.'" Lindsay grabbed his arm, and he took a deep breath before continuing. "'I'm with our neighbor Mrs. Mortimer. Please come.'" He dropped the telegram on the porch floor, and his eyes brimmed with tears as Lindsay took him into her arms.

Sarah's hand had flown to her mouth. "Father, oh, Father." She started to cry.

Faith got up, sat on her lap, and held her close. "It's all right, sweetheart. It's all right. I've got you."

Only sobs could be heard in the silence that followed.

"I'm all right now," Sarah finally murmured to Faith as she dried her eyes. She hesitated. "Is it all right with you if I bring them here?"

Faith answered promptly, "Of course it is. Your family is my family."

"Thank you, sweetheart." Sarah spoke up to the others. "We have things to do."

Scott's choked voice said, "What can we do?"

Sarah sat up straight. "I'll go. If Father's able to travel"— she took a jagged breath—"I'll bring them both here."

"Do you want me to come with you?" Faith asked.

"Unfortunately, it's probably better if you don't," Sarah said.

"I want to go, too," Scott said.

Sarah's compassion went out to him. He had always been their mother's favorite. "I know you do, but you're not strong enough yet."

He frowned at her. "Mother won't want to come with you."

Sarah lowered her voice, and it sounded flat and threatening. "I'll make her come." Everyone looked askance at her, and she returned her voice to normal. "She has to come. They have nowhere else to go." She reached over and touched Scott's sleeve. "Besides, she'll want to be here with you and Lindsay and the children."

"Sarah's right, darling," Lindsay said to him. "Your parents have to come here if they can. And since you're in no condition to travel, Sarah will have to get them."

And that's what was decided. Sarah sent a telegram to her mother and left that evening.

* * *

Mrs. Mortimer ushered Sarah into the drawing room where Cynthia was waiting, and politely left. Out of deference to her mother, Sarah had once again donned a dress, this one an orange-rust in color.

Cynthia sat on a beautifully upholstered settee that was embroidered with a hunting scene. She plucked a handkerchief from her sleeve and dabbed at her eyes.

"Mother," Sarah said, "I know you're angry with me, but this isn't a time for us to be fighting with each other. We need to get through this together."

Cynthia pursed her lips. "Scott didn't come?"

"He wanted to, but he couldn't. He's very weak. His recuperation will take a long time."

Cynthia seemed lost, and Sarah's heart went out to her. Her parents deeply loved each other. Sarah could imagine how she would feel if something so traumatic happened to Faith. "How is Father?" she asked.

Cynthia dabbed again at her eyes. "At first, he was unconscious. He didn't even know I was there. I stayed overnight, and when I awoke the next morning, he was awake, too. He was confused about what happened, but we spoke about the fire. That disturbed him, so I changed the discussion to pleasanter subjects."

Cynthia stopped talking and took a deep breath. Sarah examined her more closely. The fine lines around her eyes and mouth were more pronounced than they normally were, and her usually impeccable appearance showed some lack of attention. Several tendrils of hair hung loosely on her forehead, and she hadn't applied the lip coloring she usually favored.

"Mrs. Mortimer came to the hospital, and she insisted that I leave with her and stay at her home."

"That was kind of her. Perhaps we can borrow her buggy and go together to see how Father's doing today."

"I'm sure she would allow us to use it." Cynthia tucked her handkerchief into her sleeve and rose. "I'll ask her and we can do that now." She left the room and swiftly returned. "We can go as soon as we want to. Are you ready?"

"Give me half an hour. I need to wash and change. I always feel grimy after a train trip."

"Very well. I'll freshen up and be waiting for you."

* * *

Sarah changed into a brown dress with amber piping around the button placket. Cynthia had combed her hair and applied some color to her lips and cheeks. She and Sarah stopped at the nurse's station, introduced themselves, and inquired about Prescott's condition. The nurse picked up a folder and opened it. "Doctor Rouman saw him about twenty minutes ago. His heartbeat is thready and erratic." She closed the folder and raised her gaze to meet Sarah's. Unspoken words passed between them.

"Is he awake?" Cynthia asked in a tremulous voice.

"He woke when Doctor Rouman stopped to see him, and they talked. He's in Room 14." She pointed. "Right over there."

They entered Prescott's room, and Sarah's heart plummeted when she saw how pale he was. His skin had a bluish tinge. He seemed to be sleeping.

His eyes fluttered open when Cynthia took hold of his hand. "Prescott, Sarah's here to see you," she said.

Her father's voice was whispery and his words halting. "Sarah. I'm glad you came. Your mother needs you."

Sarah laid her hand on top of the one Cynthia held. "Scott wanted to come, too, Father, but he's not yet strong enough to make the trip. He and his family send their love. So does Faith."

A tear trickled down Prescott's cheek. "Our home burned down."

"Yes," Cynthia said, "but we both survived, and that's a blessing."

He grimaced. "I suppose we'll have to rent somewhere until we can rebuild."

Sarah was pleased that his mind appeared to be clear. "Father." She leaned closer. "If you're able to travel, I want to take you and mother home with me. You can recuperate there among your family." Sarah didn't hold much hope that he would recuperate enough to live on his own again. But she knew he would try to.

A flush covered Cynthia's face, and she bounced about in her chair. Her raised voice sounded shrill. "We will not go to live with you!"

"But you must," Sarah said. "You have no real choice."

"Your father is lying in the hospital, and here you are bullying me to do something I don't want to do. You should be ashamed of yourself."

Prescott wiggled the hand the two women were holding. His voice sounded a little stronger. "Cynthia. Don't be so hasty. I believe we should consider Sarah's offer."

The nurse came in. "I'm sorry to interrupt you, but I think you should leave. Mr. Coulter needs his rest."

Sarah wondered whether the nurse overheard their discussion, thought it was elevating to an argument, and decided to intervene. At any rate, it was good timing. She had learned that her father wasn't resistant to the idea of living with her, but her mother needed more persuasion.

"Goodbye, Father. We'll be back as soon as we can." She kissed her father's cheek and went into the hall. While she waited for her mother to rejoin her, she saw a doctor at the nurse's station and approached him. "Excuse me. Are you Doctor Rouman?"

"I am." He was an inch or two shorter than Sarah, and gray strands flecked his dark, wavy hair. He stood with hunched shoulders as though carrying a heavy weight.

"I'm Mr. Coulter's daughter, Sarah. What can you tell me about his condition?"

Dr. Rouman's dark eyes grew kinder. "Your father's heart is very weak. We have no medicines to help him other than laudanum to keep him comfortable and out of pain."

Sarah explained the circumstances. "Can he travel by train to Missouri?"

"I don't see why not. As long as you make sure he stays comfortable and gets plenty of rest. Be aware that he'll tire easily. You can pick up laudanum at the grocer's. Start with 10 drops and don't surpass 30 for each occurrence of pain."

"Can I move him tomorrow?"

Dr. Rouman touched a finger to his chin. "I'd like to see him in the morning, and if his condition hasn't worsened, I'll sign him out and you can be on your way."

"Thank you, Doctor."

* * *

Sarah and Cynthia went back to Mrs. Mortimer's house and were once again in her drawing room.

Cynthia sat on the settee. "I will not go to live with you!"

"Mother..." Sarah hesitated. Should she wait until morning and see her father's condition first? No, it would save time to settle the situation now. "I refuse to argue with you. If Father's able to travel, you will come home with me. Tomorrow."

"Your father wouldn't be pleased to hear you dictating to me."

Sarah sat in a high-backed chair whose embroidered cushions matched the settee. Her voice caught for a second before she finally freed it. "Father would want me to do exactly what I'm doing. Taking care of you both."

"I believe I should have some say in the matter." Cynthia bristled. "I will not live under the same roof with you and that woman, and you can't force me to."

"Mother..." Sarah searched for words to persuade her. "We have a large house. You would live in the same wing with Scott and his family, so technically, you wouldn't be under the same roof."

"I would be in the same house. Don't twist your words to make it sound better." Cynthia sniffed. "You always were able to manipulate words."

Sarah said in a low, grating tone, "I thought you said you admired that." Feeling guilty about sparring with her mother, she waved the remark away. "All right, think about this. Scott and his family will be staying with me for years. Do you want to be away from them all that time? If Father..." She couldn't say it. "If anything happens to Father, you could be alone here."

Cynthia's chest heaved up and down. Tears slid from her eyes and ran down her cheeks. She wiped them away with her handkerchief. "I would be all alone," she whispered.

Sarah rose, stepped to sit beside her, and embraced her. When Cynthia tried to move away, Sarah held her tighter. "You'll never be all alone, Mother," she murmured into Cynthia's ear. "You have Scott and me and our families." She felt Cynthia jerk when she said "our" families. But Sarah was determined that her mother and father were coming home with her no matter what Cynthia felt at the moment. Her husband was seriously ill, after all, and she was too emotionally upset to think clearly.

Sarah held Cynthia until she physically wilted. "All right," Cynthia said. "I don't know what else to do. We'll go with you."

* * *

Sarah borrowed Mrs. Mortimer's buggy again. She stopped by the train station and made arrangements to have a separate car added to tomorrow's 11 a.m. train for her family's use. Thank goodness they had no money restraints. She walked over to the telegraph office and sent Faith information on their journey and what they would need when they arrived. When she left the building, she noticed a bulletin about the president's health was taped to a window. It reported that President Garfield had experienced no change in his condition.

Sarah got in Mrs. Mortimer's buggy and went to the hospital office. With their help, she hired a nurse to accompany them on their journey and a bed and wagon to transport her father to the train.

She went to Red Oak Manor and spoke to Matthias about her parents' decision to give the property to him and his family.

"Your daddy already told me about that, Miss Sarah. Bless their hearts. I was always proud as could be about serving your parents. All my family was."

"And you have all been wonderful about it. Matthias, it's unlikely that Father will ever be able to return here. I think you and your family should assume the place is yours. When Father is a bit better, I'll have him sign and send the papers to you."

Matthias fought against his grief. "I'se sad for your mama and daddy. Losing their home and having them move away...probably forever...this be a hard day for us, too."

Sarah put an arm around his shoulder and patted his back. "I understand, my friend. Father and Mother were lucky to have you and Pearl to take care of them. Scott and I were lucky, too."

When Sarah stepped back, Matthias took a handkerchief from his pocket and blew his nose. "It was our honor and pleasure. How's Mr. Scott doing? Your daddy said he was mighty sick with lung trouble."

"He's a bit better since he's getting more fresh air and sunshine. We're very hopeful he'll have a full recovery."

"Good to hear that. Healing takes time."

Yes, Sarah thought, all healing takes time. Grief and anger and even prejudice. She hoped time would heal her mother.

Chapter 10

Sarah was glad Lindsay brought Jessie to the station to meet the train. Her presence perked Cynthia up a bit as they talked back and forth. That gave Sarah time to oversee Prescott's transfer from the train car to the bed and wagon she had wired ahead for. Phillip and his son-in-law, Franklin Schmidt, carefully moved Prescott to the bed and then jumped down from the wagon.

Sarah thanked the nurse who had accompanied him and paid her a bonus for her services.

"How are you feeling, Father?" Sarah had been at his side for every second of the relocation. He seemed to take everything well.

"Tired, I guess, but that's not surprising, is it?" A faint smile curved his lips. "I slept most of the way, though, so I'm not exhausted."

Cynthia and Jessie approached him. Cynthia kissed him and squeezed his arm. "Look who came to welcome you," she said and pulled Jessie forward.

"Hello, Grandfather." She patted Prescott's arm. "I used to hate having to leave you, and now I'll be able to see you all the time. I'm excited about that."

"Hello, my sweet Jessie. You are so much like your...like Aunt Sarah. You remind me of her when she was your age." He stopped and took a deep breath.

"Everyone tells me that."

Cynthia said, "Is that Phillip I see?"

Phillip and Franklin had stood aside to wait until everyone was ready for the wagon to get underway. Now Phillip strode forward.

"Yes, ma'am." He gestured toward Franklin. "And this is my son-in-law, Franklin Schmidt. When Sarah wired Faith for a wagon and drivers, we couldn't pass up the chance to be of assistance. Welcome to Bonneforte."

Cynthia hugged him. "Thank you, Phillip. And you, too, Franklin. It's good to see a friendly face."

Sarah figured that was a dig at her. She'd have to work on feeling friendly to her mother. "We better get going now. People at home are expecting us. Phillip, we'll go ahead with the buggy. You and Franklin take your time and make sure Father's trip is smooth, please."

"We'll do our best, Sarah."

She gave him a hug. "I know you will."

"Can I ride with Grandfather?" Jessie asked.

Sarah gave her a quick smile. "I think that's a great idea."

Prescott added, "I do, too. Thank you, Jessie."

* * *

For Sarah, the ride home with her mother didn't have one bright spot in it. Not one unnecessary word passed between them. Part of this, Sarah tried to console herself, was because of her mother's grief over Father's health problems and the loss of her home. But some of it was mean-spirited ill will, and that hurt.

At the house, Scott and Lindsay and Pres welcomed Cynthia, who brushed past Faith as though she weren't there. They ushered Cynthia into their wing of the house.

Sarah rushed into Faith's open arms like a long-lost lover returning home. Which she was, except for the long-lost part.

"How was your trip?" Faith asked quietly.

"Bad." Sarah held her tightly. "We'll talk about that later. Phillip and Franklin will be here soon with Father and Jessie." She released her hold and stepped back.

"Jessie?"

"Yes, she wanted to ride in the wagon with Father. I don't blame her. It had to be a happier ride than the one in the buggy. Do you remember the children's game where you tried to see who could keep quiet the longest? I bet Mother probably won every game she was in."

Faith leaned in and gave Sarah a quick kiss.

Sarah said, "I'll be so glad when this is all over, and we can get back to a normal life."

"Good luck with that," Faith said in a wry tone. "Your mother didn't appear too happy to see me."

"She'll have to adapt."

"Uh-huh. Adapt."

"We'll have to adapt, too."

"Uh-huh. Adapt."

Sarah managed a tiny grin and poked Faith in the side with her elbow. "We can do this."

When the wagon carrying Prescott arrived, Phillip and

Franklin moved him with a stretcher into the room on the ground floor that he and Cynthia would share. He promptly went to sleep. Sarah gave Cynthia a sedative in a glass of iced tea that Faith had prepared ahead of time—not that Sarah told Cynthia about the sedative. At any rate, Cynthia went off to her room to rest with Prescott, and Sarah joined Faith on the living room sofa.

"Thank you," she said to Faith, "for having that sedative ready. Mother desperately needed something to calm her down."

"I'm sure. Her anxiety and concern must be near crippling. She and your father have been married for a long time."

"And they truly do love one another. As different as they are, their love has always been strong."

Faith twined her fingers in Sarah's. "Like us."

"Like us." Sarah turned her head toward Faith. "Do you think we're as different as they are?"

"Mmm. That could be a dangerous question. You're definitely very much like your father. I'm not sure I'm that much like your mother."

"Both of you are more emotional and more sociable. You like people and enjoy mingling with them."

"Your mother seems to enjoy mingling only with those who share her views."

"Mother has a lot of good points. Unfortunately, she's allowing her bigotry to override them."

"That's too bad," Faith said. "I think we could have been good friends."

Sarah patted her arm. "I'm sure you would have been. She's missing out on that possibility by not getting to know you better. Let's hope she eventually changes her mind about us." She hesitated for a moment. "Life will be a lot easier for all of us if she does. But don't hold your breath waiting for that to happen."

* * *

Over the next few days, Prescott rallied. He was able to get out of bed and take care of himself. Because of his weakness and fatigue, he had to use a cane for balance. Other than that and suffering periods of chest pain that the laudanum controlled, he tried to return to his normal self. He and Cynthia spent the good-weather days sitting on the porch or strolling around the backyard. Scott usually accompanied them. And so did Paddy.

At first it surprised Sarah that Paddy would leave his resting place beside her in the pagoda and follow along with her mother and father for their stroll. Granted, the first time her father had been out for a walk, he called to the dog and made over him when Paddy answered the call. Ever since then, Paddy had gotten up from his spot at Sarah's feet and loped over to join Prescott and Cynthia as soon as he saw them come down the back porch steps. He had never run to Scott when Scott paced around by himself. Sarah figured Paddy loved her father as much as she did. She loved Scott, too, but she had to admit she loved her father more.

It pleased her that she could see her parents from her chair in the pagoda and know they were all right. She noticed her father had to stop periodically, and she supposed it was to catch his breath. Still, the exercise was good for him and also good for Scott.

No one knew of a cure for a weakened heart. Sarah understood her father was living on borrowed time, and she was grateful for however much of that he had left.

Chapter 11

One Saturday morning near the end of August, Faith approached the porch stairs as Cynthia and Prescott came outside. "Good morning," Faith said.

"Good morning, Faith," Prescott said. "It looks like another beautiful day." Cynthia ignored her. Prescott waved Faith on ahead of them with his cane.

"Indeed, it does," Faith answered, and she ambled down the stairs with them behind her.

Partway down, Prescott stumbled. Faith grabbed the banister with one hand and Prescott's arm with the other. "Sarah! Help!"

Prescott's weight wrenched her shoulder, but she held on and halted his fall. Sarah ran outside with Paddy following her. Faith released her hold as soon as Sarah grabbed Prescott and lowered him to a step. Lindsay, Jessie, and Pres showed up almost immediately.

Lindsay put her arm around Cynthia, whose voice wavered. "I tried to stop him, but I couldn't reach him."

"That was probably good," Faith said. "You might have fallen, too." She rubbed her shoulder.

Sarah sat next to Prescott. "Father, are you all right?"

He looked rattled and was breathing heavily. "I'm not sure." He still had hold of the cane, and he shook it as though it were the culprit. "This consarned thing missed the step, and my momentum pitched me forward." Sarah took the cane from him and handed it to Jessie.

Prescott raised his gaze to Faith who stood on the sidewalk below him. "Thank you, my dear. You may have saved my life." He put his hand over his heart and grimaced. "For the moment, anyway."

Sarah asked, "Can you make it back up the stairs with our help?"

"I'll try."

Sarah and Faith got him up, and Faith said, "Pres, would you take your Aunt Sarah's place, please?" Sarah suffered constant pain even when walking or standing on her weak leg, and Faith saw no need to put a further burden on it.

"Of course."

Sarah seemed surprised, but she moved out of the way so Pres could put Prescott's arm over his shoulder. They got him up the steps and sat him in a chair on the porch. Cynthia fussed about him.

"Mother," Sarah said, "why don't you turn down the bed, and Faith and Pres can take Father there? I'm sure he could use the rest."

"I'll help," Lindsay said. Sarah nodded and went back inside.

While Cynthia and Lindsay attended to that, Faith and Pres helped Prescott to his feet and bolstered him on his journey through the house to the bed. They set him on the side of it, and Cynthia shooed them away. "I can take care of him, now. Thank you for your help." Her gaze never met Faith's.

"Thank you both," Prescott said. He patted Faith and Pres on the arm.

Lindsay, Pres, and Jessie returned to the sitting room in Scott and Lindsay's part of the house, while Faith continued on into the quarters she shared with Sarah. She put a hand to her shoulder. It hurt. Maybe she should use a sling for a while. She stood a moment in the sitting room rubbing the injured part.

Sarah heard Faith come back so she entered the sitting room. "Sorry I deserted you. When you yelled, I got up so fast I overturned a bottle of ink. You seemed to have everything under control, so I wanted to clean that up before it dried. Is everything all right?"

"Once we got your father situated on the bed, your mother insisted we leave. She never even looked at me."

Sarah put an arm around Faith's waist. With her other hand, she joined Faith in rubbing her shoulder. Faith winced and Sarah stopped. "It hurts that bad?"

Faith nodded.

"I'll get some liniment." Sarah started toward the kitchen and Faith followed. "Stay here. I'll bring it to you."

Faith shook her head no. "I'm after a sling. I think I'll need one for a while."

Sarah applied the liniment, and Faith slipped her arm into a sling formed from a tied towel. Sarah said, "I'm sorry you got hurt. You barely know my father, but you didn't hesitate to endanger yourself by helping him. And my mother didn't even thank you."

They went back to the sitting room. Faith said, "I didn't do it for your mother. I did it for your father. And for you. I know how much you love each other."

Sarah hugged Faith and spoke against her hair. "He's more than my father. He's always been my ally." She let go of Faith, and they sat together on the sofa.

"I've told you about my travels through the forests when I was a youngster, but I didn't tell you the whole story. Mother would have forbidden me to travel alone if Father hadn't stuck up for me. She was so disapproving that I stopped telling her when I was leaving. I told Father instead. He would tent his fingers by his lips and say, 'Your mother isn't happy about your going out on your own.' But his eyes would be twinkling." Sarah laughed.

"I told him I needed some time to myself, and the trees were my friends. I'd much rather be with them than with girls my age. I thought their talks were silly—all about boys and clothes and hairstyles. I think he knew then why I was different from other girls— long before I did. In a way, he's had to dance to Mother's tune, but I knew all along that he wasn't judgmental. He's always been supportive of me."

Faith laid her free hand on Sarah's thigh. "He's a remarkable person."

"That he is."

"Like his daughter."

Sarah grinned. She clasped the hand that rested on her thigh and lifted Faith up with her as she stood. "On that note, I think we should see about lunch."

"I'll fix plates for your mother and father so they can eat in their room."

Sarah raised the hand she still held and kissed Faith's fingers. "I'll help. I love that you're always so thoughtful."

* * *

Three days later, Prescott rejoined the family for breakfast after having taken his meals in his room since the near-fall. The grayness around his mouth and eyes worried Sarah. After breakfast, she followed him and Cynthia to the porch where they settled in chairs at one of the wooden tables. Lindsay and Pres and Jessie were settled at the adjoining table. Faith came out and Sarah lifted a hand to suggest Faith sit next to her. Her mother's pinched-mouth expression sent a message, but Sarah ignored it. She looked up at

Faith, nodded her head toward the chair, and Faith sat.

Prescott seemed sad when he spoke to Faith. "I hear you had a sling on your arm. I'm sorry I was the cause of that."

"Not to worry, sir. I'm glad I was there to help."

"You saved me from a nasty fall, and I'm quite grateful. Thank you."

Faith inclined her head. "You're very welcome. I took the sling off yesterday evening. My shoulder healed quickly, so please don't be concerned about it." She moved her arm around. "It's as good as new."

A soft smile tilted the corners of Prescott's mouth. "I wish I could say the same about me." He gave a short cough and then a longer one. He didn't seem able to stop.

Faith jumped up. "Let me get you some water."

"Wait," Prescott choked out. He lurched forward in the chair, and Cynthia grabbed his hand. He gazed over at her and lifted their entwined hands to his chest. Going completely limp, he slid toward his wife and carried them both to the ground.

"No!" Cynthia landed heavily next to him. She put an arm around his neck and held his head to her breast. "Please don't leave me," she called to him. Tears ran down her cheeks. "Please don't leave me."

Sarah knelt at his side and felt for a pulse. "He's gone," she whispered, and her chin dropped to her chest. Her heart felt like it had a hole in it. Faith's hand touched her shoulder and kneaded the muscle there. She would take time to mourn later. Right now, they had to tend to her father.

She straightened up and saw that Lindsay and Pres and Jessie were consoling her mother. Everyone except Faith was crying, and even she had tears in her eyes. "We have to get Father into a bed," Sarah said. "Lindsay, we can put him in the extra bedroom in your wing."

"Of course," Lindsay said. "I'll get the bed ready. Pres, you and Jessie stay here and help Aunt Sarah. I'll tell your father."

"I want to come with you to tell Father." Pres put his arm around his mother's waist.

"I'll stay here and help," Jessie said.

"All right." Lindsay and Pres hurried away

"Sarah," Faith said, "perhaps you and Jessie could lay your father on the porch, and I'll get the short ladder from the barn. We can carry him on that."

"We'll do that, Faith. Thank you."

Faith went off to the barn, and Sarah and Jessie gently

arranged Prescott's body. Through it all, Cynthia held her husband's hand.

Sarah and Jessie moved around her and knelt to straighten his limbs. Tears ran down Jessie's face as she gently smoothed the front of her grandfather's linen shirt.

Silently, Sarah kissed her father's forehead. Over and over, she smoothed her palm against his cheek.

Scott came out the door with Lindsay and Pres, knelt next to Cynthia, and embraced her shoulders. "Oh, Father," he said. He touched his father's arm and wept.

Faith came back with the ladder, and the others lifted him onto it. Scott tried to help, but he didn't have enough strength yet. He loosened his mother's hand from his father's, rose with her, and they moved aside.

Faith said, "Jessie, suppose you and Pres take the foot of the ladder and lead the way. Your Aunt Sarah and I will take the head."

So that's what they did, though Faith tried to take on more of the weight than Sarah.

Sarah realized that Faith was trying to save her from carrying too heavy a load, but this was her father. Her leg didn't matter. She moved Faith's hand away and took her share of the weight. "I can do this," she said through clenched teeth. "Mind your sore shoulder." Faith glanced at her, but she didn't say anything.

With Scott and Cynthia following, they moved into the house and finally arranged Prescott on the bed Lindsay had stripped. She'd left a folded sheet at the bottom to cover him.

To Faith, Sarah said, "We need to let Benjamin know. By the time he gets word, he won't be able to be here for the burial, but at least he'll be aware."

"Do we have to notify any authorities of the death?" Scott took a handkerchief from his pocket and wiped his eyes.

"Not in this state," Sarah said. "I checked with Sheriff Schmidt quite some time ago about that."

Scott had been in such poor health when he came to Missouri that she'd thought it best to find that out. Missouri didn't have any laws about informing the city or state, although some states did. Some states also had laws about undertakers and cemeteries, but Sarah had discovered those requirements didn't apply in Missouri.

"We're free to do as we choose. I think I'd like to have him laid out here in the house and bury him on our land." Sarah looked to her mother who seemed at a loss about what to do. "Is that all right with you, Mother?"

Cynthia wrung her hands, but her voice sounded stronger. "I think your father would like that."

"So do I," Sarah said. "We'll have to lay Father to rest quickly, though. I would say day after tomorrow after the viewing. Mother, if you'll pick out the clothes you want to dress Father in, Lindsay and I can wash... him." She couldn't say "the body." Not yet.

Pres said, "I'll go with you, Grandmother." He took Cynthia's arm and they left the room.

Faith said, "I can help with the washing."

"What can I do?" Jessie asked. Her tears had finally stopped.

Sarah had forgotten Jessie was in the room. "We need water and washcloths and towels. You can help me gather those." Sarah turned to leave, and Faith put a hand on her arm.

"Why don't you let us take care of this while you go into town and purchase a coffin? Maybe Scott would go with you. Maybe even your mother."

"That's a good idea." Sarah silently thanked Faith for her suggestion. Better to keep busy for a while at something that needed to be done anyway. "But I'm pretty sure Mother will want to stay here with Father as long as she can." She gazed toward Scott and raised an eyebrow.

"Yes, I'll go with you."

"Sarah." Faith let go of her. "Please stop and tell Reverend Leland about your father. You might want to invite him to say a few words at the end of the viewing before we close the coffin. And tell Herman, too."

Sarah put a hand to her mouth. "I have to let Leah and Phillip know. Phillip knew Father all of his life. I'll stop there, too."

Sarah reached an arm out to Faith and embraced her. She kissed Faith's temple. "Can you and Lindsay do the actual washing? I don't think Mother or Jessie should do that."

"Of course we can."

"Thank you for taking care of..." Sarah's throat clogged up.

Faith hugged her. "Even in such a short time, I loved your father. It's my privilege to take care of him." She gave Sarah a little nudge and stepped away. "Go now."

* * *

Sarah hitched Drummer to the wagon and brought the

wagon to the side door. Scott came out, carrying a cane, and Sarah gave him a hand using the step up into the wagon seat. She recognized that it bothered him to need her help, but he couldn't manage by himself. He probably shouldn't come, but Sarah knew he wanted to be part of the preparations, and so she tried to overlook his weakness.

She untied the reins, climbed onto her seat, and started Drummer ambling down the road.

Now that she was away from all the hustle and bustle of her father's passing, the loss struck her more strongly. Visions of her father from the past marched through her mind.

"It's hard," Scott said after a prolonged silence.

Deep in her own thoughts, Sarah jumped at the sound of his voice. She glanced over at him. He was staring straight ahead.

"It's hard losing Father," he said. "Even though we expected it. The reality hurts a lot."

"Yes, it does." Sarah rubbed her chest, trying to ease the ache in her heart. "I've been thinking. There's a lovely clearing about 500 yards from the house that would be a perfect spot for Father's grave. How does that sound to you?"

"I like that idea."

"Good. Then Mother will, too."

"Probably," Scott said. "You know, Father always loved you more than he did me."

Sarah turned her head and gazed squarely at him. "I think that might be so, but Mother has always loved you more than she does me."

Scott huffed a laugh. "You're right. That seems kind of backwards, doesn't it?" He gave Sarah a speculative glance. "In a way, though, I think he considered you more of a son than I was. You were always such a tomboy—much bolder than I ever was. And he seemed to like that."

"And you've always been the perfect gentleman, and Mother likes that."

"Still, I'm going to miss him mightily. We grew closer together in the short time we spent here." He nodded toward Sarah. "Thanks to you."

"And to Faith. None of you would be here without her agreeing to it and doing a lot of extra work to accommodate everyone."

Scott stiffened in his seat and stopped talking.

That didn't bother Sarah. He had his nose so far up their mother's... *Stop it, Sarah!* She had her own mourning to do.

* * *

When Sarah and Scott informed Leah and Phillip of Prescott's passing, they expressed their sympathies. Phillip blinked quickly, and his eyes filled with moisture. He hugged Scott, then he grabbed Sarah and lifted her against him. He held her tight, not speaking, and Sarah cried and buried her head into the crook of his neck. Phillip kissed the top of her head and rubbed circles on her back. He sat down on the sofa with her and held her next to him until she stopped crying. After she quieted down, he handed her his handkerchief. "Are you   all right?" he asked.

"Yes, thank you." She dried her face and handed the handkerchief back to him.

"You look so forlorn, and of course you are. I'm so sorry you lost your father. I loved him, too."

"I know you did, and he loved you. He used to hint that I was crazy to turn you away." Sarah laughed shakily. "He eventually realized I would never marry any man, and he was all right with that. He never reproached me for it."

Phillip nodded. "He was a wise and generous man."

Phillip gazed at Scott, who sat in a chair across from them. "I'm sorry, Scott. I know you'll miss your father. I'll miss him, too. He was a good man."

Scott blinked his eyes rapidly. "Thank you, Phillip."

Leah had gone out of the room, and she returned with a tea service and cookies that she put on the table next to the sofa. "I think we're all ready for a cup of tea." She poured and fixed a cup for each of them, handed them around, and sat in a chair next to Scott.

She looked at Sarah. "I didn't know your father well, but I can see where you got your strength of character. He was a true gentleman. Will you and Scott please accept my condolences?"

"Thank you," Scott said.

Sarah got up and Leah rose from her chair. They embraced and Sarah held on to her for an extended time. She finally released Leah and said, "Thank you." She returned to the sofa, and they all sipped their tea and reminisced about Prescott.

Leah said, "If there's anything I can do to help—"

Sarah cut her off. "I think Faith and Leslie and I and the rest of the family can take care of most that needs done, but thank you."

Eventually, Sarah said, "The viewing and the burial will

happen at our home the day after tomorrow. We have yet to speak to Reverend Leland, but we're going to ask him to say some prayers before we close the coffin. I'd appreciate your being there."

"Of course, we'll be there," Leah said. "And I'm sure Amy's family will attend, too."

Phillip spoke and all gazes turned to him. "Have you chosen a gravesite?"

"We have," Scott answered. "Sarah offered to have him buried on her property. That seems more fitting than a cemetery at a church he didn't attend."

"I agree," Phillip said. "I can have a couple men take care of digging and preparing the site, and I'll assist in putting your father in the coffin and sealing it for you. Maybe even drive the wagon if you want me to."

"Thank you, Phillip," Scott said through tight lips. "I know Father would be pleased with your help."

"I surely am, too," Sarah said in a heartfelt tone. "I had visions of taking care of all of that myself."

Phillip brought a pencil and paper, and Sarah drew a diagram for where the gravesite would be. She had decided on a clear site in the woods about five hundred yards from the western side of the house. She noted on the diagram that the head of the grave would be on the west side of the site, and the headstone would face east. An area wide enough for two graves would be prepared, and Prescott would be buried on the south side of it. Customs differed as to which side a wife should be buried on. Sarah had taken it upon herself to choose the grave on Prescott's left for Cynthia's eventual use.

"Phillip," Sarah said, "will you please come over the day after the burial and help me decide what to do with the area around the gravesite? I'd like to put some kind of fence around it."

"I'll be there."

"Thank you. Around nine o'clock would be good. Now," she said, "Scott and I have to see Reverend Leland about the prayers." She took a deep breath. "And Mr. Ehrlich about a coffin." And Herman. I can't forget Herman.

* * *

"Scott," Sarah said from her seat next to him in the wagon, "I need to go first to the post office and send Benjamin a telegram about Father's passing. Sadly, he won't be able to get home before the burial. Perhaps I should tell him not to come home, in case he tries. No sense in interrupting his studies when he can't get home in time to say goodbye."

Scott didn't reply.

After leaving the post office, Sarah inquired about local funeral customs from Reverend Leland and made arrangements for him to come to the house and say some prayers. At the carpenter shop, she assured Mr. Ehrlich that they only needed to purchase a coffin; that she and her family would take care of the burial. Scott remained silent through all of this, so Sarah carried on alone in making the necessary arrangements. She bought a plain, pine wood coffin, and Ehrlich and a helper loaded it in the wagon.

She stopped in the sheriff's office to tell Herman the news, and he assured her that he and his family and some of the deputies would come to the viewing.

After they returned home, Sarah asked Scott to gather the family in the parlor so she could tell them of the arrangements. Meanwhile, she took care of Drummer and the wagon. Rather than struggle to remove the coffin, she left it in the wagon bed. When finished with the horse, she joined the family in the main sitting room. Faith wasn't there, so Sarah went after her and found her seated on Sarah's writing bench, thumbing through a pile of drawings in progress.

"Why aren't you in with the others?" Sarah asked.

"I didn't want to intrude on the family during their grief."

Sarah reached out a hand. "You're part of the family. Come back with me."

Faith jogged the drawings together and set them down. She took the offered hand, and Sarah tugged her up and closed her arms around her. "Remember, I consider you as much my wife as Lindsay is Scott's, and you belong with us. Don't let Mother's snide glances and rude remarks keep you away. Don't let her win."

"Since you put it that way..." Faith rose up on tiptoes and kissed Sarah. "Let's go join our family."

* * *

Sarah said to the gathered family, "Reverend Leland will be here the day of the viewing at five o'clock and will hold a short service for Father. He offered to pass the word about the viewing. He said we should expect people to arrive here around three, and most will bring food to be served after the burial. We'll need to supply some of that, too, and enough places to sit and eat."

"We'll need extra chairs," Scott said.

Faith said, "I can pick some up at the church."

"I'll help you." Jessie blushed when they all turned to regard her.

Faith gave her a smile. "I'd appreciate that. Thank you."

"Mother," Sarah said, "Scott and I think Father should be buried here on this property. I have in mind a lovely spot for that. Is that all right with you?"

Cynthia hesitated.

Sarah bit her lip and was grateful when Scott spoke up.

"Father never attended the church here, so Sarah and I thought it better to bury him on this land. The place she described to me is close enough for us to walk to his grave whenever we want to."

Cynthia gave him a wan smile. "That sounds like a fine choice."

Sarah continued. "Phillip will send two men to dig the gravesite, and he'll prepare it. He'll also help us put Father into the coffin, seal it for us, and drive the wagon carrying it."

Faith asked, "Did you find out what people around here usually do when there's a death in the family?"

Sarah peered at each of them as she spoke. "Reverend Leland tells me that it's customary for the deceased to be laid out in the parlor on a flat surface that's covered with a sheet—usually a door placed on wooden sawhorses. The deceased is usually wrapped in a sheet, too, but I like the idea of having Father dressed as you've done and letting people see him. Death isn't pretty, but it's part of reality. Is that all right with everyone? Mother?"

Cynthia nodded and the others also agreed.

Jessie said, "I can gather flowers to put around the room, too, if you like. Even though autumn is nearly over, a lot of beautiful flowers are still blooming."

"That's a wonderful idea," Cynthia said. "Your grandfather always loved flowers." She dabbed her eyes with a handkerchief.

"The more flowers, the better," Sarah said to encourage Jessie. Their aroma would help cover the scent of death.

"We have a ton of vases," Faith said, "and also various tables to put them on. They're in the basement under our part of the house. Remind me, and I'll take you down to pick some out."

"Thank you, Aunt Faith."

Sarah saw her mother cringe, probably at Jessie's saying "Aunt Faith." That made her sad—and angry. Now that she didn't have her father to work at persuading her mother to accept Faith as

Sarah's partner, would Cynthia ever come to that acceptance on her own?

* * *

On Monday, prior to the viewing, Eric Grunder delivered a telegram to the Coulter house from Benjamin. He expressed his deep sadness at Prescott's passing and his distress at not being present to support the family.

People started coming to the viewing shortly after three o'clock, as Reverend Leland had predicted. Some lingered only for a while before leaving, and some stayed for the five o'clock prayer gathering. Leah, her daughter, Amy, and Amy's husband, Franklin, came with their children. And Herman came with a couple of deputies.

Afterward, Phillip gathered several men, including Franklin, to aid in putting Prescott's body in the coffin. Sarah cringed inwardly. This was the last she would ever see her father. As Phillip hammered the pine box closed, every strike of the hammer drove a nail of pain into Sarah's heart. She reached blindly for Faith who grasped her hand. Sarah leaned toward her, and Faith slipped an arm around her waist. Sarah fought hard to control the grief that threatened to overwhelm her.

With Faith at her side, she approached her mother, who was being attended to by Scott and Lindsay. Sarah couldn't speak. She and her mother embraced each other, then Sarah embraced Scott and Lindsay. She turned to Pres and Jessie and gave them each a hug.

The men lifted the coffin into the wagon, and Phillip drove it just ahead of the column of mourners, who trudged toward the gravesite. He led them through the forest to a natural clearing, surrounded, and seemingly protected, by maple, elm, and dogwood trees.

Scott and Lindsay, who held Cynthia's arms, led the group, followed by Sarah and Pres and Jessie. Faith came next, accompanied by Herman Schmidt.

When everyone reached the site, Phillip and the other men unloaded the coffin and lowered it into the grave.

Sarah stood between Faith and Herman. She said to the sheriff, "I didn't expect to see so many people. Half the town must be here. They didn't know my father."

Herman took her arm and steered her closer to her mother. "That's a testament to how much they care about you, Sarah.

They're here in your honor. And Faith's."

"Thank you for pointing that out. I'm constantly grateful for all the people who have accepted Faith and me as their neighbors and friends. When we're finished here, Herman, would you please announce that people should return to the house for refreshments? Reverend Leland said that's the custom here, but I want to make sure everyone knows they're welcome to be there."

"I'll do that." He beckoned Faith and backed away to let her take his place next to Sarah.

Sarah linked one arm with her mother's and one with Faith's as Reverend Leland prayed aloud. Scott supported his mother from the other side, with Lindsay and Pres next to him. Jessie dropped an armful of flowers onto the coffin, and the men shoveled dirt into the grave. A soft sound of crying filled the air. Sarah's knees almost buckled, but Faith tightened her grip on Sarah's arm and gave her support.

A terrible sense of loss wrenched Sarah's heart. She would never in this lifetime see her father again, never feel his arms around her. Never hear his voice, his laughter. *Goodbye, Father. Safe journey.* She already missed him terribly.

* * *

The next morning, Phillip arrived as promised. Sarah met him outside as he tied his horse to the hitching rail. They sat at one of the tables on the porch, and Sarah laid down a sketch of her ideas for fencing in the site.

"We'll need sand, cement, gravel, and chain. And wood and nails. And water. And we'll need the right tools, of course."

Phillip tapped her sketch. "I think we can get ready-made posts with holes for the chains at Bindell's Cement Store. And I'm pretty sure he has a concrete bench, too. He might even have chain. We'll need to measure how much chain to buy."

"Good," Sarah said. "That will save us a lot of time and effort."

"And…"—Phillip touched the outline of the concrete base Sarah had drawn to cover the area adjacent to the grave—"I'll have Franklin bring a couple of my men out here to do this for you."

"Work up a price for me on all of that, Phillip. I want this to be a gift to Father from me."

"How about I charge you half the price, and it can be a gift from both of us?"

Sarah's throat closed. She nodded and squeezed Phillip's arm.

"All right," he said, "let's go do the measuring. Then we can get the wagon and pick up what we'll need. We can stop by where Franklin's working. I'll fill him in on what we're doing and tell him to bring his crew out here tomorrow morning."

"Yes, and could we pick up one of his men to help us with the loading and unloading of what we're buying today?"

"We sure can."

* * *

Sarah oversaw the building at the site. After the men cleaned up and left, she stood among the trees and gazed at the finished project.

Four feet from each corner of the double gravesite stood a three-foot-tall concrete post with chains draped between them to connect three sides. Entrance could be made at the foot of the grave. With input from her, Phillip's men had poured concrete on the surface between the posts, except for the grave itself and the empty gravesite next to it. In about a month, a double headstone would be placed across the top of the site with Prescott's birth and death dates inscribed on the right side of a double headstone. Cynthia's name and date of birth would be inscribed on the left.

A concrete bench sat outside the chained-in area, waiting for the newly surfaced area to cure.

Sarah heard a noise and saw Jessie approaching with an armload of flowers.

She touched a hand to Jessie's arm to halt her. "I'm sorry, but you can't walk on the concrete until it sets."

Jessie's eyes filled. She sat on the bench and placed the flowers on the ground near her. "When will that be?" she asked in a quiet voice.

"It takes about a month to fully cure, so the bench can't be set on it until then. But you can walk on it maybe tomorrow. Maybe not until the day after."

"Then I'll bring flowers both days if need be."

Sarah was touched by Jessie's attentiveness. "I think we have some vases with points on them that can be stuck into the ground. I'll try to find them for you."

"Thank you, but Aunt Faith said she would find them for me."

"Good. I'm going back to the house now. Coming?"

"I think I'll stay here for a while. Grandfather took a great interest in my drawings. And in me."

"I'm glad you two got a chance to know each other better."

"Thanks to you. If you hadn't brought all of us here, I'd never have had that chance."

Sarah admired the sincere expression on Jessie's face. "I'm glad I was able to do that. I'm sure your grandfather appreciated it, too."

"You were his favorite."

Sarah blinked. "Did he say that?"

"No, but I could hear it in his voice whenever he spoke of you."

Sarah wondered what Jessie heard in her grandmother's voice when she spoke of Sarah, but she couldn't ask that. "Your grandfather was always very supportive of me. We loved each other very much."

Jessie's head dipped. "We all loved him. We'll all miss him."

Sarah patted Jessie's shoulder. "Yes, we will."

Before Sarah left, she once again surveyed the finished site. The stolid simplicity and quiet beauty of it suited her father's personality.

She was pleased.

Chapter 12

As the summer waned, the reports on President Garfield's health had grown more ominous. Dr. Bliss, the man in charge of the president's treatment, asked Alexander Graham Bell to use his newly invented metal detector to try to pinpoint the location of the bullet, but they didn't find it. Garfield went from 210 pounds to 130 pounds. On September 6, in an effort to remove Garfield from Washington's heat, he was taken by a special train to his seashore cottage at Long Branch, New Jersey.

On September 20, the country's worst fears were realized when they learned the president had passed away at 10:35 pm on September 19 from infection and internal hemorrhaging. The succeeding president, Chester A. Arthur, declared several days of mourning. Garfield's body was taken to Washington, where it lay in state for two days in the Capitol Rotunda before being taken to Cleveland, Ohio, where the funeral was held on September 26.

"At last," Faith remarked, "his suffering is over and the man is laid to rest."

* * *

When the new school year had started and Faith returned to teaching, Sarah and Lindsay established a routine of alternating the preparation of breakfast, lunch, and dinner, and taking turns cleaning up.

With young Pres boarding at college, and Benjamin away, too, that left Jessie as the only child in the household. At nearly seventeen and in her last year of high school, Jessie was close to being a young woman.

She apparently had adjusted well to the relocation of her family and going to a new school, Sarah mused. In fact, very well. She seemed unusually excited to go to school each morning. Sarah wondered why, but she pushed the question aside. That wasn't her concern.

In the weeks after Prescott Coulter was laid to rest, Sarah hoped her mother would fit into their routine with as little disruption as possible. That turned out to be wasted hope. She wouldn't eat breakfast and dinner with the rest of the family during the week because Faith was there. Used to being waited on all her life, Cynthia had no idea how to prepare her food. She wandered into the kitchen about an hour after the others had eaten and asked Lindsay or Sarah to fix it for her.

After two weeks of this, Sarah called Cynthia into the kitchen one evening before dinner for a showdown. "Mother, I'm not fixing your meals for you anymore. And neither is Lindsay. We're not your servants."

Cynthia sidled over to the kitchen table and sat down. "I'm your mother. You could at least show me some respect."

Sarah leaned against the kitchen counter and crossed her arms. "Is that what you expect? After you called me a daughter of Satan? And Faith a whore? We deserve some respect, too."

"You'll get no respect from me as long as you're living with that woman. And look at you"—she flung her hand toward Sarah—"dressed in men's clothes. See how she's corrupted you."

Sarah thrust her fists down at her sides. She kicked her boot back against the lower cupboard with a bang, and Cynthia jumped. "Don't you say another word about Faith corrupting me. She's a better woman than I've ever been or ever will be. Or you, too, for that matter. She's one of the finest women I've ever met, and by far the kindest."

"Demand all you want to." Cynthia crossed her arms. "I will not sit at the same table with her for my meals."

Damn, Sarah thought, I must have gotten my stubbornness from her. "You have that choice, but from now on, Lindsay and I aren't serving any but the regular dinners. Either you join us, or you fix your own meals." As Sarah finished speaking, she heard the buggy arrive outside.

Cynthia looked troubled. "I've never made my own meals. And you expect me to now?"

"Yes. Faith teaches school each day, I work all day on my writing and illustrating, and Lindsay has Scott and Jessie to take care of. You, on the other hand, have no one to worry about but yourself."

Faith entered through the door and came to a quick stop. She gazed back and forth between Sarah and Cynthia but didn't say anything. Sarah, ignoring her mother's crabby expression, gave Faith a hug and kissed her cheek. "Hi, sweetheart."

"Hi." Faith's shining green eyes were asking questions. She attempted to move past Sarah, but Sarah held her arm.

"Stay," she mouthed.

Cynthia pursed her lips. After a moment, she gave a sly smile. "Jessie will bring me supper."

Sarah released Faith's arm and in two long steps was at the table. She slammed her fists down on it and shouted, "Jessie will not bring you your supper. If I find you asking her to, I will sit your judgmental carcass outside and shut the door, and you can live out there on the porch."

Cynthia's face paled. "You wouldn't do that."

"Like hell I wouldn't."

"I taught you not to disrespect your mother."

Sarah tapped the table with her fist. "And you taught me not to disrespect anyone because they were different. That burden is on you, too."

Faith touched Sarah's sleeve. "Please calm down. Don't upset your mother."

Sarah shook off Faith's hand and kept yelling. "I'm sick and tired of not upsetting my mother. Who worries about her upsetting us? We share our home with her, and what does she do? She calls us names and slanders your reputation. She upsets everyone's routine and expects us to pander to her every need. She thinks God has given her the right to judge how we live. Never mind that he made us the way we are or that we're good, decent people."

She turned back to her mother and said in her normal voice, "I'm not going to change the way I live, no matter how mean you act. I will never leave Faith. So you might as well get used to it, Mother. You'll take your meals with us. Be as nasty to me as you want, but you will be civil to Faith, or I swear, I'll put you out the door." She struck the table again. "And that's the way it's going to be." She waited at least ten seconds. "Do you understand?"

Once more, Cynthia produced her pursed-lips expression, but she nodded.

"Good," Sarah said quietly. "Supper will be ready in about half an hour. Be there."

Cynthia stood, raised her chin, and left the room.

Sarah plopped into a chair. She reached for Faith, who sat on her lap and wound her arms around Sarah's neck. Half-afraid that Faith would scold her for how she had addressed her mother, Sarah held her breath.

"Disturbing, huh?" Faith said.

With a huge sigh of relief, Sarah leaned her head against Faith's and twisted one of Faith's long curls around her finger. "Why are emotional scenes so exhausting?" she murmured.

Faith dropped one hand to Sarah's wrist and rubbed her skin. "I think maybe it's because your whole body gets involved, from the top of your head to the tips of your fingers and toes. Strong emotions take a lot of energy." Her eyes crinkled as she grinned. "Even good ones."

"Heh." Sarah grabbed Faith's waist and set her feet on the floor as she stood up. "Go change and wash, and I'll finish getting supper ready."

Faith touched Sarah's hand. "Do you think your mother will show up?"

Sarah's face hardened. "She damn well better."

"Let's try to be especially nice to her. You know, kill her with kindness. Does she have any special foods she likes?"

"I don't know." Sarah felt more relaxed. Having Faith by her side helped. If anyone could win her mother over, Faith could. Sarah gave a short laugh. "Maybe you could ask her tonight."

"I think I will." A smile was growing on Faith's face as she turned around and left.

Lindsay came into the kitchen right after Faith's departure. "I heard some yelling clear over in our sitting room. Are you okay?"

Sarah rubbed the back of her neck. "Yeah. I kind of lost my temper."

Lindsay opened the cupboard and counted out the plates to set the table.

Sarah nodded toward the plates Lindsay had gathered. "Set a place for Mother, as well."

"Good. Scott wants to join us tonight, too. He's feeling better today." Lindsay added another plate to the pile she held. She cocked her head toward Sarah as she set a dish at each place. "Is that what the yelling was about?"

Sarah lifted a lid to baste the beef roast and stir the juice around the potatoes and onions. "Yes. I told Mother she wasn't getting special treatment anymore. She has to take meals with us and behave better toward Faith."

"And?"

Sarah's lip twitched. "She argued with me at first, but after I lambasted the table a few times, she gave in."

Lindsay laughed out loud. "You big bully."

After the table was set for dinner, Lindsay went to fetch Scott. She returned with both Scott and Cynthia, and Jessie followed them. Faith wound up mashing the potatoes with plenty of butter, the way she preferred them. She and Lindsay helped Sarah put out the food, and they all sat.

With Sarah's place always at the head of the table and Faith's at the foot, Cynthia seemed indecisive as to where to sit, but she finally chose the chair on Sarah's left. Jessie sat next to her, and Lindsay and Scott sat opposite them, with Scott nearest Sarah. They served themselves and began eating.

"Scott," Faith said, "I'm pleased you feel well enough to join us. Today was glorious. Did you get a chance to enjoy the sunshine?"

Cynthia glared at Scott, and he fidgeted in his chair. "Thank you. Yes, I sat on the porch for a while. I felt chilled at first, but Sarah brought me a quilt and that made me comfortable enough to stay outside for several hours."

"Wonderful," Faith said. She turned toward Sarah. "I see you picked some apples and pumpkins. Maybe we can make a pie or two."

"That's the idea." Sarah waved her fork in the air. "You and Lindsay can fight over who makes what. You both make scrumptious pies."

"We'll do that," Lindsay said. "Is apple pie still your favorite, Mother Coulter?"

"Yes, it is."

"Then," Faith said, "we'll definitely make some apple pies. And a pumpkin one for you, Sarah."

Sarah patted Scott's arm. "Scott favors pumpkin, too."

"How about you, Jessie?" Faith asked.

About to put a forkful of meat into her mouth, Jessie paused. "I like them both. Maybe I can help."

Sarah swallowed her bite of mashed potatoes and gravy. "How about you help me make the ice cream, instead?"

Jessie's face lit up. "I'd love to."

"We can make vanilla or peach. I'll let you decide that."

"Thank you, Aunt Sarah. I love vanilla."

"So does your Aunt Faith." Sarah heard a low snort from her mother, but she ignored it. "That's settled, then. Vanilla it is."

Sarah was happy to note that the rest of the meal passed in a congenial atmosphere. Probably because Cynthia didn't say another word. While Faith poured coffee for the rest of them, Cynthia went out to sit on the porch, and Jessie helped her father return to their wing of the house. Sarah picked up her coffee cup and joined her mother while the other women cleared the table.

"You and Lindsay fixed a very good meal," Cynthia said. She lifted a sweater from the arm of the chair and put it on.

Sarah leaned against the porch railing near the steps and took a sip of coffee. "Thank you. I'm glad you decided to join us." Sarah watched her mother's face closely. "Faith helped, too. She mashed the potatoes."

Cynthia wrapped the sweater tight against her chest. Her clipped voice sounded sour. "Had I known that, I wouldn't have eaten them."

Sarah straightened up so fast some of her coffee spilled from the cup. "I've had enough of your bitterness. I'm leaving." She took a step, and her foot slipped on the wet spot where the coffee had landed. Since she was moving with a hard twist, she couldn't stop her momentum. She pitched down the steps, dropped her coffee cup, and almost hit face-first on the stone walkway. Her outstretched hands broke her fall, but her right hand landed at an awkward angle on top of the broken coffee cup.

Cynthia's scream brought Faith and Lindsay on the run.

"Oh my God," Lindsay said. She and Faith hurried to Sarah's side. She writhed on the ground holding her wrist as blood poured from her palm. Cynthia disappeared back into the house.

Faith grabbed Sarah's wrist away from her and pushed the skirt of her dress against the raw wound. "Let us help you into the house."

"No way," Sarah said through gritted teeth. "I twisted my bad leg, and it pains me too much. Please do what you need to do here. Give my leg a chance to quiet down."

Faith nodded. "Lindsay, please get my healer's kit from under the sink, and bring a glass of water and a bottle of whiskey. Sarah, did you hit your head or your back?"

"No, I fell forward. Busted up my damn hand pretty good, I think. It sure hurts like hell."

Faith examined the fingers as gently as she could. Sarah's reflexes kept jerking them away from her. "Your middle finger might be broken, but maybe it's not. At best, it and the ones on each side are stove in."

Lindsay showed up with the kit and water and whiskey. "Thank you," Faith said. "That was quick."

"Mother Coulter already had the kit out. I merely got the water and whiskey."

Faith glanced toward the porch and saw Mrs. Coulter standing at the top of the steps wringing her hands. "Thank you," Faith called to her, but she received no answer.

Faith opened the kit and removed a morphine pill from an envelope. "Take this." She put it in Sarah's mouth and held the glass of water for her to wash it down. She opened the bottle of whiskey. "This will hurt, but I have to clean the wound, sweetheart."

Sarah's jaw clenched. "Go ahead." She whispered her usual mantra in a grinding voice, "I can do this."

Faith flushed out the gash on Sarah's palm, flushed it again, and set the bottle down. Sarah picked it up and took a long swig.

Faith placed a pad of lint-matted charpie roll against the wound and told Sarah, "Hold this as tight as you can."

"Got it." Sarah pushed against the roll with her other hand. Lindsay used her handkerchief to wipe the sweat that was gathering on Sarah's brow.

Faith removed a clean rag from the kit and laid a curved needle, forceps, silk thread, and morphine powder on it. She threaded the silk through the needle and closed the forceps over the eyed end. "You can let go of the charpie roll now." She moved it away and dusted the wound with the morphine powder to numb the hand. "This will help a little, but it will still be painful."

"I can do this," Sarah said again. The muscles in her jaw stood out in graphic relief.

Faith grasped the forceps and pushed the curved needle into the side of the cut. Hearing Sarah's slight gasp at each needle prick brought tears to her eyes that she brushed away with the sleeve of her dress. She sewed the skin together with five stitches and tied off the thread with each stitch.

"No more sutures," she whispered.

She cut a piece of wire screen and molded it around Sarah's bent fingers. "This will give them support and protection," she said. Using a long roll of cotton, she wrapped the fingers and bound the hand.

"There. All finished." Sarah's eyes drooped. "Don't fall asleep yet, Sarah. We have to get you in the house." But her words were in vain. Sarah had passed out from the morphine.

"Lindsay, do you think Jessie could help us carry Sarah in?"

Cynthia surprised Faith by saying, ""I'll go get her, and I can help, too."

She returned with Jessie, and eventually, between the four of them, they got Sarah inside and settled her on the sofa. "Thank you all," Faith said. "I can take care of her now." Faith washed off her hands in the kitchen and sat in a chair in the living room. She leaned her head back and rested it against the chair. Oh, Sarah, she thought, you were right. You busted up your hand pretty damn good.

* * *

Sarah slept through the rest of the day and spent the night on the sofa. As soon as Faith got home from school the next day and put away her school paraphernalia, she hurried in to check on her. She nodded to Cynthia who looked up from her reading in an armchair at the far end of the room. Cynthia ignored the nod and went back to her book.

Was there a hesitation there before she ignored me, Faith wondered? At least there were no pursed lips.

She sat on the sofa next to Sarah's sleeping form and gazed at her. Sarah's eyes fluttered open, and Faith greeted her with a smile. "Hi, sleepyhead." Pain flickered across Sarah's face, but a smile followed it.

"Sleepyhead? How long have I slept? Are you back from school already?"

"Yes."

"So I slept all day. Good morphine."

"I doubt it was the morphine. I think you were exhausted. Especially after this morning's struggle with the chamber pot."

"Sorry about that. At least Lindsay was able to help us out."

"Yes, bless her. She's a good woman to have around."

Sarah blinked her eyes. "Why are you smiling at me that way?"

Faith brushed Sarah's dark hair back from her face and let her fingers linger on Sarah's cheek. "I was sitting here thinking about how beautiful you are."

"Hmmm. You're the beautiful one. Plus, you have a beautiful soul. I'll never be able to match you there." She reached her good hand up behind Faith's neck and splayed her fingers into her hair. They gazed into each other's eyes for a long moment. Sarah raised her head and tugged against the back of Faith's neck, but Faith resisted and glanced toward Cynthia.

Sarah wet her lips. "This is our house. If we want to kiss, we can kiss."

Faith gave a slight shake of her head. "Yes, we can. But let's respect your mother's sensibilities."

Sarah dropped back against the sofa. Her voice sounded quiet but hoarse. "She doesn't respect yours."

"Don't worry about that." Faith patted Sarah's cheek. "How are you feeling?"

Sarah sniffed. "Sweaty." She moved her sore hand and made

a face. "The hand hurts a lot." She attempted to bend her knee but gasped. "My damn leg hurts even worse. I must have twisted it badly when I slipped and fell." She paused. "I'd like to sit up."

Faith put her hand on Sarah's arm and stroked it. "Let me get you sitting up, and then I'll get some ice for your leg." She rose and stood at the end of the sofa nearest Sarah's head. "Don't try to help. Stay still, and I'll pick up your shoulders. After I get you up, I'll swing your legs out and put the sore one on the hassock." She wound her arms around Sarah's shoulders and wrestled her up. "Ugh. You're heavier than you look."

"You said not to help, so you were picking up dead weight." Sarah grinned. "You're stronger than you look."

The hassock scraped across the rug as Faith pulled it closer to the sofa. "Okay, now you can help. Don't use your bad leg. Ready?"

Sarah drew in a deep breath. "Go ahead." She planted her uninjured hand against the sofa seat cushion to help move her body.

Faith swung Sarah's legs around and put the sore one on the hassock. "How's that?"

Sarah's lips were pressed together. She had laid her injured hand across her waist and pushed her good hand against the sofa so hard it left an imprint in the fabric that slowly lifted back into shape. A beaded string of sweat lay against her hairline.

Faith sat down next to her and clasped Sarah's good hand in both of hers. "I should have given you some morphine before we did that."

"No." Sarah rested her head against the sofa back. "I don't want to be drugged again and not know what's going on." Her chest moved up and down as she sucked air into her lungs. "I can do this," she whispered. "I can do this."

Faith started to rise, but Sarah closed her eyes and held onto Faith's hand. "Stay here a minute with me. Please."

Faith settled back down. "I'll do better than that. I made arrangements to take off tomorrow and Friday."

Sarah's eyes popped open. "What? Why did you do that?" Her voice held a harsh edge. "I have Lindsay and Mother here to help me. You don't need to take time off."

Faith jumped up. "Are you crazy? Do you think they can support your weight?" She strode back and forth and waved her arms. "I'm bigger and stronger than either one of them, and I struggled with moving you." She stopped in front of Sarah, bent over toward her, and practically shouted. "Who's going to help you to your drawing board? To the table to eat? To the bathroom? Besides, you're my responsibility, not theirs."

The corners of Sarah's mouth curved down, and she frowned. "Your responsibility? Am I a burden now, redhead?"

Faith snapped upright like a soldier at attention. "I'll get the ice for your leg," she said and flounced out of the room.

Sarah squeezed her eyes shut and slowly reopened them. *Why did I do that? I should have known better.* She glanced toward where her mother had been sitting and saw that she had left the room. At least she hadn't witnessed their minor tiff. Or had she? Sarah didn't really give a damn.

Faith returned with chipped ice in a towel. She pushed up Sarah's trouser and packed the towel around her leg over the red and swollen area between her knee and ankle. When she finished, she sat again next to Sarah and took her hand.

"I'm sorry," she said. "Here you are in pain, and I go and lose my temper." She rubbed Sarah's arm. "That was very inconsiderate."

"I'm sorry, too, sweetheart. I shouldn't have been so ungrateful. I should have realized you're upset about me. Truly, I'm thankful that you've taken off for a couple of days. I'll be needing you. I didn't want to interfere with your teaching schedule."

"I can manage. Do you want to go to your work desk?"

Sarah raised her injured hand. "And do what? Too bad Benjamin isn't here. I could use his help with the drawings that I need to finish for my latest book."

"I can help with the writing while I'm home." Faith snapped her fingers. "And I bet Jessie will be willing to help with the drawings. From what I've seen, she has a lot of talent. Suppose I ask her tonight when she gets back from choir practice?"

"That's a good idea. I've seen some of the things she's drawn, and you're right, she is talented. Do you think she'll be willing to?"

"I don't see why not. She obviously loves to draw, and maybe helping her Aunt Sarah will appeal to her. You might be able to give her some suggestions to improve."

"All right. Ask her, please. Would you help me over to the desk when she gets home? I should be up to moving by then, at least with a crutch. I can block off some sketches for her to fill in if she agrees."

"Asking you if you wanted to go to your work desk was a

little premature. Let's wait until morning and see whether the swelling of your leg goes down first. You don't want to be aggravating it. Do you want to dictate any part of your story now?"

"No, that can wait. The pictures take the longest, and if Jessie will help with that, we can work on the story while she finishes them. Besides, you need a rest. We both do."

"Thank you." They smiled at each other.

Sarah put her good arm across Faith's shoulders, and they settled closer on the sofa.

* * *

The next day, Sarah's leg had improved, but not much, so she spent most of her time on the sofa. That afternoon, Jessie, who had agreed to help, returned home after school eager to get started. With the crutch Faith retrieved from the bedroom closet, Sarah managed to hobble to the bench at her desk in the studio.

Jessie sat beside her and leafed through the pictures already finished for Sarah's current book, another war story. "These are wonderful, Aunt Sarah. I hope I can draw this well some day." She glanced up, her face aglow with excitement. "How many more do you need?"

"About five more. I'll block them off for you—I think I can manage that left-handed—and you can fill in the fine details. I'll tell you what they are as we go. Does that sound all right?"

"I'd love to try."

"Good. Let's get started then. I'm sure we'll be working on these for more than a week." Sarah stowed the finished pictures in the bin connected to the side of the work area for that purpose. She put a fresh piece of paper on the desk and chose a pencil from the holder at the top right of the drawing surface. "I do everything in light pencil, and when I achieve what I'm aiming at, I use black ink to trace all the lines for the finished picture."

She bent her head to her work. She found using her left hand to sketch even a rough shape was unwieldy and uncomfortable. Jessie must have sensed this.

"If you want," Jessie said, "I can do the blocking, too. Point out the boundaries with your good hand, and I'll sketch it. That should help me get the perspective right, too."

"That's almost perfect, Jessie." Sarah pointed to a spot between two figures. "How about putting another block there? See how the cannon sits on the bottom left and its smoke rises heavy above it? Adding another figure on the middle right will balance the rest of the scene."

Jessie leaned back from her work and examined what she had done. "Yes! I see what you mean." She bent back to the paper and sketched in the block for the extra figure. She glanced back and forth to what had already been blocked as she marked in the required spot.

"Good," Sarah said. "Now it's ready to be drawn and filled in." She awkwardly pulled two of her old pictures out of the bin. "Use these as a guide for portraying the soldiers. We don't want them to be exact matches, but their clothing and equipment have to be pretty close and consistent within each drawing."

Sarah squirmed to the edge of the bench and stood up. "I need to get this leg up onto a hassock for a while. When you get two or three of the figures drawn, give me a holler and I'll check on them for you."

Jessie didn't look up from her efforts. "All right."

Sarah limped into the living room. Instead of using the hassock, she leaned the crutch against the wall, sat on the sofa, and strained with her left arm to lift her sore leg onto the seat cushions.

Faith came into the room, drying her hands on a dish towel. "I thought I heard you. Do you need any help?"

"Yes, please." Sarah got her other leg onto the sofa and lay back on the cushions. "Can you raise my foot onto the top of the back of sofa?"

Faith flipped the towel onto her shoulder, carefully wrapped her hands around the leg, and did as Sarah asked. The relief was immediate, and Sarah groaned with pleasure. "Oh God, that feels so much better."

Faith giggled. "You keep moaning like that, and you might have to make room for me on the sofa, too."

Sarah reached out an arm and lifted one eyebrow. A grin tugged at her lips, and her eyes sparkled.

"Oh no." Laughter bubbled up through Faith's words. She took the towel from her shoulder and waved it. "We both have work to take care of. Speaking of work, how's Jessie doing?"

Sarah's demeanor sobered. "Very well, so far. I'm waiting to see how she draws a couple of soldiers. She has a sure hand."

"Have you seen her sketchbook?"

"I didn't even know she had one."

Faith tickled Sarah's face with the dish towel. "Maybe she's been shy about having you see it. But you should ask her about it. She's done some good work. I do believe she takes after her Aunt Sarah."

Sarah brushed the towel away and snorted. "Scott blames all her bad traits on me. I hope you're right about this good one. I can use the help."

"How's your hand feeling?"

Sarah glanced at the bandaged extremity. "It's throbbing, but I'll live." She tilted her head toward the chair her mother generally sat in. "Where's Mother?"

"She's sitting out in the pagoda with Lindsay." Faith grimaced. "I think she's trying to avoid me. She's not used to seeing me at home on a school day."

"Maybe not. She often sits out with Scott when he's on the porch. Sunshine's good for everyone. Though the days are turning chillier."

"That's what sweaters and jackets are for."

Jessie entered the room holding the picture she was filling in. "How does this look, Aunt Sarah?"

After a moment of scrutiny, Sarah nodded. "That's very good. I feel secure now about your assistance. You go ahead and finish this one, and show it to me again when it's ready to be inked."

"Thank you, Aunt Sarah. I'm happy you like it."

"I'm very pleased. Thank you for doing this for me."

Jessie glowed with pleasure as she left the room.

Faith said, "It's good to hear you encouraging Jessie. Sometimes you sound cool toward her."

"Her presence makes me uncomfortable. It's hard to pretend otherwise."

"You could make a stronger effort, you know."

Sarah shrugged.

Faith glanced back as she headed to the kitchen. "Don't forget to ask her about her sketchbook."

"I'll ask her after the drawings are finished. If she's shy about showing it to me, I don't want to upset her."

"That's a good idea. I'm sure you'll love what she's done."

Chapter 13

Over the next nine days, Sarah's leg and hand improved. Her palm and fingers were almost fully healed, but they were still stiff. Fortunately, she had to make only minor adjustments to the pencil drawings Jessie completed, and Jessie inked them for her. True to her promise, Faith had written the story as Sarah told it to her, and they edited it together. Everything worked out even better than Sarah expected.

Before sending the finished book to the publisher, Sarah received a request from him for several drawings to use for promotion of her book. He said she could wait and send everything together.

Things would have been easier had she known that ahead of time, but still, she had enjoyed learning firsthand about Jessie's talent and was grateful for Faith's willing help to get the book finished.

* * *

"That should do it." Sarah completed one of the newly requested drawings. She stuck her ink pen in its holder, sat up straighter on the bench, and stretched her back. As she laid her spectacles on the drawing table, she heard movement behind her and assumed Faith had come into the room.

She was startled when two hands cupped her eyes and a falsetto voice said, "Bet you can't tell who I am in three guesses."

She doubted it was Jessie trying to be funny. Besides the hands were too large. "Pres?"

"Not even close."

"Phillip?"

"Nope. One mooore guess."

"Now that she had calmed down from her initial surprise, Sarah caught a whiff of a familiar cologne. She grabbed the hands and yanked them from her eyes as she yelled, "Benjamin!"

She scrambled off the bench and threw her arms around him.

Benjamin was easily six feet tall and perhaps still growing. He had his father's features and dark, curly hair, but his tall build came from Faith's side of the family.

The two of them stood there hugging and laughing as Faith watched from the doorway.

"How wonderful to see you," Sarah said. "Are you home to stay?" She sat backwards onto the bench. Faith joined her there and Benjamin pulled up a chair.

"Not yet. I still have a bit of time to spend in Iowa, but I have some news."

"So, out with it. Now."

He laughed. "As patient as ever, I see. I don't know how Mother puts up with it." He ducked away, grinning, as Sarah made a punch toward him.

"All right," she said. "Stop teasing me. What's the news?"

"I talked to Asher Perlmann about being a partner in his medical practice here, and he agreed to it. As soon as I finish in Iowa, I'll be the new doctor in town."

Sarah opened her mouth to speak, but nothing came out. She stood and Benjamin did, too. She stuck out her hand, shook with him, then tugged him into a hug. Finally, she found her voice. "Dr. Benjamin Pruitt, I am so proud of you, and I know your mother is, too."

"Thank you, Aunt Sarah. You and Mother made all this possible, and I thank you for that, too."

They parted and stood for a moment grinning at each other. Then Sarah motioned toward the chair. Benjamin sat back down, and Sarah rejoined Faith on the bench. She smiled at Faith and twined their fingers together. "You knew this already?"

"Benjamin told me before we came in here."

Benjamin laughed. "Telling you separately gave me a chance to say it twice." He sobered. "I'm sorry I couldn't be here for you when you lost your father."

"Thank you," Sarah said. "And thank you for the beautiful card and letter you sent. That warmed my heart."

"I hoped it would. How's the rest of your family doing? Each letter I got sounded like the household has stayed pretty full."

"My mother has no real choice about moving since Scott and his family are here. Pres is away at school, but everyone else in my family will stay here for now."

"You seem pleased."

"Surprisingly, I am. Even though it presents some difficulties. Your mother got me out of my loner ways." Sarah glanced at

Faith and back to Benjamin. "She might be regretting that now."

Benjamin raised his eyebrows. "Are you, Mother? You never mentioned anything in your letters."

"Not regretting it," Faith said. "I wanted to keep my letters cheerful, so I didn't say anything derogatory about the situation here."

"But?" Benjamin said.

"Sarah's mother and brother aren't happy about our relationship. Especially her mother. She barely speaks to me."

"I don't care for the sound of that. How could anyone not like you?"

"Because," Sarah said, "your mother's a troublemaker."

Benjamin looked puzzled and his voice rose. "What?"

Sarah laughed. "I'm teasing you. Your mother couldn't be nicer to them—to everyone. She's kept that infamous temper of hers under control. The only one she yells at is me, and I usually deserve it."

Benjamin appeared to be calmer until Faith said her next words. "Sarah's mother has called me some nasty names, but I try to ignore them. She's lost her husband and her home, and that has to weigh on her a lot."

Benjamin frowned. "She better not call you names in front of me."

"If she does, you will show respect and do nothing to upset her. People are never won over by conflict and contention. Showing them kindness is much more likely to produce good results."

There was a short pause as Benjamin seemed to be thinking about that advice. Finally, he clapped his hands against his thighs, reminding Sarah of Phillip. "You're right, Mother, as always. I will be as nice as pie. I will overflow with kindness."

"Sounds to me," Sarah said, "as though you're overflowing with something a little browner right now."

He chuckled. "No, no, no. I'm serious. I shouldn't have to be reminded to show your mother respect. You've earned that much from me, whether she has or not."

Sarah inclined her head. "Thank you."

Faith stood. "All right. Put your belongings in your room and clean up. By that time, dinner should be ready."

Sarah rose. "Come in after everyone's seated, and I'll introduce you."

Benjamin gazed from Faith to Sarah. "How should I address them?"

Sarah said, "Your mother and I can't be legally married, but in our minds, we are. Address them as befits someone who is my son. If they don't like it, that's too bad."

"Should I call your mother Grandmother?"

"Yes. You'll probably get her sour prune face, but try to smile and ignore it."

"I can do that." Benjamin's eyes gleamed, and he hit his closed fist against his chest twice. "I'm only here for two more days."

Sarah twirled her finger around to include the three of them. "We can all do this. Forever."

* * *

As planned, Benjamin entered the dining room after everyone was seated. He looked quite handsome in his black linen suit with white shirt, starched collar, and green tie. Sarah rose to meet him. She put a hand on his shoulder and turned to her mother. "Mother, this is our son, Doctor Benjamin Pruitt."

Sarah let go of him and sat back down. Benjamin approached Cynthia. Appearing a bit flustered, Cynthia offered her hand. Benjamin bowed, lifted her hand to his lips for a moment, and said, "I am so pleased to meet you, Grandmother Coulter. Aunt Sarah has said many good things about you."

Sarah hoped that Cynthia's innate good breeding would take over, and she was delighted to see that it did. "I'm pleased to meet you, too, young man."

"Thank you." Benjamin moved to Scott, who sat to Cynthia's right. Benjamin stuck out his hand. "Hello, Uncle Scott."

Scott made an attempt to stand but was partly bent over when he shook Benjamin's hand. "Hello, Benjamin. You've certainly grown since I saw you last."

"Yes, sir, I have." Benjamin smiled and turned toward Lindsay. "Aunt Lindsay." He kissed the hand she offered.

"How good to see you, Benjamin." Lindsay motioned toward Jessie, who sat across the table from Scott. "You might remember our daughter, Jessie."

His face lit up into a wide smile. "Of course, I remember her." He scooted around Sarah and Faith and stood by the empty chair next to Jessie. "You kept pestering Pres to give you his toys."

Jessie laughed and held out her hand. "I confess I was too young to remember you clearly, but you describe me perfectly."

Benjamin kissed the back of her hand and held it a moment longer. "Mother wrote me that you helped Aunt Sarah with some drawings when she injured her hand."

"I did."

"You'll have to give me all the details." He squeezed and released Jessie's hand and indicated the empty chair next to her. "Since this is the only chair left, I assume I'm sitting here." With that, he sat down. He looked toward Sarah and winked at her.

Sarah winked back. That all went well, she thought. She picked up the meat platter, took a slice of roast pork, and passed the platter to Lindsay. As everyone served themselves, Cynthia surprised Sarah by saying, "Benjamin, do you have a private practice?"

"I will soon. Before the end of the year, I'll be a partner with Dr. Asher Perlmann, right here in Bonneforte."

"Wonderful!" Lindsay said. "Scott can be one of your first patients." Scott gave her a long-suffering look but refrained from speaking.

"What made you decide to be a doctor?" Cynthia asked.

"Grandfather Pruitt was a doctor, and my mother has done a lot of doctoring on her own. She was an assistant to one of the doctors in our hometown during the war."

"Your grandfather was a doctor? That's interesting." Cynthia finished cutting her pork and took a bite.

"In fact, Mother saved Aunt Sarah's leg." Benjamin sliced his meat and forked a piece into his mouth.

Lindsay set down her water glass. "Tell Mother Coulter how she managed to do that."

Benjamin swallowed his food. "A gunshot wound in Aunt Sarah's leg had become badly infected, and the doctor said the leg should be amputated. Mother had an idea of how to save it. She and I went to the compost pile to gather some maggots. When we brought a bowl of them back, Mother spooned them into the wound on Aunt Sarah's leg."

"Benjamin," Sarah said, "that's not a good topic for the dinner table."

"Nonsense," Cynthia said. "I think it's fascinating. Please continue."

Sarah nodded to Benjamin, and he went on with the tale. "I was horrified and intrigued at the same time. How could maggots help Aunt Sarah's leg?"

"And how did they?" Cynthia asked.

"They ate all the diseased flesh and left the good flesh. In a matter of days, Aunt Sarah began to recover. Even Doc Schafer was impressed. He swore he would take that treatment back to the battlefield and save numerous lives." He turned toward Faith and smiled. "I was proud that Mother had thought of it."

"And I was grateful," Sarah said. "My leg would have been as good as new if it hadn't been reinjured later on." That silenced everyone for a moment, and they continued eating. With the exception of Jessie and Benjamin, they all knew what had happened when   she'd been attacked.

"How was it reinjured?" Jessie asked into the silence.

Sarah hesitated. "I ran afoul of some Union soldiers who thought I was a Rebel, and one of them kicked me in the leg, right at the wounded spot."

"Oh, my," Jessie said. "Is that why you limp sometimes?"

"Jessie," Lindsay said, "let Aunt Sarah eat in peace."

Sarah waved her hand in the air. "I don't mind, Lindsay. Yes, it healed wrong, and it always hurts. If I overuse the leg or step wrong, it hurts even more. The weather affects it, too. But at least I still have it. My recent fall from the porch aggravated it. That's why I had so much pain."

Benjamin adroitly changed the subject. "I wish I had known my grandfathers."

Cynthia said, "I wish Sarah's father had known you. You're a fine young man, and he would have enjoyed your friendship."

"Thank you. Maybe we can visit his grave together while I'm home."

Cynthia nodded. "I'd like that. Would tomorrow after lunch suit you?"

"Yes, ma'am. That will be good. My employer and my friends don't expect me back for four more days. That gives me one more full day before I have to return."

"Sarah, speaking of friends," Faith said, "I know you said Rusty's coming soon. What day is that?"

"Unfortunately, Benjamin will miss meeting her. She'll be here next Saturday. I'm eager to see her. She's a cheerful person, and her presence should give us all a lift."

"Let's hope so," Faith said.

Dinner continued as everyone explored other lighter topics. Finally, the meal was over, and Lindsay and Jessie shooed everyone out while they took their turn at cleaning up.

The whole dinner astounded Sarah. Her mother had acted like her old self. Sarah had worried that Cynthia would treat Benjamin badly. Instead, she had acted truly interested in him and had been completely charming. Sarah decided to bask in this behavior while it lasted.

Chapter 14

The next day, after lunch, Cynthia strolled arm in arm with Benjamin to Prescott's grave. She glanced up at Benjamin as they spoke and couldn't help but admire what a handsome young man he had grown into. And how delightfully pleasant he was.

They entered the enclosure around the grave and sat on the concrete bench. Each partook of a moment of quiet before continuing their conversation.

Cynthia surmised Benjamin would wait for her to break the silence, so she spoke first. "Sarah drew up the plans for this arrangement and helped build it. She was always good with her hands."

"It's beautiful. Aunt Sarah built some of our furniture for us. Would you like me to tell you something else she did with her hands?"

"Yes, please do."

"I think I was about twelve years old. One of the older boys at school bullied me. One time he beat me pretty badly, and Aunt Sarah saw my black eye. She asked me what happened, and I told her. Over the next week, she taught me how to fistfight. Real fistfighting, like the British prizefighters do, with footwork and everything."

Cynthia tapped his arm with the closed fan she had carried outside with her. "And?"

"And..." Benjamin gazed at her with eyes alight with humor. "I never told Aunt Sarah this, but a few days later, that same bully accosted me and I beat the stuffing out of him. He never laid a hand on me again."

Cynthia's light laugh tinkled in the air. "I'm so glad you gave him his comeuppance. Good for you!"

"You mean good for Aunt Sarah. She's been a wonderful parent to me."

Cynthia grew quieter. She asked herself if it was appropriate to question Benjamin about his mother and Sarah and decided that he was a grown man and could handle it.

"I want to ask you something serious," she said.

"Yes?"

Cynthia gazed into his warm brown eyes with their thick, dark lashes, and she hesitated. How she wished Prescott and Benjamin had gotten the chance to know each other. She was honest enough to admit that her own beliefs about Sarah and Faith living in sin had kept her apart from them. But she couldn't change that. And wouldn't, even if the opportunity were to arise now.

She didn't want to alienate this lovely young man, though. He wasn't responsible for his mother's actions. But she couldn't help herself. She had to know. "Doesn't the situation between your mother and Sarah bother you? They're living in sin."

Benjamin ran his fingers through his dark, curly hair. "I know a lot of people think that, but I don't. They're good, law-abiding women, and from my perspective, they've been outstanding parents. Aunt Sarah has been kinder to me than a lot of so-called 'real' parents are to their children."

He once again met Cynthia's gaze. "And they love each other. You can see that every minute of the day, in the way they treat each other and the way they look at each other. I know I'm young, but I grew up surrounded by that love and I know it's true and solid. I don't believe God would call that sinful."

Cynthia sniffed in spite of herself. "I don't feel the same way you do."

Benjamin patted the hand lying in her lap. "I know you don't, and I respect your right to your own beliefs. But please don't expect me to change mine."

"I won't. We can have different beliefs and still get along." She felt uneasy about her treatment of Faith even as she spoke. She recognized hypocrisy, even when it was her own.

Benjamin smiled. "I definitely agree with you on that one."

* * *

Sarah and Faith stood at the kitchen window and watched Cynthia and Benjamin stroll toward Prescott's grave. Cynthia had her arm in the crook of Benjamin's.

"They look quite friendly," Faith said.

"Mother certainly fooled me. I didn't expect her to be so quick to accept Benjamin as part of the family."

"Neither did I. But I'm happy that she was. Benjamin's visit is so much nicer because of it. I wish he were staying longer."

"So do I. He could have served as a buffer between you and Mother. But he'll be back after the end of the year. Maybe sooner, on another visit or two."

"Sarah, do you think he'll still be staying here when he goes into practice with Asher?" Faith's voice sounded almost mournful.

"Hmm. That's a good question. He's a grown man, and he might decide to live in a boardinghouse downtown."

Faith licked her finger and rubbed at a spot on the window. "Did you see his face light up when he spoke to Jessie?"

Sarah laughed. "I wondered whether you noticed. I suspect any young man's face would light up when he spoke to Jessie. She's an attractive girl." Sarah wet her finger and rubbed it on Faith's cheek.

Faith grabbed her hand. "What are you doing?"

"You can go ahead and rub the window. I'd rather rub your cheek." Sarah closed her arm around Faith and drew her close. "You and I are the only ones in this side of the house. Let's take advantage of that." She dipped her head, and they kissed until Sarah's knees weakened.

"I think we need to continue this in the bedroom," she whispered.

"I agree."

Chapter 15

Benjamin's visit was over far too soon, and Sarah was sad to see him go. She and Faith hugged him repeatedly until he laughed and nearly ran to the wagon. Even Cynthia sent him off with a hug and a hand-embroidered handkerchief.

After his departure, Sarah continued to work on the new drawings.

On the following Saturday afternoon, she went to pick up Rusty at the train station. Drummer seemed unusually perky on the buggy ride, maybe picking up on her excited mood. Sarah pulled him back to a slow trot a couple of times. Bonneforte hadn't had rain for a while, and every time Drummer broke into a fast trot, his hooves raised whorls of dust from the road. Sarah sneezed a time or two.

When they got to the station, Sarah tied the wagon to the hitching rail and hopped up onto the raised platform next to the train tracks, where people arrived and departed. She stomped her boots and brushed the powdery dust off her yellow shirt and brown pants. She sat on a bench and waited in eager anticipation of Rusty's arrival.

A few other people waited, too. She was surprised to see Della Kumber there. Della noticed Sarah at almost the same time and hurried over. "Hello, Miss Coulter. May I join you?"

Her father must not be anywhere nearby, Sarah thought. "Of course. And please call me Sarah." She waved at the bench and Della sat and smoothed the skirt of her gray gown. "How are you?"

Della's lip twitched. "I'm all right."

"Are you waiting for someone?"

"No. I come to the station every once in a while to watch the trains arrive and depart. My father doesn't mind. He knows I don't have enough money to go anywhere. But he still stops by occasionally to check on me."

She got a faraway look in her eyes. "I daydream about being on one of the trains and going to exotic parts and starting a new life." When Sarah didn't respond right away, Della blushed. "I guess that sounds silly."

Sarah patted her shoulder. "No! No. Not at all. Your comments made me recall how I used to daydream when I rode my horse, Redfire, all over the mountains of Virginia."

"Did you daydream of meeting someone like Mrs. Pruitt?"

"No. I didn't know then that a woman would make me feel the way she does. I only knew I didn't want to get married to a man. I dreamed of being a world-famous traveler and writer."

Della turned in her seat so she faced Sarah directly. "When did you learn you preferred women?"

"When I met Mrs. Pruitt. Her name's Faith."

Della clapped her hands. "She was your first love? How romantic. Will you tell me about it?"

Sarah stood up. "Uh, here comes the train." Thank goodness. Sarah treasured her privacy.

Della's shoulders slumped a little, and she seemed disappointed, but she jumped up and stood beside her. "Are you meeting anyone I might know?"

A light went off in Sarah's brain. Maybe Della would enjoy getting to know Rusty. "As a matter of fact, I'm meeting a friend who also prefers women. Perhaps you'd like me to introduce you?"

Della stood up straighter, and her demeanor changed dramatically to a gleeful one. "I'd love to. I haven't met anyone here like us. Except you."

Sarah gave a rueful grin, and Della stumbled over her next words. "I-I m-mean, I'm so happy I met you, b-but I haven't met anyone else."

"That's about to change." The train eased into the station with several clangs, hisses, and belches, and Sarah blinked against the soot and ash that accompanied the behemoth. Her nose wrinkled at the smell of smoke mingled with oil from the wheels and the odor of metal-on-metal as the wheels screeched against the rails.

When Sarah spied Rusty and moved quickly to intercept her, Della trailed behind.

"Rusty," Sarah called. Rusty turned her way and set down her three suitcases. She wore a light-green dress that complemented the red in her strawberry-blonde hair.

"Sarah-Bren!" Rusty threw her arms around Sarah's neck, and Sarah lifted her up and kissed her cheek. Rusty gave Sarah an extra squeeze. "I'm so happy to see you. I thought I'd never get here. That train ride seemed to take forever."

"I'm happy to see you, too."

Sarah set her down, and Rusty reached a hand toward Della.

"Is this your Faith?"

Della shook hands. "No, my name's Della. I'm a friend of Sarah's."

Rusty grinned. "I should have known you weren't Faith. Sarah told me she was a redhead."

Della said, "A beautiful redhead."

So Della had noticed Faith's looks, Sarah mused. She picked up the largest of Rusty's suitcases.

Della quickly grabbed the other two. "I've got these."

One of them had an odd shape, long and narrow with a circle at one end. Sarah pointed at it. "What's in that funny-looking case?"

Rusty winked. "That's a secret. I'll show you later."

"Okay. Meanwhile," Sarah said, "Faith is dying to meet you." She inclined her head toward the hitching rail. "Our buggy's right over there."

Della helped Sarah strap the luggage onto the tail board. She gave Rusty a hand up to the step and into the buggy as Sarah untied the reins and got in the other side. Della reached up and she and Rusty shook hands.

"Thanks for your help," Rusty said.

"You're welcome. I live here in town, so maybe I'll see you around. Are you here for long?"

"Probably a week or so. Sarah and I haven't seen each other for a few years, so we have a lot of catching up to do. She stayed with my brother and me in Wyoming for a few months. Helped us out a lot. She even gave us sketches of ourselves before she left."

Sarah gave Rusty's skirt a tug. "You can tell Della your life story the next time you see her. Right now, I'm taking you home."

"Ha-ha," Rusty said. "You know I'm a talker, so don't go getting smart-ass with me."

Sarah grinned. "Sorry. I guess I should wait a day or two before tormenting you." She gazed down at Della. "I'm sure you'll see each other again. I'd invite you over if I could. Goodbye."

"I understand. Goodbye. Good to meet you, Rusty."

Sarah clucked and shook the reins, and Drummer started off.

Rusty gave Sarah a strange look. "Why can't you invite her over? Would Faith object?"

"Not Faith. Della's father. He thinks Faith and I are living in sin. Della favors women, too, and he beats her for it."

"Beats her?" Rusty was obviously shocked. "Why doesn't she leave him?"

"She says she has no skills and wouldn't know how to fend for herself."

"Hmmm. I wonder if she'd like to dig for gold."

Sarah laughed. "Don't go getting ahead of yourself. Wait until you know her better before committing yourself to a situation that might not work out."

"You're right. Let's go meet Faith."

* * *

When they got back to the house, Rusty insisted on accompanying Sarah into the barn to help her. Sarah set Rusty's luggage next to the door, and they unhitched Drummer and the buggy.

After the women pushed the buggy to its usual resting spot, Sarah pointed at the odd piece of luggage. "Is that a banjo case?"

"Oh, it's just like you to guess right. I wanted to surprise you. I've been taking lessons for a year or better, and I've gotten pretty good with it, if I do say so myself." Rusty led Drummer into his stall and came back out. "I thought maybe I could entertain you one evening."

Sarah checked the feedbag and pumped a little more water into the pail. "That sounds like a wonderful idea. I'll pretend I didn't guess, so you can still surprise the others. Do you sing?"

"I used to sing pretty bad. But I've been practicing a lot, and I sound better now. Not as good as you do, but it's passable."

Rusty stood in the middle of the barn and turned slowly in a complete circle.

She stuck her hand into a sunbeam that shone through the tall doorway and sparkled against the motes of dust floating within it. "This is a nice barn. I get so used to ours that I sometimes forget most barns are completely open to the sun and pretty airy."

"Doesn't keep them from smelling, though," Sarah said with a snicker.

"Yeah, they both smell, but even that's a little different here than it is at home. This smells better, almost pleasant. Don't you think so?"

"I have to agree with you, though probably only horse lovers like us would think this smell is pleasant."

Sarah tilted her head toward the house. "Come on. We're finished here."

She led Rusty into the house through the back door. Faith had set three places at the table and put a plate filled with cake slices and cookies in the middle. When they entered, she rose from a chair and moved quickly toward them. By coincidence, Faith's green dress almost matched Rusty's but was darker.

"Rusty," Sarah said, "this is Faith."

Faith reached out with both hands and clasped Rusty's. "I'm so happy to meet you. Sarah told me how welcoming you and your brother were to her."

Rusty beamed. "I sure am glad to meet you, too. Me and Mel enjoyed having Sarah stay with us. She more than paid her keep by helping with the gold mining." Rusty gave a little laugh. "She was too tall to dig without breaking her back, so she took on the job of clearing out the rubble and dumping it. Mel kept her pretty busy."

Faith said, "You're here on a visit, and I want you to relax. Please join us for some coffee and cake and cookies."

"Ummm," Rusty said. "My three favorite C's."

Sarah grinned. "Mine, too."

Sarah and Rusty sat at the table. Before she joined them, Faith asked, "Do you want a sandwich, Rusty? I have some sliced ham and cheese, if you're hungry. We're having chicken for dinner in an hour or so."

"If dinner's that soon, I can make do with the cookies and cake. But I'm about as hungry as a bear waking up after a long winter."

"How was your trip?" Faith dropped into a chair.

While Rusty doctored her coffee with copious amounts of cream and sugar, she said, "I had a good trip, I guess. I'm not used to riding trains for so long or making so many transfers from one train to another. I had trouble sleeping, and that's made me tired. Seeing so many different kinds of people was kind of fun."

She took a bite of cake and a drink of coffee before continuing. "The most exciting thing was the day they tried to load a mustang on one of the train cars, and he didn't want to go. They wrassled him around for a while, and he kicked a couple of the men and knocked a big dent in the side of one car before they got him tied down and settled."

She took another bite and swallowed. "I think the noise upset him. I know it upset me. Trains are too danged noisy and dirty. I'd rather travel by stagecoach if it didn't take so durn long."

"I have to agree with most of that," Sarah said. "Horseback would be my first choice."

Faith passed the cookie plate to Sarah. "I'm with Rusty. I'd choose the stagecoach."

"Yep," Rusty said. "The thought of sitting a horse for all

that time makes my bottom hurt."

Sarah shrugged. "I've been riding horses since before I could walk, so my bottom's tougher, I guess."

Faith tapped her head. Sarah made a face and Rusty laughed.

When they finished eating, Rusty offered to help clean up, but Faith shooed her away. "Sarah can introduce you to the rest of her family and show you around. I'll take care of this."

* * *

At the other end of the house, Lindsay answered Sarah's knock.

"Hello, Sarah," she said, and her gaze went to Rusty. She smiled warmly and opened her arms. "You must be Rusty."

Rusty embraced her and gave her a good squeeze. "I am. Sure is nice to meet someone closer to my size." She laughed as the embrace ended.

"Mother's your size, too," Sarah said. "But the rest of us are tall."

"It's the Coulter heritage," Lindsay said. "Come in and meet Scott. Jessie should be home soon." By the time Rusty met Scott and was taken out onto the porch to meet Cynthia, Jessie arrived home and joined in the introductions.

"By golly," Rusty said to her, "you're the picture of your Aunt Sarah."

"I hear that a lot," Jessie said.

Rusty gave Sarah a wink. "Sarah-Bren's a fine-looking woman, so you can take that as a compliment."

"Believe me, I do." Jessie and Sarah smiled at each other.

Sarah said, "Jessie's very talented. I injured my hand and she helped me finish some illustrations my publisher was waiting for."

"That's wonderful," Rusty said. "How did you injure your hand?"

"I fell. Stoved a couple fingers and had a nasty cut on my palm." Sarah flexed her hand. "But it's fine now."

The porch door opened and Faith stuck her head out. "Dinner's ready."

* * *

After dinner was cleared, Rusty asked if they all could

gather in the sitting room. "I have something I want to show you." She went toward the bedroom Sarah had designated as hers for the visit.

Everyone sat, and Rusty soon returned with the oddly shaped case Sarah had remarked on earlier. Rusty set the bag on a chair, unsnapped it, and drew forth a musical instrument.

Lindsay clapped her hands. "A banjo! Will you play something for us?"

"This is a surprise," Sarah said. "So the music lessons you spoke of were about this."

Rusty moved the case onto the floor and sat in the chair. "Yes. A colored minstrel show came to town—real colored people, not the pretend ones. I was so excited about the music. I talked to one of the players, and he said his mama taught him to play. I asked him if he would teach me, and he did."

She strummed the banjo and tuned it by tightening the pegs. Giving them a final strum, she said, "I wanted to show you that I brought this, but to tell the truth, I'm tuckered out from traveling. How about I play one tune and promise to play more tomorrow?"

Everyone nodded and Sarah said, "Of course. What are you going to play?"

"I'll play a slow one for now. 'Beautiful Dreamer.' I'll save the bouncier ones for later." Rusty gave a quick smile, bent her head, and plucked the banjo strings.

A sweet love song, Sarah thought as Rusty played and sang. She glanced toward Faith, who gave a tilt of her head in Sarah's direction. Her body warmed, and she gave a tilt of her head back.

Everyone clapped when Rusty finished with a flourish of notes. "I added those myself," she told them.

Sarah gave another clap of her hands. "That was wonderful."

Lindsay said, "I'm looking forward to tomorrow. That sounded like a good tune to waltz to."

"It is." Rusty's expression became more animated. "My...friend used to dance to it all the time. By herself, of course, since I had to play the music."

"Maybe," Sarah said, "you could teach one of us to play a song or two. Or would that take too long?"

"I think I could teach at least one to somebody. But right now, I'm ready for bed." She rose and placed her banjo in its case.

Jessie jumped up. "Let me do that for you." She closed the case, snapped the lid down, and picked it up. "Lead the way, Rusty."

"Thank you, darlin'. How about I follow you so I don't trip you with the case?" Rusty gave a wave. "I'll see you all tomorrow."

Chapter 16

Sarah and Rusty spent most of Sunday on horseback touring the fields and woods. Before the sun went down, Sarah took Rusty to Lake Respite.

"How beautiful," Rusty said. "This is part of your property?"

"Yes. It's one of our favorite spots for swimming and picnics. Sometimes fishing."

"I love our Wyoming property, but you saw it's mostly all mountain. You have a lot more flat areas than we do. And it's so gorgeous." Rusty turned in the saddle and gazed right at Sarah.

Sarah raised an eyebrow. "Why are you looking at me like that?"

"Like what?"

"Like you're a starving wolf and I'm your next dinner."

Rusty rubbed her hand over her face. "I'm sorry about that. But you are a very attractive woman."

"Who's taken."

"Yeah, yeah. I keep telling myself that about every fifteen minutes."

Sarah laughed. "Maybe I should invite Della Kumber out and the heck with her dad."

Rusty's expression lightened. "Can you do that?"

Sarah shook her head. "No. He's mean enough to hurt her over it. Or me. Or Faith. I don't want to take that chance."

"You're right. I wouldn't want you to get in trouble for my sake." She turned her horse. "How about we go back now? I'm getting hungry."

Sarah guided Redfire next to her. "Okay. You feel up to playing more music tonight?"

"Once my bottom gets feeling back in it."

"Food should help with that problem. Let's go."

"Yes, ma'am!"

* * *

After dinner, Rusty did offer to play more music in the living room and everyone seemed delighted.

"Let's clear an area for dancing this time," Faith said. So she and Sarah and Jessie moved the furniture against the walls while Rusty tuned her banjo.

Rusty began with a bouncy tune and followed it up with a slow one. Jessie and Lindsay paired together while Scott and Cynthia sat and watched. As they danced, Faith whispered into Sarah's ear, "Ask your mother to dance the next fast one with you."

Sarah tensed. "Why?" she whispered back.

"Because her toe was tapping the whole time Rusty played the first song. I'm sure she'd like to join in."

"I don't know whether my leg can take another fast one."

"Do you want to stop dancing for the night?"

"No." Sarah grinned. "I'm looking for an excuse to say no."

Faith pinched her side.

Sarah jumped. "Ow. All right, I'll ask her."

The very next tune was a fast one, and true to her word, Sarah approached her mother. Cynthia watched her coming, and Sarah bowed in front of her. "May I have this dance, Mother?"

Cynthia seemed flustered and didn't answer. In a low voice, Sarah said, "Pretend I'm Father."

Cynthia raised her hand, Sarah took it, and Cynthia rose from her chair. They joined in the dance that Jessie and Lindsay were already taking part in. A slow one followed, and without asking, Sarah pulled her mother close and continued to dance with her. Cynthia leaned her head against Sarah's chest. "I miss your father so much."

Sarah gave her a little squeeze. "So do I, Mother. So do I. He's probably watching us now and smiling."

When the tune was finished and everyone had clapped, Sarah took her mother's arm and led her back to her seat. Cynthia looked up at her before she sat down. "Thank you, Sarah. I'm sure if your father could have seen us, he would have been very pleased."

"You can thank Faith. She's the one who noticed you were eager to join in."

Cynthia didn't say anything, and Sarah returned to her seat. Rusty took a break, and Jessie brought out a tray with a pitcher of apple juice and glasses.

Rusty came over to sit with Sarah. "Looks like everyone's enjoying the music."

"We certainly are. I think I can handle one more fast one and maybe a slow one to finish the evening. Is that all right with you?"

"Perfect," Rusty said. "It's been a long day." After a few more minutes of rest, she went back to her banjo strumming and delivered the fast and slow dances then announced that would be all for the night.

When everyone had said their goodnights and left for bed, Faith moved the furniture back into position. When Sarah stood to help her, Faith waved her off. "I know your leg's bothering you. I can manage."

Sarah said, "I can at least replace my chair." She set it in its usual spot.

"Your mother seemed pleased that you danced with her." Faith put her hands on either side of Sarah's face. "And you're a very understanding daughter." She stood on tiptoe and gave Sarah what turned into a long, lingering kiss.

Sarah's arms went around her. She had been feeling sleepy, but the kiss brought her whole body into alertness.

Faith slipped her hand under Sarah's shirt. "I hope you're not too tired," she murmured.

"I'm never too tired for you." They clasped hands and headed for the bedroom.

* * *

Time flew by and soon it was Saturday.

Rusty sat on the top rung of the corral fence, facing Sarah, who stood outside the corral. "So you sell Redfire's stud services?"

"Yes. He's sired several horses in the area. Now that Benjamin will be back in the area, I want to find a good dam and have Redfire sire one for him."

"How come you didn't do that before?"

"It never occurred to me. We had the two horses, Redfire and Drummer, and that's all we needed. Now he'll need a horse of his own to call on patients."

"That sounds like a good idea. I hope I get to meet Benjamin some time."

"You will. Next time you visit, he should be here."

"Good." Rusty reached out her arms. "Help me down?"

Sarah took hold of her waist, lifted her, and ignored the twinge in her leg. Before she could move, Rusty clasped her arms around Sarah's neck and kissed her.

Startled, Sarah tried to pull her away, but Rusty wasn't letting go. When she did, Sarah set her quickly on the ground. "You know I'm in love with Faith. Why would you do that?"

"I'm sorry. It's so beautiful here, and it's a beautiful day, and you're so beautiful, I lost my head."

"If Faith's looking out the window, I'm liable to lose my head."

"I truly am sorry. I wouldn't purposely do anything that would hurt you or Faith. I'll come in with you so I can explain in case Faith is upset."

When Sarah entered the kitchen with Rusty right behind her, Faith took two steps toward her and slapped her across the face, hard. Sarah's head went sideways. She pushed her bent arms up alongside her face in reflex.

"How dare you?" Faith screamed. She raised her arm to hit Sarah again, but Rusty grabbed it.

"Please, Faith, don't!" Rusty shouted. "It was all my fault. Sarah didn't kiss me. I kissed her. Honest. She never kissed me at all. I had hold of her neck, and she couldn't move me away from her. Please, that's the truth. Don't hurt her. Slap me if you have to."

Faith tried to shake her loose, but Rusty held fast onto her arm. "Faith, I swear, I've thrown myself at Sarah a few times, but she always turned me away. She said she was faithful to the only woman she's ever loved, and she would never do anything to hurt you. That's the truth. I wish I had a woman who cared that much for me. I'd be hugging her instead of hitting her."

Faith stared at Rusty during this outburst. She finally calmed down and Rusty released her arm. Sarah plopped into a chair at the table, bowed her head, and held her hand against her cheek.

Faith said, "Is that so, Sarah? That's certainly not what it looked like."

"It looked bad," Cynthia said from the doorway. All three women turned to stare at her. "Well, it did."

"Mother"—Sarah's voice sounded rough—"have you ever known me to break my word?"

Cynthia shook her head, but her eyes seemed sad. "No, not before now."

Sarah gazed toward Faith and posed the same question. "Have you ever known me to break my word?"

Faith repeated Cynthia's words. "No, not before now."

Sarah's free hand came down in a fist against the kitchen table. "I haven't broken it now, either. I didn't kiss Rusty. She kissed me. And like she said, I didn't kiss her back. I promised you I would forsake all others. I've always stood by that, and I always will."

Faith's voice shook. "You're right. You've never lied to me, and I accept that you're not lying now. I'm sorry I lost my temper." Tears welled in her eyes. "I'm so sorry I hurt you."

She reached toward Sarah, but Sarah leaned away.

"I'll get you some ice."

Rusty took a seat next to Sarah and kept mumbling, "I'm sorry. I'm sorry."

Faith shaved some ice from the block in the icebox, wrapped a towel around it, and handed it to Sarah who gently held the ice to her face, which was hurting like hell.

Rusty said, "I guess I should go back home. You probably don't want me here now."

Sarah shook her head no. At the same time, Faith touched Rusty's shoulder and said, "Don't feel like you aren't welcome here. I can't fault you for being attracted to Sarah. I'm well aware of that feeling. As far as I'm concerned, you can stay as long as you like. But please keep your hands to yourself."

"You mean my lips."

Faith didn't smile, but it seemed like she wanted to.

Rusty stood. "Thank you, Faith. That's more than generous. I hope I've learned my lesson. I think I'll go out to the barn for a while. Get my head in order."

Cynthia left the room when Rusty did.

Faith sat next to Sarah. "Are you terribly angry with me?"

"Not terribly. I'm more hurt."

"I feel bad that I slapped you—and about how hard I hit you."

Sarah set the towel full of ice on the table and kept her gaze down. "I don't mean my face. My heart hurts that you could think I would cheat on you."

Faith took Sarah's hand. "Look at me, Sarah." When Sarah's gaze met hers, Faith said, "When I saw that kiss, my temper flared. It appeared to me that the woman I loved was kissing someone else, and that scared me. I lost control. I love you. I've always loved you. I know I've made mistakes, like now, but I've never fallen out of love with you." She rubbed Sarah's hand. "Please, please forgive me."

One side of Sarah's mouth turned up. "It's kind of ironic. I'm the one who got kissed, and you're the one asking forgiveness."

"But I struck you and I shouldn't have. I should have given you a chance to explain."

"Yes, but we both know what your temper's like. I warned

Rusty that you'd probably take my head off if you saw us."

Faith gave a wry grin. "And I proved you right. You know me well."

Sarah reached around, put a hand on the back of Faith's head, and brushed her lips with a kiss. "But I still love you," she said with a smile. She let go of Faith and put the towel with ice against her cheek once more.

"Are we all right, then?" Faith asked.

"We will be."

* * *

Rusty slunk into the barn berating herself for her actions. "You shoulda known better," she said aloud. "Sarah warned you once, and you ignored it. Now you messed things up."

She flopped down on a bale of hay and sat there. After a moment, she heard a noise different from the ones horses made. It sounded like it came from the loft. "Is someone there?" she called. She stood and strode to the bottom of the ladder that led up to the loft. "Hello?" She heard a scuffling noise and started up the ladder. Halfway up, she stopped. If someone was up there, they might be dangerous. She climbed back down, opened the barn door, and called back. "I know someone's there. I'm going to get Sarah. She'll be armed. You better get going before I come back."

"Wait!"

Rusty peered toward the loft. A woman emerged from the darkness into the dim light. "It's me, Della Kumber. I don't mean any harm."

"Come on down here, Della." Rusty shut the barn door.

Della climbed down the ladder. Rusty could see she was moving slowly and her shoulders were hunched. When Della stood before her, Rusty asked, "Are you all right?

"No."

"Here, sit down."

Della sat on a bale of hay. "No, I'm not all right. My father beat me again. I mentioned Sarah's name, and he went berserk. He was the angriest I've ever seen him. I was scared he would beat me to death. I couldn't stay there one moment longer."

She sniffled and when she tried to shift position on the bale, she cried out and put a hand against her back.

"What's the matter?"

"My back hurts something awful."

"Maybe Faith will have something to ease the pain."

"I don't think anyone can help me. I don't know how I'll make a living, but maybe I can borrow enough money from Sarah for a train ticket so I can get out of here before he kills me."

"I think I can help you," Rusty said. "I live in Wyoming. We have a small gold mine on our property. If you're willing to help dig the gold, you could come with me and live in my house, just as a friend, mind you. Digging's not easy, but I can do it, so you should   be able to, too."

Della's look of startlement turned to one of caution. "Who do you mean by 'we'?"

"My brother, Mel, and me. We used to live on the property together, but he's married now and living in the nearest town. I live by myself, and I sure would appreciate the company. I'll even pay for your ticket to get there. Nobody will bother you about who you like. Your work would pay for your keep and probably even more—extra spending money."

Della put her hands together as if praying. "You're an answer to my prayers. Thank you so much. I'll be beholden to you forever."

Rusty shook her head. "Let's not be talking about forever. You might change your mind once you're there. In that case, you can work off your train fare and go your merry way. Fair enough?"

"More than fair. When are you going home?"

"Let's get you up to the house and fed. Maybe Faith has something for your back. Then we can talk about traveling." Rusty stood and offered Della a hand up. Della was taller than Rusty, but most people were. She tucked Della's hand into the crook of her arm and escorted her to the back door. She liked this woman. Who knew what the future might bring?

She opened the door and pulled Della in behind her. Sarah was sitting at the table, still holding the ice compress against her face, and Faith was setting flour on the table.

"Guess who I found in the barn," Rusty said. Faith and Sarah looked surprised.

Sarah laid down the ice and stood. "Della, what are you doing here? My God, what's happened to you?" She gestured toward a chair. "Please sit down, both of you."

They sat and Della said, "I ran away from my father. He beat me again. I can't take it anymore. Rusty said Faith might have something to help my back."

Faith moved behind her. "Let me take a look at it." She unbuttoned the back of Della's dress and sucked in a breath. "Your whole back is bruised and swollen. I have some liniment that should help the pain." She crossed to a cupboard and removed a bottle and a soft sponge. "This might feel cold at first." She spread the liniment on Della's back. "Let that dry and then we can button your dress back up."

Della closed her eyes and reopened them. "Mmm. That feels so much better. Thank you."

"Does your father have any idea of where you are?" Sarah asked.

"I didn't tell him anything. I hid in your barn so he wouldn't see me at your house in case he looked. I wanted to borrow some money from you for train fare, but Rusty came up with a grand offer." She gazed at Rusty and smiled. "She offered to pay my way to Wyoming and let me work off the fare digging in her mine. She said I can even live with her until I get settled."

When Della wasn't looking, Sarah winked at Rusty. "That does sound like a grand offer."

Rusty blushed. "There's no promises being made except a place to live. I was thinking we better get on our way before Della's father catches up to her. Maybe leave tomorrow morning."

"That sounds like a good idea," Faith said. "Though I bet Jessie will be disappointed that you aren't able to give her banjo lessons."

"Maybe next time I come."

"Do you play the banjo?" Della asked with wonderment in her tone.

"I do," Rusty said. "Maybe you'd like to learn it."

"I would." She gazed at the other women. "My future's getting brighter and brighter. I have to thank you, Sarah, for encouraging me to step out into the world. And I have to thank you, Rusty, for making that possible."

"We couldn't be happier for you," Sarah said.

"I better get packing," Rusty said. "Come on, Della. You can help me."

Chapter 17

In the early evening of the day Rusty and Della departed, a pounding came on the front door. Faith answered it, and Elias Kumber was on the porch. "Where's my daughter?" he shouted. "I know she must have come here. Where is she?"

Sarah heard the commotion and moved to stand beside Faith. "She's not here. And you've no business pounding on our door. Go back to town or wherever you belong. Under a rock, maybe."

Kumber's red face turned almost purple. "You abominable piece of dung, if I see my daughter anywhere near either one of you, I'll kill you all." He stomped off the porch, got on his horse, and took off like something was chasing him.

"Whew," Faith said, "Rusty and Della got away in the nick of time."

"Yes, and I hope that ignorant, brutal man never sees his daughter again."

* * *

On Mondays, Sarah and Lindsay did the household laundry, an all-day undertaking.

The house had a separate laundry room with its own door to the outside. Inside sat a long sorting table, woven clothes baskets, and several washtubs on wooden benches. The washtubs had wringers attached to their sides and wooden rods to mix the clothes. One wall held a large fireplace with a mantel on which resided bars of laundry soap and bags of bluing, starch, and salt. Straight, wooden clothes-pegs rested in a cloth bag that could be thrown over the shoulder or put in one of the clothes baskets.

Near the edge of the cleared back lawn, rope had been fed from post to post to make four long lines to hang clothes. Three of those lines would have drooped with the weight of the clothing if notched poles hadn't propped them up. A brisk breeze hastened the drying process during good weather. In bad weather, they had to rely on the fireplace and drying racks inside the laundry room.

Early in the day, they'd hung out three tubs of white and light clothes which were almost dry. Two tubs of colored clothes were about ready to run through the wringers.

"Whew!" Sarah dropped the wooden rod into the tub of her colored clothes and put a hand to her back as she stood up straight. "I'm always glad when this chore is over. I don't know which hurts more, my back of my leg."

Lindsay stopped, too, and brushed a strand of black hair away from her face. Both women were sweating around their hairlines. "This isn't any worse than gardening, though maybe it's more intense."

"But the garden produces food to nourish us. Doing laundry doesn't produce much of anything. And like housecleaning, you have to do it over and over and over..."

Lindsay laughed. "I get the message. We could all go nude. Then we wouldn't need clothes."

"Hmmm." Sarah gave that some thought. "No, that won't work. I can think of a few people I wouldn't want to see nude. On the other hand..." A picture of Faith jumped into her mind, and she turned away so Lindsay wouldn't see her leer.

Lindsay smacked her arm. "Behave yourself, Sarah Coulter."

"Hey!" Sarah rubbed her arm. "I was thinking of my woman. That's not bad behavior, is it?"

"Not if you're telling the truth." Lindsay suddenly grabbed Sarah in a hug. "Oh, Sarah, I'm so sorry Scott and Mother Coulter are being mean to you and Faith. You've both been so good to all of us, sharing your home and everything. I'm ashamed of both of them, especially the way Mother Coulter treats Faith. And Faith is always kind to her. And to Scott."

Lindsay barely came to Sarah's shoulders. Sarah clasped Lindsay tighter and kissed the top of her head. "You've nothing to be ashamed of. You've always been on my side. You and Father." Tears stung Sarah's eyes at mention of her father. She clasped Lindsay tighter.

"Ahem." Faith's voice came from the doorway. "Should I be jealous?"

Lindsay gave Faith a huge smile and lifted an arm to her. "Never. I have a hug for you, too." She and Faith met and embraced. "Thank you for everything you've done and continue to do for us." Lindsay dropped her arms. "Please remember my gratitude every day in case I forget to tell you."

"Thank you for saying it," Faith said.

Lindsay picked up a basket and put the empty clothes-peg bag on her shoulder. "I'll get the clothes off the line. I'm sure they're dry by now with that breeze blowing." She went outside.

Faith flung herself into Sarah's outstretched arms, and Sarah kissed her soundly. Faith rubbed her forehead against Sarah's chin. "It's so nice to be able to kiss you without having to check the perimeter like a sentry."

"Yes, it is. Why are you home? I was going to pick you up at school when we finished the laundry." She lifted up an empty woven basket and went outside with Faith following her. Faith helped Lindsay fold a sheet while she answered Sarah.

"The Town Council's planning a Founders' Day Celebration two weeks from today, on a Friday. Some of the children were recruited to help with making the programs and decorations, and the School Board gave us the rest of today off."

"Founders' Day?" Lindsay gathered the corners of the sheet. "I wonder what kind of celebration the council's working on."

"I heard about a few items of interest." Faith grabbed the other corners and handed them to Lindsay when they met. "Different establishments are going to offer different values. For instance, the bakery will make half-price cookies and cakes with the Founders' theme. The bank's offering higher interest rates for a month or two on new accounts. And some of the shops are discounting certain merchandise. It sounds pretty good."

"It does," Sarah said. "Maybe we should start a new bank account for entertainment. We could save up for a vacation and actually go some place."

"Omigosh." Faith paired socks and rolled each into a ball as Sarah handed them to her. "Did you hear that word, Lindsay? Vacation? Will you be my witness?"

Sarah grabbed a pair of the balled-up socks and tossed them at Faith. They bounced off her chest and right back into the basket Sarah had set on the ground. She made a growling sound. "I never said we couldn't take a vacation." She handed Faith a dry undershirt.

"I know." Faith folded the shirt and carefully placed it in the basket. "But we've never had one. And I'm so in need of a break now. I know school's not out, but maybe we could take a weekend trip."

Sarah gave her a crooked grin. "We can at least talk about it, redhead. A weekend to ourselves sounds good to me."

Lindsay had taken down the first two rows of clothes and filled her basket. She returned to the laundry room while Faith and

Sarah finished the third and fourth rows. Sarah hefted the basket. "We still have two loads of dark clothes to wring out and hang. Let's get them done and start dinner."

"What are we having tonight?"

"Pork roast, peas, sweet potatoes, and baked apples for dessert."

"Mmm."

"And maybe some smart-aleck remarks to my mother to spice it up."

"Sarah!" Faith hit her with a hip as they entered the laundry room, laughing.

Chapter 18

Sarah finished the extra drawings that her editor requested, and on Saturday, Jessie came to the studio to help pack the manuscript and the art for mailing to the publisher.

Sarah opened an empty box to put everything in and lined it with several layers of old newspaper. "Jessie, thank you again for helping me with this. I couldn't have done it without you."

"You're very welcome, Aunt Sarah. I was happy to get the pointers you gave me. I learned a lot, especially about perspective." She slipped the manuscript inside a large envelope Sarah gave her and put it in the box.

Sarah put cardboard backing above, below, and in between the twelve drawings. She tied the bundle with string, wrapped it in newspaper, and added it to the manuscript box. She included a letter she had written to her publisher and sealed the box.

"Would you please address this for me?" She read the address and Jessie printed it on the box. "That's it," Sarah said. "Now all we have to do is mail it. We'll take care of that on Monday." She stole a glance at Jessie and caught a satisfied smile on her face. "I hear you have a sketchbook full of pictures that I've never seen."

Jessie turned bright red and smoothed down the skirt of her dress. "I have a lot of sketchbooks. I've been drawing since I was little."

"Would you mind showing one to me?"

"All right. I'll go get it."

When she returned, she set a sketchbook on the desk's drawing surface. "This is the newest one." She sat next to Sarah on the bench. Sarah opened the cover and found a nearly perfect illustration of Scott lying on the sofa.

"Jessie, this is fantastic." She turned several more pages, and Jessie described when and where she drew the subjects. Sarah reached a page near the end of the book, and her jaw dropped. Stunned at the image of a young man she saw, she could barely speak. "Who is this?" Her mind screamed at her: Perry Hager!

Jessie peered at her sharply. "Are you all right?"

Sarah nodded. She fought for her breath, which came heavily. She put her finger below the portrait and said again in a raspy voice, "Who is this?"

Jessie stared at her. "He's a boy I go to school with." She turned red again. "He's sweet on me. Do you know him?"

Sarah grimaced. "I'm not sure. Are you sweet on him?"

Jessie obviously was upset. She said, almost belligerently, "I am. What does that matter?"

"What's his name?"

"Perry."

Sarah felt like she'd been struck in the stomach with a hard fist. Please, please don't let his last name be Hager. Please. "What's his last name?"

"Wycoff. What's wrong with you, Aunt Sarah? You're acting like he's someone awful, and you've never even met him. That's not fair."

Sarah breathed a little easier but not much. "You're right, and I apologize. He reminds me of someone from my past, someone I hated. I suppose it's a coincidence." Oh God, please let it be a coincidence. "Are we going to get a chance to meet this young man?"

"The school's giving a barbecue dinner for the students next Saturday afternoon on the school grounds. Our families are invited, so yes, if you want to come, you can meet him."

Sarah stood. "I'll be there." Nothing could keep her away. "Jessie, your sketchbook is beautiful. I had no idea you were so advanced in your drawing. Thank you for showing it to me. I'm sorry if I upset you."

She hurried out of the room. Her thoughts clanged against her skull, bouncing from brain to bone and back again. She had to talk to Faith right away.

* * *

Sarah led Faith out to the pagoda behind the house and sat with her only for a moment. She jumped up to pace, almost stomping until pain told her she couldn't overuse her leg like that. So she sat back down and drummed her fingers on the table that filled the center of the structure.

Faith watched all this with a wrinkled brow and a rather bemused expression. She covered Sarah's drumming fingers with her hand. "What's this great mystery that's got you so upset?"

"Jessie showed me her latest sketchbook."

"And?"

"She's very good. Her drawings of Scott look like Scott. Her drawings of Lindsay look like Lindsay."

"I told you she was good. But why is that upsetting you?"

"Near the end of the sketchbook, I saw a drawing of one of the men who attacked me years ago."

Faith grabbed Sarah's hand in a tight grip. "What? That's impossible." She shook her head. "Are you sure? Which man was it?"

Sarah took a deep breath and let it out slowly. "Perry Hager. Jessie's father."

Faith put her hands together and raised them to her mouth. "But how could that be? They're all dead."

"You know how much Jessie resembles me except for her eyes. She has Hager's eyes. So does the drawing." She ran her hand through her hair. "He must be Hager's son. He's the exact image of him."

Faith took hold of Sarah's hand again. "That could be a coincidence. Lots of people resemble someone they don't even know. You haven't seen Hager since he got killed. Maybe your eyes are fooling you."

Sarah jumped up again, but she winced and sat right back down. "For God's sake, Faith! The man attacked me. His face is burned into my brain. I'm not making a mistake. Besides, the boy's name is Perry. How many Perrys do you know? He has a different last name, but maybe he has a new father."

"All right, let's say he is Hager's son. No one needs to know his father is Jessie's father. Let's keep quiet about it."

Sarah's shoulders slumped. She leaned her head on her hand and stared at the table. "He and Jessie are sweet on each other."

Faith gasped. "Oh my God."

"Exactly." Sarah lifted her head and met Faith's gaze. "I'm not going to say anything to Scott and Lindsay until I'm sure."

"And how do you expect to be sure?"

"Jessie's school is having a barbecue dinner next Saturday for the students and their families. I'm going. I want to meet this boy's mother. I saw Perry Hager's widow once, and if that's who she is, I'll know her."

"This is going to be a long week."

"Yes, it is."

* * *

That afternoon, Lindsay approached Sarah in her studio. "Sarah, do you have a minute to talk?"

"Sure. I'm trying to work the stiffness out of my fingers by drawing a picture." She patted the bench next to her. "Sit down, and we'll talk."

Lindsay sat and studied the nascent drawing. "That's Redfire, isn't it?"

"Yes. I guess my dexterity is returning after all." She nudged Lindsay with her elbow. "What did you want to talk about?"

Lindsay folded her hands in her lap. "Jessie tells me the picture she drew of one of her classmates upset you, and she's worried about that."

Sarah's fingers tightened on her pencil. "I'm worried about it, too. I should have told you and Scott about it right away."

Lindsay sat up straighter. "Your tone sounds ominous. Whatever is the problem?"

"You know the picture she drew of Perry Wycoff?"

"Yes. She said that's the one that bothered you. What's wrong?"

"Did you notice his eyes are similar to Jessie's?"

"Yes, I did notice that. Jessie said that was what first caught her attention about him. What of it?"

Sarah shifted on the bench and ran her hand through her hair. "Lindsay, I don't know how to say this except to blurt it right out. That picture of Perry Wycoff is a perfect duplicate of Perry Hager, the man who was Jessie's father."

Lindsay's mouth dropped open, and she blinked several times. They sat in silence. Sarah thought her heart would break at the pain she saw in Lindsay's face. She put down her pencil and placed her hands over Lindsay's. "I'm so, so sorry. I know this is a shock."

Lindsay gazed at their clasped hands, and her shoulders slumped. "Could you be mistaken?"

"I suppose I could be, but I feel pretty sure. Jessie said the school's having a party for the students and their families next Saturday. I figure I'll go and meet the boy's parents. I would recognize Hager's widow. She might recognize me, too."

Lindsay snapped upright, and her voice got firm. "No, let's not wait. You and I and Scott need to visit the Wycoff's tomorrow. Sunday's visiting day, so I'm sure they'll see us. We must meet this head-on, Sarah. Jessie likes this boy, and we might have to tell her that's all it can be—friendship."

Tears came to Sarah's eyes, and she tried to blink them away. "You do realize what this could mean, don't you? Jessie would have to be told that I bore her. That you and Scott adopted her."

"Yes." Lindsay started to cry, and she and Sarah touched their heads together and put their arms around each other as their tears poured forth.

Chapter 19

Sunday afternoon, Sarah drove the buggy toward the Wycoff property, with Lindsay and Scott in the backseat. According to Lindsay, Scott hadn't had too much to say, other than, "Damn, damn, damn." Sarah supposed he was too shocked at the time to think straight, but she figured once the shock wore off, she would hear more from him. She was right. As they rode, she couldn't shut him up. Trouble was, he kept saying the same things over and over. Here it came again.

"You can't be right about this, Sarah. You saw this man, what, fifteen or sixteen years ago? And the boy has a different last name. Wouldn't a boy keep his father's name?" Sarah heard him slap his thigh. "You're getting Lindsay all upset over nothing. But you're good at getting people upset, aren't you? Maybe one of these days you'll realize the world doesn't revolve around you."

Sarah had given up discussing the matter with Scott after the third or fourth attempt. She wished he would shut up and give Lindsay a break. The poor woman was overwrought with nervous energy. What was it she said to Sarah as they parted earlier? "You'd never be wrong about anything this important, Sarah." She probably already accepted that the boy and Jessie were half-brother and half-sister.

Scott finally quieted when they reached the Wycoff's house. Sarah tied the buggy to the hitching post, climbed the steps to the porch, and approached the door. After she knocked, a short, slender man with black hair and a neatly clipped beard answered the door.

"Mr. Wycoff?" Sarah said.

He looked her up and down and frowned a moment, but then he raised his eyebrows and said, "Yes. What can I do for you?"

"My name's Sarah Coulter." Sarah pointed toward the buggy. "My brother and his wife and I have some important questions we need to ask of your wife. Could she spare us a moment, please?"

"I'm right here, Arthur." Mrs. Wycoff stood in front of the doorway as Mr. Wycoff made way for her. "I'm Doris Wycoff. Do I know you?"

Sarah's heart fell into her shoes. She had hoped against hope that she was wrong. But the woman in front of her definitely was Perry Hager's widow.

Sarah removed her hat and got closer to the doorway. "I know who you are, ma'am. I'm Sarah Coulter. You might remember me from a long way back." She stood still, waiting.

Doris Wycoff's brow furrowed. Suddenly, it cleared. "I remember now. You were there when Perry was killed. You shot the man who killed him."

"Yes, ma'am." She pointed once more toward the buggy. "My brother and his wife and I have important information concerning your late husband. Do you have time right now to speak with us?"

"Yes, I do. Please come in."

"I need to help my brother, Scott. He's been ill and isn't fully recovered yet."

"I'll give him a hand," Arthur Wycoff said. Sarah moved out of his way as he came out onto the porch. "You go on in and make yourself at home."

Sarah entered the house and followed Mrs. Wycoff to the sitting room. "Mrs. Wycoff—"

"Please, have a seat." She indicated the sofa to Sarah and sat in one of the stuffed chairs. She gave a slight smile. "I see you're still wearing men's clothes. When I saw you with Perry, I thought you were a man, but someone explained to me that you were a woman."

"I was always very active, and I did a lot of traveling on horseback. I discovered that men's clothes were much more comfortable for that than women's were. I've stayed with them over the years." She glanced around the pleasant room and saw photographs of two boys on the mantel. She rose to examine them. Scott and Lindsay entered the room, followed by Arthur Wycoff. Arthur introduced them to his wife, and they sat on the sofa Sarah had vacated. Arthur stood at the other end of the mantel.

"Did we miss anything?" he asked in an agreeable tone.

"No," his wife said. She waved a hand toward Sarah. "Miss Coulter was looking at the photographs of the boys."

Sarah picked up the one of Perry and said in a somber tone, "He bears a great resemblance to his father."

"Yes," Mrs. Wycoff said. "That made it difficult for me for quite a while." She smiled at her husband. "Until I met Arthur."

Lindsay spoke up. "Has Perry ever mentioned a classmate, Jessie Coulter?"

"Yes, he has," Mrs. Wycoff said. "I recognized your last name immediately. Are you her parents?"

"Yes, we are," Scott said. He put his arm through Lindsay's and hugged it to him. "That is, we're her adopted parents," he added in a raspy voice.

"Perry speaks very well of your daughter. He seems quite taken with her." Mrs. Wycoff glanced back and forth from Scott to Lindsay, and her voice sounded more reserved. "Is that why you're here? Do you object to that?"

"That's why we're here," Scott said, "but we have nothing against your son. Unforeseeable circumstances have forced us to object to his being interested in our daughter." Scott nodded toward Sarah. "My sister will explain our dilemma."

Sarah set Perry's photograph back onto the mantel and turned full-face toward the three seated people whose gazes were fixed on her. She gestured toward her clothing with both hands. "I disguised myself as a man and served in the war as a scout for the Confederacy. I was captured by three Union soldiers, Angston, Wertz...and Hager. When they discovered I was a woman, they didn't turn me in to the authorities. They staked me out on the floor of the forest and took turns assaulting me."

Mrs. Wycoff put her hand to her mouth and shook her head.

"To give Perry his due, he was forced into assaulting me by Angston, his sergeant, who held a gun on him and threatened to kill him if he didn't join in. All the time he was on top of me, he cried, and said over and over that he was sorry." She stopped and cleared her throat.

"Wait, Miss Coulter," Arthur Wycoff said. "Let me get you a drink. What would you like?"

"Water, please." She waited until he returned to hand her a tall glass filled nearly to the brim. She drank deeply. "Thank you."

Wycoff nodded and sat in a stuffed chair. "Please continue."

"When the assault was over, Hager was told to kill me." She heard Mrs. Wycoff gasp. "But he purposely faked my death. He tilted the pistol barrel when he shot, and the fire coming out of it burned me. That's how I got this." Sarah touched the scars on the upper right quadrant of her face and ran her fingers back over the white part of her hair. "I hated those men. I hated all three of them. And I swore I would hunt them down and kill them. Wertz died in the war. Turns out the only one I got rid of was Angston. He and Hager tricked me. Hager had the drop on me, but he refused to fire at me, so Angston shot him. Angston turned his gun on me, and I shot him." Sarah took another drink of water. Retelling this story brought back every wretched moment of the worst experience in her life, and she felt sick to her stomach.

But I can do this, she told herself. The Wycoffs were hanging on every word. So were Scott and Lindsay.

"I've skipped over the most important part of this revelation, the part that concerns all of us." She took a deep breath and pushed it out noisily. "A few weeks after being assaulted in the woods, I found out I was pregnant...with Jessie." She stopped to let that information sink in and held up her hand to forestall any questions.

"I was unmarried, consumed with hatred, and determined to chase down those soldiers. I had no room for a baby in my life. So Lindsay and Scott offered to adopt her. And I wholeheartedly accepted their offer. So that brings us to where we are today." She took a sip of water.

"Jessie doesn't know she's adopted. She thinks her features come from her father, Scott. But they actually come from me. Except she has Perry Hager's eyes and hair color." Sarah gazed toward the Wycoffs, who seemed astounded. "And she's very attracted to a young man who happens to be her half-brother. What do we do now?" Sarah sat in a third stuffed chair that nestled with the other two in a semicircle in front of the sofa. "What do we do now?" she repeated harshly.

Arthur Wycoff looked around at each of them. "Perry knows I'm not his father. Our job won't be easy, but it's going to be a lot easier than yours."

"Yes," Doris Wycoff said. "I feel sorry for you." She gestured outwardly. "I feel sorry for all of us."

"And our children," Lindsay added in a voice that trembled.

"And our children," Sarah whispered.

Scott said, "I don't think we should tell them together. It's going to be hard enough on them to be told separately. But I do think we need to tell them at the same time. We don't want one knowing and one not knowing."

"Suppose we tell them tomorrow, when they come home from school?" Lindsay said. She glanced from Scott to Sarah and back. "That will give us time to calm down and put our thoughts together."

"That's all right with me." Scott gave Lindsay's arm a squeeze.

Mrs. Wycoff inclined her head toward her husband, and he said, "That's all right with us, too."

"Sarah?" Lindsay asked.

Sarah nodded. Tomorrow, she thought, with a feeling of doom. Tomorrow will change us all.

* * *

Sarah told Faith everything that happened at the Wycoff's. Later, she went to bed and tossed and turned all night while phantoms from the past trailed wispy fingers through her dreams. Grateful for the arrival of dawn and the light glimmering through the window, she lay in bed and soaked in its warmth. She gathered her thoughts, groaned, and rose with trepidation to face the new day.

Faith stirred and lifted a hand toward her. "Come back to bed," she murmured. "It's too early to get up yet."

Sarah took Faith's hand and kissed her knuckles. "I can't sleep. Figured I might as well get up and get moving." If someone had told Sarah she would be this disturbed about how Jessie might look upon her, she would have scoffed. The only deep feeling she had about Jessie was her disgust at how she had been born. Wasn't that the truth? She didn't even like having her in the same house as a constant reminder of that horror. Wasn't that also the truth? Sarah's innate honesty forced her to admit she no longer felt that way. Jessie was her daughter, and she loved her.

Faith drew Sarah's hand against her cheek before she let go of it. "I know you were restless. Your family meeting doesn't happen until after Carey Gilson brings Jessie home from school. Try to keep busy until then."

"I'm grateful Carey's able to take her back and forth, even though it's a little out of his way."

Faith smiled. "I'm sure the money Scott and Lindsay give him makes it worthwhile."

"True, but he has a horse to feed and care for and a buggy to keep in good shape, so it evens out. Otherwise, someone here would have to take her, probably me."

"I hadn't given that much thought. But I see what you mean."

"Right now," Sarah said, "I'll fix breakfast as usual. I can drop you off at school and mail out my manuscript. Maybe pick up some groceries. After that, I'll come home and start on my next book if I can stay focused. I already have the beginning in mind. I'll pick you up when school's out."

"That sounds good to me."

"Go back to sleep. I'll call you when breakfast is ready." Sarah realized that she was jittery. Although she considered Faith the more emotional of the two of them, sometimes their roles seemed reversed. This was one of those times.

But Faith didn't have a daughter who would probably hate her by the end of the day.

Chapter 20

Sarah mailed the manuscript to her publisher, folded the receipt, and stuck it in her shirt pocket. She checked for mail and finding none, left the post office. The coming talk with Jessie weighed so heavily on her that she barely noticed the beauty of the day. She strode up the boardwalk, and as she passed the sheriff's office, she heard Schmidt shout.

"Miss Sarah, wait up." He came to the doorway and beckoned her in. "I have something I want to show you."

Sarah entered and followed Schmidt to his desk where he sat down. "Bring that chair around, Sarah, and sit where you can see this map." The map showed Missouri and the states surrounding it. Large black X's marked on it were connected by a black line. "I've been trying to keep an eye on Litchfield." He ran his finger along the black line. "These marks are all bank robberies. I don't have any proof, but the robberies started as soon as he broke out of jail. I'm assuming he's involved. They hit banks in Arkansas, Illinois, Iowa, Kansas, Kentucky, Nebraska, and Tennessee. Now they've moved into Missouri."

"And they're getting closer," Sarah murmured.

"Yep, they are. He's within two days' ride of here. I filled Ed Bristow in, in case they plan to rob his bank." Schmidt's brow creased. "I'm concerned. I'm not sure whether our bank is on his list, but I'm pretty sure you and Faith are."

"I have to agree with you there, Herman." As if she didn't have enough on her mind already.

"We all know his face, so we'll be on the lookout for him." Schmidt pointed a finger at her. "You be careful, too."

"I'm not worried about me." Sarah removed her hat, set it on her knee, and ran her fingers through her hair. "Five days a week, Faith's at the schoolhouse and I'm at home. Litchfield's so obsessed with her, he's crazy enough to try to grab her in town."

Schmidt shifted his bulk. His size made the chair look small. "Or on her way back and forth."

"That's a good thought. I'll take her to school and back now." Sarah put on her hat and stood.

Schmidt rose, too. "I can't be everywhere, Sarah. I wish to hell I could."

Sarah strode to the doorway and turned around. "I know that. I'll keep my eyes peeled for anything suspicious."

"Me, too." He gave her a wave. She touched a finger to her hat and exited out onto the boardwalk.

Sarah laid her hand on the butt of the gun riding in the holster tied to her right thigh.

I hope the bastard does show up. If he comes near my woman, I'll shoot his blasted balls off.

* * *

Lindsay, Scott, and Sarah congregated in the living room to talk over what to say to Jessie. Lindsay's eyes kept filling with tears, but she managed to keep them at bay. Sarah had always admired Lindsay's strength. That strength would soon be sorely tested.

Sarah cleared her throat. "I'm so sorry you both have to go through this."

"Oh, Sarah," Lindsay said, "it's not your fault. You gave us a daughter, and we've had sixteen years of a wonderful relationship with her. We'll get past this. I do worry about how hurt she might feel that we never told her."

"Strange, isn't it?" Sarah said. "That family could have settled in a thousand other places, but they chose here."

Scott said, "Sometimes fate has a way of punishing us for what we do wrong."

Sarah rose and paced. "And what did I do wrong, dear brother? Did I ask those bastards to attack me?"

Scott snorted. "First of all, you shouldn't have pretended to be a man and joined the army. And second, you shouldn't continue to pretend to be a man. You don't understand the harm that does."

"I'm not pretending to be a man," she ground out evenly. She halted in front of him and jammed her fists on her hips. She desperately wanted to crash one into Scott's face. "Are you serious? My 'pretending,' as you put it, hasn't harmed anyone except bigots like you who think you have the right to tell everyone else how to act. And if I hadn't joined the army, Jessie wouldn't exist and we wouldn't be having this discussion."

Lindsay rose and tugged on Sarah's arm. "Please sit back down. Everyone's upset, but please don't fight with each other. We have Jessie to worry about."

Sarah reluctantly resumed her seat, and Lindsay sat, too.

"Thank you," Lindsay said. "Now here's what I think we should do..."

* * *

Sarah picked up Faith after school, and the ride home was relatively quiet. In answer to Faith's one question, Sarah said, "We're about as prepared as we could be. No one knows how Jessie will react, so we could only do so much."

Faith put her hand on Sarah's thigh and gave a little squeeze. "You'll be fine."

"I hope you're right."

* * *

Jessie met Lindsay and Scott in the kitchen after Carey dropped her off. She glanced back and forth between them. "Is something wrong?"

Scott said, "We need to have a talk with you, sweetheart. Put your things away and come to the living room."

Jessie seemed alarmed. "Are you all right, Father? Is your sickness worse?"

"I'm fine. This has nothing to do with my health. We'll explain in the living room. We'll meet you there."

Jessie ran toward their part of the house and disappeared. Scott leaned a little bit on Lindsay as they walked arm in arm to the living room and sat on the sofa. Sarah, already there, was in one of the wingback chairs. The weather hadn't cooled enough for a fire in the fireplace, but they all wore sweaters.

Jessie came hurrying into the room, and Scott waved her toward the chair next to Sarah. Jessie perched on the edge of the seat, clasping and unclasping her hands. She turned toward Sarah. "Is it you, Aunt Sarah? Are you all right?"

Sarah felt her muscles tightening as she inclined her head toward Scott. "Your father has something to say to you." Jessie's gaze swerved to Scott.

Scott cleared his throat. "There's something we maybe should have told you a long time ago." He covered his eyes for a moment with a trembling hand but quickly dropped it into his lap. "Your mother and I"— he swept his gaze to Lindsay and back to Jessie—"love you very much, but we aren't..." He faltered, and his lips twitched. "Your mother isn't your mother. She isn't the woman who gave birth to you."

Jessie sat speechless for a moment, apparently stunned. When she found her voice, she said, "She's not my mother? You had me by another woman?"

"No!" The word erupted from Scott like cannon fire. "I would never cheat on your mother." His tone turned poignant. "I'm not your father, either."

Jessie gasped and frowned and her voice quavered. "But you must be. I resemble you." Her head moved slowly back and forth as she searched his face, but Scott couldn't bring himself to say anything more. "I must be your daughter. How could I look so much like you if..." After an awkward pause, Jessie's expression changed as though she had found an answer. She turned to Sarah.

"It's you," she said, sounding like a prosecutor. "It's you I get the drawing talent from. You're the one who gave birth to me."

Sarah said, "Yes."

"So am I *your* love child?"

"No. There was no love involved. Let me explain."

"Oh, please do. I can't wait to hear it."

Sarah realized that Jessie's anger and sarcasm arose from the startling revelation of her birth, but she had no forewarning that Jessie's attitude would feel so hurtful. She glanced at Lindsay and saw tears rolling down her cheeks. She sucked in a breath. This had to be hurting Lindsay—and Scott—even more than it did her.

"I didn't know your father. I was attacked."

"Attacked?" Jessie looked doubtful.

"Let me start from the beginning."

Sarah told Jessie the whole sordid story. She tried to emphasize that Perry had been forced at gunpoint to go along with his superior's order. She also stressed that Scott and Lindsay had eagerly asked for the chance to raise her as their own daughter.

Jessie's face crumpled more than once during the recitation. "You gave me away? Without a care?"

Sarah rubbed her face with both hands. "Please understand, Jessie. Every time I looked at you, I relived that ordeal. I hated those men, and innocent though you were, I hated you, too." There, she had said it.

"I knew it. I knew you didn't like me. I didn't understand why. The only time I felt comfortable with you was when I helped you with your book. Now I wish I hadn't done it." Jessie jumped up from her chair. "I hate you, too!"

"But I don't hate you anymore." Sarah wanted to convey her change of heart. "I know you now as a person, not as the issue from that terrible time."

"Issue? Issue? I don't suppose you know which one was my father."

"But I do. You have his eyes. That's why we're here, why we're having this discussion." She reached behind her chair and brought forth Jessie's latest sketchbook.

"That's my sketchbook. What are you doing with it? How did you get it?"

"Your mother got it for me."

"My mother? I thought you were my mother."

Sarah stopped with the sketchbook in her lap. "Jessie, when I bore you, I was angry and sick at heart and full of hatred. I vowed to kill the men who had attacked me, and I went after them. I was in no condition to take care of a child. Lindsay and Scott did me—and you—a huge favor by taking you and raising you in a loving family for sixteen years. They deserve to be called your mother and father."

"We love you, Jessie," Scott and Lindsay said almost together.

Jessie glanced toward them, but her mind was focused on Sarah. "Did you kill my father?"

"No." Sarah explained what had happened to Perry Hagar. "At the time all this occurred, I saw his wife, too. That's important for you to remember."

Sarah leafed through the sketches until she reached the one she wanted to show Jessie. She pointed to the picture of Perry Wycoff. "This is an exact picture of the man who was your father. Especially notice his eyes. They're like yours."

Jessie hovered over Sarah's shoulder to see the sketchbook, and her whole body sagged. "No. Oh no. That can't be." Her expression brightened for a moment. "Perry's last name is Wycoff, not the name you said."

"That's why I told you to remember I met Perry Hagar's wife. Your parents and I went to see them on Sunday. Mrs. Wycoff is the former Mrs. Hagar. She remarried."

"But... but... that means Perry and I are half-brother and half-sister."

"Yes, it does, and the Wycoff's are telling Perry about it right now. I'm sorry. Under different circumstances, Perry would probably be happy to learn he has a half-sister."

Jessie abruptly straightened up. "First you threw me away, and now you're ruining my life." She stomped her foot. "How could you do that to me?"

Sarah stood and raised her voice. It had an edge to it. "I didn't ask to be assaulted. I didn't ask to be pregnant, and I sure as hell didn't ask for a baby. So whatever I did to you wasn't planned. It happened against my wishes."

They were together, nearly nose to nose, and Jessie started shaking. She shouted, "I didn't ask to be born, either. I didn't ask to have you for a mother. I didn't have anything to do with what those men did to you. But you blame me for it. And you've completely torn apart my feelings for Perry. I hate you!" She gestured wildly. "I hate all of you!" She dashed out of the room.

Lindsay leaped up to follow her.

Sarah felt like shards of ice had entered her chest and were piercing her heart.

Scott said, "That didn't go very well."

Sarah stared at him. She had to keep telling herself that he was hurt, too. "Did you expect it to? She was hit by two big revelations at the same time. None of us would react in a good way to that. She took it better than I thought she would."

Scott coughed and inhaled several short breaths. "But she hates us. You think that's all right?"

"When she calms down, she'll remember the life you and Lindsay have given her, and she'll get over her hatred for you. Her hatred for me might be a different story. I've never done much to win her over." Sarah rubbed her chest, but the pain was still there.

"Most of the time you seemed like you barely tolerated her. Even I noticed that."

"I know, and I was wrong. It took me sixteen years—and this jarring situation—to admit that she's my flesh and blood and I care for her. I don't know what to do to make up for that lack of attention."

"Perhaps all you can do is keep trying, I guess. Same as us."

"I guess. Do you need help getting to your rooms?"

"No, I'd rather sit here in the quiet and think. Lindsay will come after me when she's ready to."

"Remind Lindsay and Mother there's a pot of stew on the range. I don't feel much like eating."

"Neither do I," Scott muttered.

Sarah took a good look at him. He seemed to have shriveled up in the corner of the sofa. An uncharitable thought leaped into her mind, and she chided herself for it. But it was true. She was glad Jessie had her assertiveness rather than Scott's passivity. The girl was a fighter.

Sarah leaned over and kissed the top of Scott's head as she

passed behind the sofa. "Let's hope for the best, brother. This could be a rough ride."

He seemed surprised and sat up a little straighter. "I'm afraid you're right."

Sarah hurried from the room. She couldn't wait to put her arms around Faith and be embraced in return. She needed to feel loved.

* * *

Faith wasn't in the kitchen or the studio, so Sarah climbed the steps to the second floor. She found Faith sitting in the bedroom. Faith stood, opened her arms wide, and Sarah walked into them. She held Faith close and buried her nose in Faith's hair. She always smelled so good.

Sarah started crying, and Faith held her silently until she was all cried out for the moment. When Sarah's hold relaxed, Faith took her hand and led her to sit on the settee in the corner of the bedroom.

Faith said, "Do you want to talk about it?"

Sarah tugged a handkerchief from her pocket, wiped her eyes and cheeks, and blew her nose. "Not too much to talk about, to be honest. Scott and I told her everything, and now she hates us. Especially me." She balled up the handkerchief and stuck it back in her pocket. "Can't say as I blame her. If I were in her shoes, I'd hate me, too."

"You're being pretty hard on yourself, aren't you? You did what you thought was right at the time. So did Scott and Lindsay."

Sarah grimaced. "Try telling that to Jessie. She accused me of throwing her away." Tears trickled down her cheeks again, and she wiped them away with her fingers. "In a way, I guess I did."

"That's the first I've heard you admit it."

"I know you've chided me about that before, and I've always sidestepped it. No one likes to admit their failures."

"Failures have a way of coming back to bite us in the rear end. This is a perfect example."

Sarah leaned her head back against the wall and closed her eyes. "Scott said something very similar. Are you taking her side, then?"

Faith twined her fingers into Sarah's left hand and gave it a squeeze. "My heart is always on your side, even if my mind thinks otherwise. You should know that by now."

Sarah opened her eyes and turned toward Faith. "Thank

you," she said softly.

Faith smiled. "You're welcome. I have to confess I peeked into the living room when I heard some shouting going on. You and Jessie were standing toe-to-toe and yelling at each other. You could have been gazing into a mirror with your hair and eye colors changed. She certainly is her mother's daughter, in more ways than one."

Sarah gave a rueful smile. "She is feisty." Her face fell. "But that might make her hate me more."

"Give her time, Sarah. She's an intelligent girl. She'll come around."

Sarah sighed. "I hope you're right. I had no idea this would hit me so hard. I need time to come around, too." She leaned over and ran her hands through her hair. "I have something else to tell you."

"What?"

Sarah glanced up, and Faith's expression told her she must look like hell. That was no surprise. She sure felt like hell. "When I was in town this morning, Herman called me in to his office. He's been tracking bank robberies that he thinks could be the work of Litchfield. Herman says the last bank was about two days' ride from here."

Faith grabbed Sarah's forearm with both hands. "What can we do?"

"First off, I'm going to take you to school and back each day. I don't want him swooping down and spiriting you off. He's crazy enough to try that."

"I agree. But I'm not the only one in danger. He probably wants revenge on you. And maybe Leah, too."

"I'll stay aware. And I'll let Leah know what's going on. Not much else we can do right now. I thought of riding toward him and settling it before he got anywhere near you, but I have no way of knowing exactly where he is. I could be riding around searching for him, and he could get past me without my knowing it."

"No, please don't change your mind and go after him. I want you near me."

"Don't worry. I'll stay as near as I can." Sarah patted Faith's hands. "You can let go of my arm now and let the blood flow back in."

Faith released her hold and gave a small laugh. "Sorry. The idea of Joel being so close scares me."

"Me, too. We'll have to keep alert as to where and when he could surprise us."

Sarah's mind raced through possibilities of protecting Faith. "Maybe you should carry a gun."

Faith appeared startled. "Where would I put it? Don't forget I'm surrounded by children most of the time."

"Mmm, that's right." Sarah scratched her head. "I could get you one that fits into a small holster that straps to your thigh underneath your dress."

Faith considered that for a moment. "No, I don't think so. I'm not experienced with a gun like you are. I might shoot myself in the foot. Besides, I don't think Joel wants to risk his freedom by killing me. If he shows up, I think it will be because he wants to steal me away from you. And maybe hurt you in the process."

Sarah made a growling sound. "Neither of those plans will work if I can help it. But you're probably right. Okay, no gun."

Faith gave Sarah's arm a pat and stood. "Do you want to come to the kitchen with me to get some stew?"

"Good God, no. The last thing I need is to run into my mother."

"All right. I'll get some and bring it here. I'm hungry, and I know you have to be."

"I wasn't at first. I was too upset. But you always help me calm down, and I appreciate that." She grabbed Faith's hand and kissed it. "I love you. I don't know what I'd do without you."

"I feel the same way about you, sweetheart, so don't plan on running off anywhere."

"Nah, you're stuck with me forever, whether you like it or not."

Sarah let go of her hand, and Faith waggled a finger as she headed toward the door. "Keep thinking about that. I'll be right back with some food."

When Faith returned, she put a tray on the end table near the bed. "It's getting dark," she said. She lit the gas fixture on the wall near the door.

"Ummm. That stew smells good. Thank you for getting it."

After they ate, Sarah undressed and climbed under the covers while Faith searched through the bureau for a fresh nightgown. When she undressed and was about to put it on, Sarah said, "Wait."

Faith grabbed the nightgown to her chest and turned toward at Sarah. "What for?"

Sarah tilted her head. "I hardly ever get to see your whole body at one time. Put the nightgown down and come to me. I want to feast my eyes on you." When Faith hesitated, she added, "Please?"

Faith dropped the gown on the floor, put one hand on her hip, and sauntered toward Sarah.

Faith had the most beautiful body Sarah could ever imagine, all curves and hills and valleys. And her glorious red curls were mirrored in the triangle where her legs met.

Faith said, "So you're getting a feast. Where's mine?"

Sarah flipped off the covers. She was nude. She sat up on the edge of the bed and put her hands on her knees. Gazing all the while at Faith, she pushed her knees slowly apart and smiled.

Faith's full breasts rose and fell more quickly. When she reached the bed, she fell to her knees between Sarah's legs. She slipped her arms under Sarah's thighs. "Here I come, ready or not," she said hoarsely. She lifted Sarah's legs and dipped her head.

Sarah tangled her fingers in Faith's hair, and her thighs tightened against Faith's cheeks. "I am ready," Sarah whispered. A few moments later, her body heaved and her voice sounded strangled. "You found me. You found me."

Chapter 21

Joel Litchfield and Burt Dembroke sat in the kitchen of the house on their newly acquired ranch. A bowl of peanuts rested in the middle of the table, and they were washing them down with uncorked bottles of beer.

"I got to give you credit, Doc," Dembroke said. He touched the neck of his beer bottle to Litchfield's in salute. "You picked a right nice spot for us to buy a place." He took a swig of beer, set the bottle down, and tapped the map Litchfield had spread out on the table. "And jumping from state to state to rob banks was pure genius. No one knows where to look for us."

"That was the idea," Litchfield said. He jabbed at the map as he spoke. "Now here we are in Oklahoma, with a place of our own to retire to."

"Yeah," Dembroke said, "and the boys like the idea of us hiring them to be our ranch hands. I guess they're ready to quit robbing banks, too." He had been surprised when Litchfield offered to give the members of their gang a chance to quit and work for them. And even more surprised when almost all of them jumped at it. Only one of them turned down the offer and left. The gang's share of the loot gave them enough to live comfortably as long as they held steady jobs. Of course, Litchfield's and Dembroke's shares had been ten times as much. They had enough to last the rest of their lives, whether the ranch was a success or not.

"Seems like it. We have a full pantry and larder, too, and I bet they like having good food at hand all the time. I certainly do." They hadn't bought many perishables yet. They weren't quite ready to retire in earnest.

"Me, too." Dembroke grabbed a handful of peanuts and cracked the first shell. "You going to be happy ranching, Doc?"

Litchfield rubbed his forehead and grimaced. "You know I don't know much about it. If I don't like it, maybe I can leave that up to you and open a practice in town." His expression cleared and his eyes gleamed. "Faith would like that. She could act as my nurse." He tilted his head back and finished his beer. He set the empty bottle down. "Now it's time to plan how to get her here."

"No lying low for a while?"

"We've rested for a week. That last bank we robbed in Missouri was only two or three days' ride from Bonneforte. I wanted her so bad, I was sorely tempted to go after her right then."

"So you said. I'm glad you listened to reason." Dembroke popped some shelled peanuts into his mouth.

"I realized it would take some planning. Last thing I want to do is get caught as I'm bringing her back here. But I'm tired of waiting."

"What do you want to do?"

"I have someone watching their actions."

"What?" Dembroke frowned. "You didn't tell me that. You might make them suspicious." He got up and yanked a couple more beer bottles from the tub full of ice they were packed in.

"I'm sure they're already suspicious. But they have no way of telling when or where we'll strike."

Dembroke returned to the table and set down the beers. He slid the bail over on his and twisted off the cork stopper. "When is this 'watcher' going to contact you?"

"We have a drop-off place in a hollow tree outside of town. I'll pick up his information when we get there, and I can figure out when would be the best time to grab Faith." Litchfield opened his bottle and took a drink. "Then, while a couple of us get her and that bitch, the rest of the boys can rob the Bonneforte bank." His grin was sly. "Kill two birds with one stone."

"Sounds good to me. When do we start?"

"We'll leave first thing tomorrow morning."

* * *

After Sarah dropped Faith off at school on Tuesday, she drove the buggy to Leah's.

"Sarah! Come in. I'm about to have some coffee. And I think I can rustle up a cookie or two for you. I made some yesterday."

Sarah removed her hat. "You look mighty purty today, ma'am." The words brought a flush to Leah's cheeks.

"Why thank you, kind...lady, I think." They both laughed.

Leah did look good. She wore a full-skirted cotton dress of a light yellow color covered with tiny blue blossoms. The yellow nearly matched the hair she'd plaited over top of her head and secured with blue bows the same shade as the blossoms.

She took Sarah's hat from her and hung it on a rack by the door. "Is this a new hat? I see it's different from the flat-top style you wore before." She meandered into the kitchen with Sarah right behind her. She obviously had been sorting laundry. A jumble of unmatched socks and assorted handkerchiefs lay on the table.

"Yes, and it's from Amy as usual. She's still buying me a new hat every other year or so."

Leah reached for the clean laundry, but Sarah said, "Leave it there. I'll help you sort it while we talk." Sarah sat at the table and Leah served coffee and cookies before she joined her.

"Amy told me she had kept up with buying you hats because it was so much fun. She sure is crazy about her Aunt Sarah." Leah tapped Sarah's arm. "As are we all. The whole danged family has a crush on you."

Sarah laughed. "I feel the same about all of you."

"It's good to hear you laugh, Sarah. But you don't look happy. What's wrong? Can you tell me?"

Sarah sucked in a breath and let it out slowly. She wrapped her hands around her coffee mug and blinked as her eyes got wet.

Leah seemed alarmed. "What is it? Are you all right?"

Sarah nodded and finally found her voice. "We had to tell Jessie the truth, that I'm her mother."

"Oh, no." Leah put her hand over her mouth for a moment. "Why? What happened?"

"She showed me a drawing of a boy she's sweet on at school, and he was the spitting image of Perry Hager." Sarah told Leah the whole story of the revelation. Her voice caught at the end when she said, "She hates me, Leah."

Leah scooted her chair closer and put an arm around Sarah. "I'm sure she doesn't hate you. She had a lot dumped in her lap, and it's natural to fight back. Especially for her."

Sarah swiped a hand at her damp cheeks. "What's that supposed to mean?"

"She *is* your daughter." Leah poked her in the side. "I'm glad she takes after you instead of..." Her words trailed off.

Sarah choked out a brief laugh. "I confess I had the same thought. But knowing that she hates me hurts more than I ever could have imagined. I haven't treated her well, Leah, and now it's coming back on me."

Leah gave Sarah's back a pat. "You'll have plenty of time to make up for that. Give her some space for a while. When she gets to know you better, she can't help but love you."

"Of course." Sarah gave a wry grin.

"You'll see. Mama Leah knows what's best." Leah jiggled her chair back into place. She picked up two socks. "Meanwhile, I thought you offered to help me sort these."

"You're right. About the sorting anyway." She got another poke in the ribs from Leah, then she sobered. "But I have some more unsettling news for you."

Leah set the two matched socks aside. She picked up two more but hesitated and turned her attention to Sarah. "And what might that be?"

"Herman Schmidt called me into his office yesterday and told me that Doc Litchfield is likely getting closer to the vicinity. He cautioned me to keep an eye out for him, and I offered to convey that warning to you, too."

Leah folded the two socks together and set them on the others. "That man has been nothing but trouble from day one. But I suspect he has his sights set on hurting you and stealing Faith away. He should have his hands full attempting to accomplish those two objectives. I doubt he'll have time to vent his spleen on me."

Sarah smiled. "Vent his spleen? Is that a new phrase?" Ever since Sarah had introduced Leah to the world of words through reading, Leah had assigned herself the duty of learning new words and phrases. She used them in her conversations as often as she could. She said it helped her to remember them. It tickled Sarah to hear her come up with something new.

Leah beamed. "Yes, and quite evocative, I think."

"Definitely. Evocative is a good word, too." Sarah grabbed a couple of men's handkerchiefs and worked with them as she spoke. "On a pleasanter note, will you be at Founders' Day on Friday? With school being closed for the day, everyone at home intends to go." At least they had before all this mess came up, she thought.

"Yes, we'll be there. The newspaper said some of the shops are giving discounts, and even the bank is offering an interest uptick for whatever's deposited that day."

Sarah placed the handkerchiefs on their pile. "Since this is the first celebration of Founders' Day Bonneforte has ever had, I guess everyone wants to make it special. I like the idea."

"I do, too. I think it might be fun. I'm excited about it."

Sarah picked up a cookie and took a bite. "Mmm. Is this a new recipe?"

"Yes. Mrs. Beesom gave it to me. It's nice to have a neighbor who enjoys cooking as much as I do."

"So these are gingerbread and...strawberries? Isn't it late for strawberries?"

"Yes and yes. Those were the very last ones I collected from the garden. I put them in the ice box as a test, and they kept a couple of weeks."

Sarah chose another one. "They taste great." She took a bite and, with her mouth full, said, "You better put them up before I eat them all."

Leah laughed. "Brendan is well named, Miss Sarah-Bren. I have to hide them from him."

"That's what you get for being such a good cook. Phillip and I have spent time comparing and salivating over what you fix for your family and what you fed me when we lived together. It's a wonder your handsome husband doesn't weigh more."

Leah finished the last sock pairing and set it with the others. "He tells me he's so active in his construction work that he burns it off."

Sarah patted her stomach. "I need to be more active. Maybe I'll begin walking each day."

"No! You don't want to be wandering off too far with Litchfield maybe in the vicinity."

"You're right. You stay close to home, too."

Leah reached for the last handkerchief and folded it. "Don't worry. I'll keep my eyes open."

"Please do." Sarah stood and moved toward the door. "I have to be going."

"Wait." Leah rose and got a tin from the cupboard. "I made some cookies for your family, too." She handed it to Sarah. "I, for one, hope Litchfield never shows up."

Sarah struck her fist against the door, and Leah jumped. "If the bastard's going to do anything, I wish he'd do it soon. I'm tired of waiting for the sword to drop."

Leah's hand quivered as she touched Sarah's arm. "I remember that story from one of the books you gave me. Damocles had a sword hanging by a horse's tail hair over his head and never knew when it might fall on him."

"That's exactly the way I feel. Like something's waiting to fall on me." Sarah gave Leah a one-armed hug and kissed her cheek. "Enough of that. I'll see you Friday at Founders' Day."

"Please be careful."

"I will. And thanks for the cookies. I might be persuaded to share them." She winked and went out the door as Leah shook a finger at her.

Chapter 22

On Wednesday morning, Sarah suddenly felt twitchy as she guided the buggy toward the school. She glanced around and behind them so many times that Faith finally said, "What's wrong?"

"Do you sense anything? Like someone's watching you?" Sarah asked in a low voice.

Faith sat perfectly still for a moment with only her eyes moving. "I don't feel anything. But if anyone's out there, do you think it's a good idea to let them know you suspect it?"

"Maybe I'm imagining it." Sarah jiggled the reins, and Drummer's pace increased. Several times lately she had felt as though someone was watching her, but nothing had happened. This time the watching didn't seem to stop. A shudder went through her.

Faith frowned. "You've always been more aware of what's going on around you than I have. I trust your intuition."

"I'm going to hang around the schoolhouse today."

"Inside?"

"No, I'll be outside. I'll ask Herman to put a deputy on watch, too."

"Good."

When they arrived at the schoolhouse, Sarah engaged the handbrake, jumped down, and hurried to help Faith disembark. She gave her an extra-long hug. "Take care of yourself, redhead."

"You, too, sweetheart."

They parted, and Sarah rode in the buggy to the sheriff's office.

Herman peered up from the paperwork on his desk as Sarah came through the door. "Hello, there, Sarah. Come for a friendly visit?"

"That, too, but I wanted to let you know that I think someone's watching Faith and me. I can feel their eyes between my shoulder blades."

Herman pushed the papers away and motioned for Sarah to

sit in one of the two chairs in front of his desk. "I know exactly what you mean. Only I always feel it in the short hairs on the back of my neck." He grinned. "But you don't have those short hairs. I guess your shoulder blades work the same way."

"Yes, they do, and I've learned to trust them." She explained she first noticed them when she and Faith began coming into town together to the schoolhouse. "I'm going to hang around the schoolhouse starting today, and I wondered whether you could spare a deputy to join me. I'd like to give our watcher a sense of our awareness. Maybe make him think twice about whatever he has in mind."

"You think it's Litchfield." Schmidt made it a statement rather than a question.

"I do. And I don't want him trying anything at the school."

Schmidt rubbed a finger along his nose. "Your weakest link is the trip back and forth to school."

"I know. I've been carrying a loaded rifle, a double-barreled shotgun, and extra ammunition with me. Besides my handguns. And a knife in my boot."

"He could shoot you from a distance."

"I don't worry about that. I doubt he's a sharpshooter. He'd be afraid of hitting Faith." Sarah removed her hat, ran her hand through her hair, and reset the hat on her head. "There's no way I can cover every single angle, Herman. But I'll do the best I can." She rose. "Meantime, I need to get back to the school. Who will you send over?"

"Fred Shillinger. He's a good man and has lots of patience."

"I agree. Thanks."

Sarah stopped at the Post Office first and was pleased to find a letter from Rusty. She stuck it in her pocket to read later, hurried to the buggy, and returned to the school.

On the way home that afternoon, she handed the letter to Faith. "This came in today's mail. It's from Rusty."

Faith opened it and read aloud, "Dear Sarah and Faith, we got home all right and Della loves it here. She digs more gold each day than me. She says thanks again for all your help and I thank you too. We started out really liking each other and now we are sweethearts. Two alone women are not alone now. Love to both of you. Come visit if you ever can. Rusty."

Faith folded the letter and returned it to its envelope. "Rusty's spelling has improved."

"I suspect that's Della's doing. I think she's had some education."

"I think you're right. I'm so happy for them. Della needs to have some good things happening in her life."

Sarah said, "So does Rusty. I know she felt really lonely. Let's hope it works out for them."

Faith took hold of Sarah's arm and laid her head on Sarah's shoulder. "I hope they can be as happy as we are. I wish everyone could be."

Sarah patted her thigh. "You have such a big heart, redhead. In my mind, not everyone deserves to be happy." She snorted. "But I'm not in charge of the world today."

Faith laughed. "That's probably a good thing."

* * *

Thursday afternoon, Litchfield found the hollow tree on the outskirts of Bonneforte and picked up the note. It was dated a day earlier. He read it and stuck it in his pocket.

He returned to where Dembroke and the rest of the gang had camped farther into the woods. He dismounted, tied his horse to a tree limb, and approached the group. The other men looked up at his arrival, but he waved their stares off and approached Dembroke.

Dembroke squatted next to the fire, drinking something from a tin bowl. He wiped his mouth and said, "Did you get a message?"

"I did." Litchfield took the note from his pocket and read it aloud. "Coulter drives Faith back and forth every day in a buggy. Coulter and a deputy stayed at the school today. The only other time they're together is at their home."

Dembroke poured some water into the bowl, swished it around, and drank it. He stuck the bowl into the saddlebag lying next to him.

"Sounds like the best time to grab them might be when they're in the buggy."

"I agree. I'll tell the men the plan after I get something to eat. Any of that soup left?"

Dembroke took the bowl back out of the saddlebag and handed it to Litchfield. "Yep." He nodded toward the cooking fire near the men. "Over there in that pot. Help yourself."

After he ate, Litchfield sized up the men sitting on logs around the campfire. Seven men counting himself. He stood near them and got their attention.

"Okay, men, here's what we're going to do. Two of you will

go with me to grab the women. I might have another man helping us. The other three will go with Dembroke and hit the bank." He kneaded his forehead. Blasted headaches!

Those going to the bank hadn't needed to stake it out and perhaps cause suspicion for their presence. Litchfield had drawn an exact replica of the inside of the bank for them, complete with the two teller stations and the spot where the security man would be. They were perfectly prepared.

"I'm going to go over the kidnapping plan one more time." He grabbed a twig and drew with it on the ground. "Every day, Faith gets driven to and from the schoolhouse by the Coulter bitch, and she and a deputy hang around all day. Our best bet is to grab them before they get to the school."

He marked an X on the road he had drawn. "Right here, where the road gets closest to the trees, is ideal. I'll ride out in front of them with my hands in the air saying I only want to talk." He guttered a path with the twig from the trees to the front of the X. "I expect the Coulter bitch to train her rifle on me. Then Brewster and Ruiz will come out of the woods with their guns out. They'll place themselves on each side of the buggy and tell her to drop the rifle."

He added two more paths and brought each one up along opposite sides of the X. "I'll take my gun out, too, and she won't be able to cover all three of us, so if she has any sense at all, she'll drop it. We'll snatch them both. Brewster, you and Ruiz will tie Coulter up. I'm pretty sure Faith will do anything I want her to in order to keep the bitch alive." He dug the twig into the X as though he were stabbing someone.

"Sounds good," Dembroke said, and the others murmured agreement.

"All right." Litchfield dropped the twig and brushed his hands together. "Let's get some sleep. We have a busy day tomorrow." He doubted he would sleep. All he could think about was getting his hands on Faith. First, he'd have his way with her right in front of the Coulter bitch and then get rid of Sarah Coulter. Once he got Faith back to the ranch, he'd convince her that her life with him would be a lot happier than anything she had before. Even his usual headache couldn't dampen his excitement. His whole body jerked with pleasure as he imagined them being together at last.

* * *

On Friday morning, Sarah hitched Drummer to the wagon

and led him out of the barn for the trip to town. She stood next to the wagon, waiting for the others to join her. She stomped her booted feet and slapped her gloved hands together. The morning was brisk and bright. A great day for a town shindig. Faith came out with some empty woven shopping bags, and Sarah pointed to them. "Are you expecting to fill those up?"

"One of them is for Lindsay. But I'll probably fill the one I have. You can use a new pair of pants and a shirt, and I'd like to get some material for a new dress."

"Do you have enough cash on you?"

"No, I have to go to the bank. Lindsay needs to, also. Are you still planning on shifting some of your savings to the new interest rate?"

"Yes, but I'll drop you off at the bank and go see Herman first."

"I heard the bank's putting out some cookies and coffee and other refreshments. We can dawdle over those until you join us."

Sarah's mother came out of the house followed by Lindsay and Jessie. They were all bundled up against the cold. This was the first Sarah had seen Jessie since their talk. Jessie had stayed out of Sarah's way and didn't even join them for dinner. Each night Lindsay had fixed a plate for her daughter and taken it to her room.

Sarah helped the women into the wagon. Jessie accepted her help, but she didn't respond to Sarah's nod. The rawness of their feelings toward one another stood between them like a bloody wound.

"Scott's not coming?" Sarah asked Lindsay.

"No. He figured we would be in town all day and thought that would be a bit more than he could handle. He said to go on and enjoy ourselves without worrying about him."

"He's probably right," Sarah said with a grin. "I have a hard time keeping up with you shoppers myself." She climbed up onto the driver's seat, and they departed.

When they passed the closest outgrowth of trees on their way to town, Sarah felt that same prickle between her shoulder blades. She silently picked up her rifle and glanced quickly at Faith, who was already gazing at her. Sarah opened her mouth to speak, but Faith gave her head a quick shake, and Sarah didn't say anything. The rest of the trip was uneventful, and Sarah clamped down on her misgivings. But she didn't forget them.

Chapter 23

"Son of a bitch!" Joel Litchfield said under his breath and pounded his fist against his saddle horn. He rubbed his head. Another damn headache. He whispered to his men, "We'll have to give up on the kidnapping for today. I didn't expect a whole wagonload of people."

"But they're all women," Ruiz said. "We can handle them."

Litchfield snorted. "Don't count on it. They could all be armed, and we're outnumbered. We'll have to postpone our plans." He was irate. What could have gone wrong, dammit? Why wasn't Faith alone in a buggy with the Coulter bitch as she usually was? The stupid watcher he had planted must have messed up somehow.

"What do we do, boss?" Brewster asked. "Go on into town and help with the bank robbery?"

"I can't do that. Too many people know me. We'll depend on the other men to rob the bank and meet at the bluff as we planned."

* * *

Sarah hitched the wagon to the rail outside the bank, and after she helped the others out, she strode to the sheriff's office. She was surprised to see Herman with a splint on his leg and the leg propped on a chair. "What the hell happened to you?" she asked.

"Tripped over my own clumsy feet and fell down my porch steps yesterday evening. Broke my tibia bone."

"Porch falls can be disastrous."

He tapped the splint. "Doc says it's not broke all the way through, but I'll have this confounded thing on until the swelling goes down and then a cast. Might take months to heal."

"This could be especially bad timing."

Herman's attention perked up. "Why? Has something happened? Have you heard anything?"

"I think we were watched this morning. When we passed

that stand of trees that comes near the road, my shoulder blades got uncomfortable. Maybe I'm being twitchy again."

"Doggone it, Sarah, you're not the twitchy type. I'd bet my last penny someone was out there."

"The good thing is, if they were out there, they're not here."

The door opened, and Fred Shillinger came into the office. "Hi, boss, Miss Sarah." He tipped the edge of his hat.

"Hi, Fred," Sarah said "Thanks for your help so far in safeguarding Faith. I appreciate it."

"I'm glad to be of service. Sure beats chasing town drunks." They all laughed and told a few stories of past encounters of that sort.

Next they discussed the problems that might arise with having the sheriff relatively immobile. They reached the conclusion that he probably should have a deputy constantly with him. Also, he couldn't ride a horse with a splint on.

Finally, Fred said to Sarah, "How come you aren't out enjoying the festivities? Lots of new faces in town today."

Sarah became more alert. "Any that looked out of place to you?"

Fred rubbed his jaw. "None I can think of. Acourse, I don't know everyone who lives around here."

The door banged open. "Sheriff! The bank's being robbed!" Whoever shouted the message was gone as quickly as he came. Sarah bolted out the door. She touched her pistol to make sure her sheepskin jacket wasn't blocking her holster. Damn, damn, damn, she thought. How could I be so complacent? If anything, I should have been more aware.

Men ran toward the commotion as mothers hurried their children into stores for safety. Most of the women and older people cleared the boardwalk.

As Sarah elbowed her way through the crowd, she saw a man standing in the bank's doorway with his gun trained on a woman.

He hollered, "Everyone get back and throw your guns into the street, or I shoot this woman. And I'll keep shooting people until you do what you're told. Drop them! Now!"

Sarah came to an abrupt halt in front of the men lining the street directly across from the bank. She got a clear view of the woman, and her heart almost pounded out of her chest. No. Please, God. No.

* * *

Faith and the others entered the bank, removed their coats, and hung them on a rack supplied for that purpose. Several people were gathered around tables set against one wall that were filled with cookies, doughnuts, and cakes. A female employee dispensed coffee and tea from a separate table. A small woodstove sat beside her to heat the water.

"Oh, look," Lindsay said. "What a lovely idea. Should we start there?"

Faith walked toward the teller's station. "I think I'll take care of my business first."

"That sounds like a good idea," Lindsay said. "Mother Coulter, why don't you and Jessie partake of the offerings while Faith and I get our money?"

Faith and Lindsay finished their withdrawals and were heading toward the refreshments when a man who was standing near the security guard suddenly pulled a revolver and struck the guard on his head. The guard went down, and people froze where they stood, seeming confused as to what had happened.

It's a robbery, Faith quickly realized, and she almost shouted the words aloud. But the robber turned his gun on the group and said, "Keep quiet, folks, and you won't get hurt."

Three other men materialized from the group and held guns on the people and tellers. Two of the men grabbed the cash from the tellers' drawers and stuffed it into valises.

The third robber entered the bank president's office, brought him out, and thrust him toward the vault. He held a gun to the president's temple while the vault was opened. He knocked the man out with a crack of the gun against his skull and entered the vault with a gunnysack.

A man who had opened the door a notch as though to enter yelled, "The bank's being robbed!" He slammed the door shut and ran. Outside, a crowd was gathering.

"What'll we do, Burt?" one of the robbers asked in an alarmed voice.

The one called Burt said, "Get everyone's guns and gather up the cash." Burt grabbed Faith's arm and steered her toward the door. "I'll show her to the crowd and threaten to kill her if anyone causes any trouble."

Faith was too startled to object. But the next voice she heard startled her even more.

"Wait!" Cynthia Coulter said in a rather imperious tone, and Burt hesitated. "Don't take her. She's a nobody. Take me instead.

I'm the mother of the grocery store owner. Everyone knows me. Your threat will carry more weight."

Burt stood there for a moment, frowning.

"Besides," Cynthia said as she marched toward him, "she's with child. Surely you don't want to be responsible for threatening the mother of an unborn child. It makes more sense to take me. And I can assure you, I'll be easier to handle."

"All right, all right." Burt shoved Faith aside and took Cynthia's arm.

Faith struggled to gather her wits. "But that's not true—"

"Be quiet, my dear," Cynthia said in the same commanding tone, "and let the man go about his business. Do you think he's foolish enough to listen to you?"

As Cynthia finished her comments, Burt yanked her toward the door. He curled his left arm around her neck and held a pistol against her back with his right hand. "Open the door," he said into Cynthia's ear. He steered her through it.

The crowd outside immediately hushed. "Everyone get back onto the boardwalk and throw your guns into the street," he said, "or I shoot this woman. And I'll keep shooting people until you do what you're told. Drop them! Now!"

While he was talking, Cynthia saw Sarah-Bren show up at the front of the crowd. Cynthia shook her head no.

Nobody moved. Nobody tossed out any weapons.

"Too bad they don't seem to care about you," Burt said in a loud voice.

Cynthia raised her chin. If she had to die, she would do it proudly. Burt lowered his arm from around her neck. She felt him move away from her. She barely heard the shot that hit her, and she went down in a heap.

"Mother!" Sarah yelled. She started forward, but when a bullet hit the ground in front of her, she hesitated. The robber reentered the bank, and she ran to her mother's side.

The sheriff shouted, "Stay away from the bank, Sarah." On crutches, with Fred Shillinger clearing a path for him, Herman Schmidt had gotten to the edge of the boardwalk behind her.

She nodded in acquiescence. What could she do, anyway? Nothing. Her mother lay there bleeding, her family was inside the building, and she was out here with no cover. She was completely powerless, and that reality angered and frustrated her. She struggled to pick up her mother, and Fred Shillinger ran over to help her. They placed Cynthia on the boardwalk, and Sarah knelt beside her. Fred pushed his hands against her mother's wound.

The door opened again, and the same man held Jessie in front of him. "This one's next," he yelled.

Sarah's heart compressed so hard she thought it must be bleeding. Her mother lay on the boardwalk, maybe dying, and her daughter was being readied to join her. Sarah stood, drew her gun from its holster, and tossed it into the street. She heard rustling behind her as others moved forward. Their weapons raised dust from the street as they threw them down.

"That's more like it," the man said. "Now stand back while we get on our horses and leave. I'm taking this gal with us, in case you get any ideas." He motioned with his head, and the other robbers, carrying valises and a gunnysack, exited the bank and mounted their horses. They surrounded his horse while he pushed Jessie up on it and got into the saddle behind her. They rode out of town at full speed, and no one followed them.

Faith and Lindsay came out of the bank and ran to kneel next to Cynthia. Faith tore a piece of material from Cynthia's gown. Fred moved away, and Faith used the cloth to stanch the bleeding. "Thank you, Fred," she said.

Sarah fell to her knees beside them. "How is she?"

Faith said, "She's alive. Other than that, I can't tell. The wound's bleeding profusely, and that's not good." Faith peered up with an incredulous expression. "She took my place, Sarah. She took my place."

Sarah didn't understand what Faith meant. Her mind kept bursting back and forth, from her mother to Jessie and to Faith and back again to her mother.

Faith visibly gathered her composure. "We'll get her to the doctor right away." She touched Sarah's hand. "We'll take care of her, Sarah. Please go after Jessie." Sarah stared at Faith, and an unspoken word of resolve passed between them.

Lindsay was crying as she stroked Cynthia Coulter's arm. "Oh, Sarah, please do rescue Jessie."

Sarah rose and patted Lindsay's shoulder. "I'll do my best. You and Faith concentrate on Mother." She turned to Herman, who had worked his way across the street toward her with Fred at his side.

Fred picked up Sarah's pistol from the dirt and handed it to her.

"Thanks. Can I borrow a horse?"

"Take Red Star," Herman said and pointed. "He's right there. I had him saddled this morning and tried to ride him, but I couldn't ride for any distance. You go on after them, and Fred will gather up a posse and follow you as soon as he can." Fred sprinted away to attend to that very act.

"All right. And thanks." Redfire had sired Red Star, so Sarah knew she was getting a good animal. "I'll blaze a trail through the woods to make it easier for your posse." She turned to go.

"Wait, Sarah." Herman grabbed her arm and took a badge from his pocket. "I want to deputize you."

Sarah stared at him. "You might not want to do that." She shook her arm, but he held her tight. She could have yanked away from him, but she was loath to knock him off his crutches.

"Dead or alive," Herman said. "I authorize you to bring 'em in dead or alive.

"I don't want to cause any trouble for you," Sarah said. "Sometimes the laws get in the way of what needs to be done."

"Don't worry about that." Herman slipped the badge into the top front pocket of Sarah's sheepskin jacket. "Consider yourself deputized." He let go of her. "Now get out of here."

Sarah ran for Herman's horse. She was relieved to see he had a rifle scabbard on the saddle and a canteen. She led Red Star to her wagon and grabbed her rifle and the extra ammunition from below the wagon seat. She considered the double-barreled shotgun but decided to leave it. She stuck the rifle in the sheriff's scabbard and the ammunition in her coat pockets.

She always stashed some beef jerky in a pocket, so food wouldn't be a problem. And she always carried the little packet with a lock of Faith's hair in it. That thought brought back memories of Litchfield grinding the first packet she had beneath his heel. I will kill the bastard this time, she vowed, her teeth clenched.

She mounted the horse and glanced back. Her mother, Faith, and Lindsay were gone, and the crowd had dispersed. She kicked Red Star into a gallop and took off.

Chapter 24

She followed the robbers through the forest for a day and a half. They didn't stop, and neither did she. True to her word, she blazed a trail by carving notches in trees close enough to each other to be visible to the posse. Eventually she came to a rocky segment devoid of trees. Gazing across it, she saw that shortly after the forest continued, a bluff reared into the sky. She had a hunch that the crooks might take a breather near the foot of the bluff, especially because it provided cover at their backs.

She halted and chewed on a piece of beef jerky as she contemplated her options. Working her way around the rocky area would be safer than trying to cross it and expose herself to whoever might look back. But who knew what they might do to Jessie when they stopped? They might kill her or even worse. That thought spurred Sarah on, and she rode across the rocks toward the bluff. She stopped twice and dismounted to form an arrow of stones pointing toward the direction she traveled. No one shot at her, and she reentered the woods.

She got off Red Star and tied the horse to a tree limb. She took the rifle from its scabbard and worked the lever to chamber a round. If the crooks had stopped where she suspected, they would be within walking distance. Sure enough, after about five minutes of moving through the trees, she heard talking and saw a group of men in various poses ahead of her. Her breath caught as one of the men threw Jessie to the ground and unbuckled his belt.

Sarah dropped to one knee, aimed her rifle, cocked the hammer, and fired. She didn't hit the man—too many trees were in the way, and she didn't have time to search for a clear shot—but he stopped in his tracks and dove to the ground. The others did the same.

She felt something round and hard press against the back of her head. A tough voice said, "Drop yer rifle and stand up." She did as she was told. He picked up the rifle and prodded her in the back with his gun. "Hand me yer pistol, too." When she complied, he said, "Move over there where everyone else is." He hollered ahead, "It's me. I've got the shooter." He marched her right up to Doc Litchfield, who was brushing off his coat and pants.

Litchfield saw Sarah and burst out laughing. "Well, well, well, look who you got, Ruiz. *Miss* Sarah Coulter. Good job."

Sarah heard murmurs about her being a woman.

One of the other men stepped forward, the one who had shot Sarah's mother. "So this is your bitch, huh, Doc? She don't seem so tough to me." He spat at Sarah's boot, but she jerked it out of the way.

"Yeah, Dembroke, this is the one." Litchfield reached out and slapped Sarah hard across the face. "I don't want anyone killing her until she sees me with Faith."

Sarah had swung her head when she saw the blow coming. It didn't have as much impact as Litchfield probably intended, but her lip split and bled. She spat blood on the ground. "The posse's right behind me. They might have other ideas about who gets killed."

Litchfield turned to Ruiz. "You see any signs of a posse?"

"Nope." He set the rifle against a tree and handed Litchfield Sarah's pistol. "Here's her gun."

Litchfield examined the tooled ivory grip and stuck it in his waistband. "Nice. I might save it to kill you with."

The man who originally accosted Jessie grabbed her again. "I got some business to finish with this one. How about it, Doc?"

Litchfield gave a welcoming gesture. "Do whatever you want. I have no use for her now."

The man threw her to the ground once more, and Jessie screamed, "No!" He stood over her with his hands on the buttons of his fly. "Thought you were going to miss out, huh, sweetie? Don't worry, we'll have some fun."

Crack! A rifle shot sounded, and the man fell to the ground. Blood welled from a hole in the side of his chest. Once again the men dove for cover. Sarah stayed standing and hurried toward Jessie, who had remained on the ground and was scooting herself away from the body near her feet.

"I warned you bastards," Sarah said over her shoulder.

Litchfield yanked his pistol from its holster and yelled, "Get out of here, men. Meet back at the ranch." The men scrambled away, heading toward their horses. When they reached them, they mounted and rode off.

Litchfield had grabbed Ruiz's arm and held him back. He jerked his head toward Sarah. "Help me with this one, and kill that one."

Ruiz drew his gun, aimed it at Jessie, and squeezed the trigger.

"No!" Sarah dove sideways in front of Jessie. The bullet hit Sarah in the chest with the power of a horse kick, and she blacked out.

"Aunt Sarah!" Jessie pulled her onto her lap and started crying. "Aunt Sarah, please be all right," she sobbed.

Ruiz backed up to fire at Jessie again. Crack! Another rifle shot rang out, and Ruiz crumpled to the ground. His pistol landed next to Jessie. She picked it up and aimed it at Litchfield, who laughed at her. "You think you can shoot me, little girl? You can't even hold the gun steady."

A man rode up, leading another horse.

Jessie hesitated. The heavy gun bobbed up and down.

The man dismounted and ran to Litchfield. He brought the other horse with him and seemed oblivious to what was happening.

Litchfield gave a quick glance his way. "What's going on, Dembroke?

Dembroke gave him a shove toward the horse he was leading. "Come on, Doc. We ran into the posse and had to turn around. Get on your horse and let's go."

Litchfield mounted his horse and turned back to Jessie. "Tell Faith I'll be back for her." He laughed and rode off.

Dembroke started toward the horse he had ridden up on.

Sarah revived as Litchfield left. *I got shot in the chest. I should be dead. How can I feel that my chest and left arm hurt like hell? Dead people don't feel anything.* She sat up and Jessie gasped. Her face was tear-streaked. Wincing, Sarah grabbed the gun from Jessie's hands. Jessie let go and stared at her.

Sarah yelled, "Hey, you. Stop." Dembroke turned toward her. He had a dumbfounded expression on his face.

"You," she said in a harsh whisper, "are the man who shot my mother and kidnapped my niece."

Dembroke raised his hands and went to his knees.

Sarah stood with difficulty. She nearly doubled over with the pain in her chest and arm, but she managed to straighten and keep the gun trained on him. "Stand up." She waited.

Dembroke rose with his hands in the air. His voice shook. "I didn't mean to shoot your mother. I swear. My finger slipped."

"I'll give you a fighting chance, you sorry bastard. That's more than you gave my mother." Sarah holstered the pistol she held. "Draw."

Dembroke grabbed for his gun. Sarah grabbed for hers. One shot rang out. Dembroke crumpled on the spot. Sarah had shot him between the eyes.

She forced her words out in a guttural tone. "Oops, my finger slipped."

Suddenly, she saw movement in her peripheral vision. She swung the gun that way, ready to shoot, then realized it was Jessie rising from the ground. With relief, Sarah quickly holstered the weapon. That damn Litchfield had her ivory-handled pistol.

"Aunt Sarah, Jessie," a man's voice called out from the trees, "thank God you're both all right."

"Benjamin," Sarah shouted. "Oh my God, Benjamin, it's so good to see you." Benjamin engulfed her in his arms. When Jessie came nearer, he included her in his grasp.

Sarah lifted her head as she heard horses go by.

"It's the posse," Benjamin said. "They're running down the rest of the gang." The embrace ended, and Benjamin peered around. "I see you accounted for one of them. I shot the man who was attacking Jessie plus another one."

"Yes, you got two of them," Sarah said.

Benjamin frowned. "I'm supposed to be saving lives, not taking them." He saw Jessie shiver. "Jessie, you must be freezing." He shucked off his coat. "Put this on." He helped her into it.

"Now, you'll be freezing," she said.

"Not for long." He strode over to Dembroke, removed the thief's coat, and donned it. "Not a bad fit," he murmured.

Sarah sneered. "Who knew he'd be good for anything." Her breathing became ragged, and she felt a little dizzy.

Benjamin must have noticed. "Let's all sit down a minute," he said.

"Aunt Sarah should be dead," Jessie said. "She threw herself in front of a bullet and saved my life."

Sarah sat on one of the logs. She gulped in air and forced her breathing back to normal. Her mind cleared, too.

Benjamin pointed toward her chest. "Let me check that wound."

Sarah looked down at her coat. The bullet had torn a furrow from the chest pocket to across the arm. Blood covered part of the arm material. She reached in the pocket and lifted out the badge Herman had given her. A badge she had tried to refuse. The bullet meant for Jessie had scarred the front of it. She shuddered. It was over. Jessie was all right.

"Humph," she said. "This is the second time a 'gift' from a

friend saved my life. Sheriff Schmidt gave me this. I didn't want to take it." She gave a wry grin. "Good thing Herman was more hard-headed than I was."

Jessie asked, "When was the first time?"

"You've seen the vest with the silver dollars on it?"

"Yes."

"Rusty made that for me. A man who blamed me for his son's death shot at me, and the shot hit one of the dollars. I'll tell you more about it later. We have to get going after Litchfield."

Sarah grimaced when she moved her left arm.

"Wait," Jessie said. "Let me help you with that."

Jessie unbuttoned Sarah's jacket and helped her remove it.

Sarah reached in her boot for the knife she always kept there and handed it to Jessie. "You can use this to cut off the arm material."

Jessie ripped the shoulder seam out of Sarah's shirt, pulled off the sleeve, and exposed the wound. She sat next to Sarah on the log while Benjamin examined the arm. Blood still oozed from the furrow that ran across her bicep.

"Jessie," Benjamin said, "give me the knife, please. And would you get the canteen off my horse and give it to Aunt Sarah?" Jessie hastened to follow his request.

While Sarah drank her fill, Benjamin cut the torn shirt material into a long strip. He used the material as a bandage and wrapped it tight over the wound to slow the bleeding. "You're lucky. The bullet only dug a groove on the outside of your arm."

"Lucky, huh?" Sarah handed the canteen to Jessie and slipped the knife back into her boot. She tugged the front collar of her shirt away from her body and looked down at herself. "I've got a red mark the size of a fist on my chest, but no broken bones. You're right, I'm lucky. That mark could have been a hole."

Benjamin clasped her hand and swallowed hard. "We're all lucky you're still with us."

Jessie murmured, "Yes, we are." She took a drink from the canteen and gave it to Benjamin when he reached for it. He took a long swallow and set it on the log next to Sarah.

Sarah forced a laugh. "Tell me that a month from now."

Benjamin gave her hand a squeeze and let go. "I'll give your arm a better dressing when we get home. Meanwhile, we need to get you there."

Jessie helped Sarah put her jacket back on. Sarah's eyes drooped. She suddenly felt very tired. Blood loss, she would guess. Then, too, she wasn't getting any younger. After all, she had a grown-up daughter.

She blinked at Benjamin. "How were you here in the nick of time, anyway?"

"I came in on the train right after you left. When Mama told me what happened, I hurried home and got Redfire and trailed after you. Thanks for those blazes, by the way. I caught up to the posse, and when we got to the rocky area and didn't see you anywhere, they decided to go around it. I talked Mr. Shillinger into letting me go ahead across the rocks to check out the situation. I convinced him that if the posse descended all at once on them, the robbers might kill Jessie—and you, if they had you."

He turned toward Jessie. "I saw what was going on, and I shot the man. I didn't give it a lot of thought. I saw he was going to hurt you, and I fired."

"That's exactly how they caught me," Sarah said. "They had a sentry out, but like you, I didn't have time to think about that or to get a clear shot. I opened fire. I didn't hit anyone, though, only a tree nearby. That scared them, and they dove for cover. Then the sentry caught me."

Benjamin said, "I was lucky enough to get away with it. I didn't know what was going on when that man shot at Jessie. But he moved back, right into my sights, and I fired."

"You both saved me," Jessie said with a sob in her voice.

"Now it's time to get you and Aunt Sarah home," Benjamin stood. "I'll get Redfire. I almost ran right into your horse, so I can bring him, too. Isn't that Sheriff Schmidt's Red Star?"

"Yes. He's strong and younger than Redfire. You and Jessie can ride him together." Sarah's body tipped a little as she spoke, and Benjamin picked right up on it.

"No," he said. "You're probably weak from blood loss. You'll need someone to hold you on the horse, and I know you want to ride Redfire. How about you and Jessie ride Redfire, and I'll take Red Star?"

"I swear, Benjamin, you're as hardheaded as your mother." She noted that he didn't look the slightest bit abashed.

Jessie said, "I'll be happy to ride with Aunt Sarah."

Sarah tapped Jessie's thigh. "I admit, I will welcome the assistance."

"Good," Benjamin said. He pointed at the three bodies lying near them. "What about these fellows?"

"The posse can take care of them," Sarah said. "I want to get home and see how Mother is."

"Of course. I'll be right back."

When Benjamin left to get the horses, the posse came back through. Sarah saw three bound men, but they weren't close enough for her to identify them. She couldn't make out Litchfield's black coat, and that got her attention in a hurry.

Fred Shillinger rode up. He tipped his hat. "Miss Sarah. Thanks for blazing that trail. We'd still be hunting them."

"Did you get all four?" Sarah asked. "I only see three."

Fred took off his hat and scratched his head. "We got three and all the money."

Sarah strained to make out the features of the gang members. None of them looked like the one she was searching for. "Was Litchfield with them?"

Fred put his hat back on. "No, ma'am. We didn't see hide nor hair of him."

"Aren't you going after him?"

"Well, ma'am..." Shillinger glanced everywhere but at Sarah. "Doc Litchfield wasn't at the bank, so we got nothing against him. And we got all the money back. I can't ask the men to do any more than they already done."

"Fair enough," Sarah said. "When you get back, tell the sheriff I went after Litchfield. He'll understand." Sarah pointed at the bodies lying on the ground. "Your posse can take them back. They were all at the bank."

"Yes, ma'am. We'll do that." He whistled to his men to get that task organized.

Benjamin returned with the horses while Shillinger and his men dealt with the bodies. Sarah approached him. "You heard all that?"

Benjamin said, "I did." He handed Sarah the reins for Redfire. "Do you need help getting on?

"No, I can manage." She swore she wouldn't give in to the chest and arm pain her wound caused her. Thank goodness her leg hadn't acted up. Maybe she'd been too preoccupied to notice if it did. She mounted Redfire and patted his neck.

"Litchfield's escape changes things. I'm going after him," she said. "I'm not sitting around waiting for him to show up to steal your mother away."

Benjamin put a hand on Sarah's knee. "I'm going with you."

Sarah rested her hand on his. "No. I want you to take Jessie back to Lindsay and Scott. I'm sure they're worried sick about her."

"I'm sure they are, but Mama will be worried about *you*.

She would want me to go with you," he said firmly. "Jessie can go back with the posse."

As the posse tied the dead men to their extra horses, Sarah nodded toward Jessie, whose blue eyes were wide and troubled. Benjamin followed her gaze, and his face softened.

Sarah said, "Jessie has been through a lot. She needs a friend to take her home."

"Please, Benjamin," Jessie asked. She opened her arms toward him, and he clasped her to him. She sniffled.

"All right," he said. "Please don't cry. I'll go with you."

He turned to Sarah. "As soon as Jessie's home, I'm coming after you."

"No. Please stay with your mother. Protect her." Sarah lifted Redfire's reins. "I have a strong suspicion that Litchfield is heading toward her right now. I've got to be going." She clucked to Redfire and took off.

She rode directly toward her home. If she was right, she should encounter Litchfield before he could harm anyone. He had to be more cautious about approaching the house than she did. If she was wrong, and he wasn't going near Faith, then she was safe for the moment and they could deal with Litchfield later.

Chapter 25

Litchfield drove his lathered horse toward Faith's home. He had been riding for hours and hours. Having to stop several times to rest his horse had fanned his anger at what had happened at the camp. Ruiz was dead, and Litchfield hadn't seen hide nor hair of Dembroke. His gut told him the Coulter bitch was still alive.

He knew she'd be after him, and he had given up on capturing her along with Faith. Too dangerous for him to try that alone. He'd kill her instead. That thought filled him with glee and was almost enough to stop his throbbing headache.

He would get Faith himself, and when the bitch followed them, he would ambush her.

He kept an eye out for places to set up an ambush, but nothing so far had appeared. He cursed whoever had taken his rifle from its scabbard—but when you came right down to it, he wasn't much of a shot with one anyway. All he had left was a handgun. He had put his pistol in a saddle bag and stuck the bitch's pretty one in his holster. If he played his cards right, a pistol was all he would need. He was bigger and stronger than that faker and certainly he could best her in a hand-to-hand fight. She couldn't stand up to a real man.

Thinking about killing her with his bare hands so entranced him that he almost passed the perfect spot for an ambush. A tight stand of trees branched out from the forest on a short rise next to the trail he was on. He could easily shoot her from there, but the more he thought about strangling her, the more the idea intrigued him. He could use Faith as a shield and stop Sarah Coulter as she rode up. As he spurred his horse on, he entertained himself by imagining what he would do to the bitch.

* * *

Sarah alternated galloping and walking Redfire so he wouldn't tire to the point of exhaustion. The situation was dire, but Redfire wasn't young anymore, and killing him wouldn't help anyone. Riding

Red Star would have been wiser, but she wasn't thinking straight at the time. She and Redfire had been through some bad times together, and she automatically chose him. She calculated getting home would take the better part of a day.

She followed a regular trail and noticed evidence that someone had preceded her down the path recently. She hoped that "someone" was Litchfield.

For the last few days, the weather had been outstanding. Light, puffy clouds chased across a big sky background of robin's egg blue. Nights had been clear with a bright sliver of a moon backed by undimmed star fields that stretched from horizon to horizon.

If the weather had mirrored the enormity of events, it should be stormy and dark with mucky ground pulling at Redfire's hooves. The contrast between the beauty of the day and the ugliness of what had transpired made Sarah's heart ache.

Saving Jessie and the arrival of Benjamin had been two bright spots. But the ugliness hadn't ended yet. Her encounter with Litchfield could be the ugliest of all.

* * *

Faith drove the buggy toward home and was relieved when the house came into view. She needed a respite. She had been at the hospital for two solid days with Cynthia. Her prognosis was still uncertain. The bullet hadn't hit any vital organs, but Cynthia's age and loss of blood made her recovery difficult and tenuous. Sedatives and pain medicine kept her unaware of what was happening except for an occasional lucid moment that quickly passed.

How Faith wished Sarah could be there with her. For herself, but also for Cynthia. Any mother would want her child near her at such a time. Scott and Lindsay had come yesterday for a visit, but Scott wasn't able to stay long, so their time at Cynthia's bedside had been short.

Faith wasn't certain that Scott's condition caused an inability to prolong a visit to his mother. She suspected he had trouble facing the possibility of losing her and didn't have the gumption to face up to his fears. Sarah had proved over and over again that she was the stronger of the two. But Faith had to admit she might be thinking unfairly of Scott. Sarah's absence had her mind in turmoil.

And her heart hurt. She was the cause of Joel Litchfield's obsession. If only she had never met the man—or at least never paid any attention to him—none of this would have happened. Sarah would be safe. Jessie would be unharmed. Cynthia would be all right. Their world wouldn't be turned topsy-turvy.

Her chin rested on her chest as she castigated herself for her leading part in this nasty business. Slowly she became aware that the buggy had stopped. She raised her head and gasped. Joel stood in the middle of the dirt road with a pistol aimed at her. In her peripheral vision, she saw a horse tied to a tree limb off to the side.

How did he get here? Where was Sarah? The implications of his presence... Was Sarah dead? She gasped and held her hands to her chest against the pain that surged through her heart. She couldn't bear that thought.

Joel said something to her.

"What?" Faith tried to calm herself.

He waved the pistol. "Get out of the buggy."

"What do you want with me?"

"You'll find that out soon enough." He sneered. "Do as I say or you'll get the same thing your girlfriend got."

Faith's heart plummeted, but she didn't want Joel to know that. She turned her face away, climbed out of the buggy, and stood on the road. She wanted to run, to escape, to get as far from him as possible. But she knew he might kill her, and until she knew what happened to Sarah, she would fight to stay alive. Sarah, where are you? her mind screamed. Was Joel connected to the bank robbers? Of course he was. Where was Jessie? Fear wrenched her stomach.

When she was able to look at him without throwing up, she met his gaze. He pointed with his free hand. "Walk toward my horse."

Faith did as he said, and he followed behind her. When he got near her, she quivered with anger. She swallowed hard against the bile that rose in her throat. Rage built in her. She wanted to rake his face with her nails, to scratch his eyes out. She struggled not to show her feelings.

He whispered in her ear, "When I get you to my home, you'll forget all about that Coulter bitch. You'll remember how much more pleasure a real man can give you."

Faith's fury built until her temper finally got the better of her. She spoke when she knew she should have kept quiet. "I don't see a real man anywhere near here."

That was the last she remembered saying. Something hit the back of her head and blackness closed in on her.

* * *

Litchfield tied Faith's hands and feet with pieces of rope he cut from the coil attached to the side of the saddle. He took a handkerchief from the pocket of Faith's apron that she wore over her dark-green dress. As he stuffed it into her mouth, he noticed the embroidered FPC on it, and it infuriated him. He shouted at Faith's unconscious form, "Faith Pruitt Coulter, eh? I'll make you forget you ever knew Sarah Coulter." Using one of his own handkerchiefs to cover her mouth, he tied it at the back of her head.

He shoved her into the saddle, climbed up behind her, and settled her against him. Returning to the trail he had ridden in on, he was eager to get to the ambush site and settle things forever.

So far, so good, he thought when he reined in his horse in the stand of trees. He placed Faith on the ground where he could keep an eye on her and waited patiently for the Coulter bitch to show up. Of course, she would. He had a good view of the trail and would have plenty of time to grab Faith and get in the right spot with her.

His timing was perfect. After about half an hour, he heard hoofbeats along the trail. He glanced at Faith who was making groaning and gasping noises. He was pleased that she might be conscious soon. He wanted her to see what he had in store for her lover.

After moving her into a sitting position and getting a firm grasp of her waist, he lifted her against him, drew his gun, and moved out to block the path.

The horse slowed to a walk, and he grinned. The Coulter bitch was making it easy for him. Faith made a muted sound.

"Stop right there," he called out. She was about thirty feet away. "And throw down your gun. With two fingers."

Sarah's heart leaped into her throat, and for a moment, she couldn't speak. The bastard held Faith in front of him. Would Litchfield hurt her? Sarah couldn't take the chance that he wouldn't. Besides, she couldn't get a shot at him without endangering Faith. She halted Redfire, lifted her pistol from its holster, and tossed it onto the ground.

"Your rifle, too. Slowly."

Sarah yanked the Spencer from the scabbard and dropped it next to the pistol.

"Now get off your horse and come toward me."

What was he up to? Maybe he wanted her closer so he wouldn't miss when he shot at her. She gazed into Faith's eyes and had a glimmer of hope. Faith would do what she could to spoil Litchfield's aim. Sarah's muscles went on full alert as she inched forward. She might get only one chance to stay alive.

"Stop," Litchfield said. He surprised her by setting Faith down on the trail and moving past her. He kept his gun trained on Sarah as he took the five steps that separated them.

She took a deep breath and coiled to jump him, but he lunged forward and slugged her with his fist. Though caught unawares, she didn't fall, but the punch jumbled her brain. She shook her head to clear it. Litchfield holstered his gun and grabbed her throat with both hands. "I'm going to squeeze the life out of you once and for all."

Sarah yanked at his arms, but they didn't budge. His clutch tightened on her throat. She had no air. She tilted her head back and snapped it forward as hard as she could. He was near her height, and she caught him right in the nose. Blood spurted everywhere. Sarah's eyes closed reflexively and reopened immediately.

"You bitch!" Litchfield's hands loosened. He went for his gun. When it came out of the holster, Sarah gripped his wrist with both hands and pushed it skyward. A battle of strength broke out between them. Litchfield tried to bring the gun to bear on Sarah, who was struggling mightily to shift the barrel toward him.

Sarah's wounded arm hampered her. Litchfield managed to get the gun down between his body and Sarah's. He fought to turn it in her direction.

Her good leg skidded in the dirt, and her bad leg screamed with pain. The gun was agonizingly close to sending a bullet into her.

It's now or never, Sarah thought. *I can do this.* She slid both hands around the gun barrel and grabbed against it for leverage to hit Litchfield in the groin with her knee. That didn't work. A split second later, she thrust her body weight against her arms with all her might.

The gun went off, and they both fell.

Faith screamed, but the gag damped the shriek to a whimper. Litchfield lay on top of Sarah. Blood leaked from between their bodies. Neither moved. Faith squirmed up on her knees and inched toward them by swiveling her hips to move one knee at a time. She grimaced against the pounding in her head from the blow she had taken. In seconds that took forever, she closed the distance while avoiding most of the pooling blood. At last she reached their inert forms.

She bent to get her shoulder against Litchfield's body and shoved as hard as she could. He partially moved off Sarah, and Faith fell across her. She put her throbbing head against Sarah to get some leverage to twist off of her. When she managed to sit up, she saw Sarah's jacket was torn and it and her stomach and chest had blood on them. Was she even breathing?

Faith fought against panic and frustration. Fear overwhelmed her mind. What could she do with her hands and feet bound? *Think!* She searched around. Litchfield's pistol lay on the ground nearby, but that wouldn't do her any good. She needed a—

Oh my God. In all the turmoil, she had forgotten that Sarah carried a knife in her boot. She pushed herself along on her bottom with her bound feet until she came close enough to get her fingers under one leg of Sarah's pants. Fumbling around the top of her boot, she managed to grasp the knife's handle and work it out of the boot. She tried to hold the handle and cut the ropes binding her hands, but that didn't work very well. Her wrists were more endangered than the rope.

A solution came to her. Pointing the knife toward the ground, she used her body to push it until it held firmly in the hard soil. She moved her hands up and down with the rope against the blade, and finally it let loose. She untied the gag and threw Litchfield's handkerchief to the ground. Her own handkerchief was wet with spit, but she stuck it into her apron pocket.

She yanked the knife from the dirt and freed her legs. She dropped the knife to the ground and pushed Litchfield the rest of the way off of Sarah. He lay on his back right next to Sarah. The pistol lay between them, and Faith picked it up and threw it off to the side.

She knelt beside Sarah and almost passed out from relief when she heard her groan. Or was that Litchfield?

They both moved their heads. Litchfield's hands came up to his stomach and pushed against it. Sarah's came up and patted her chest as Faith finished unbuttoning her jacket and pushed her clothes out of the way.

Sarah's eyes blinked open, and when they focused, she grinned. "Hi, redhead." Then Sarah sobered. "You have blood on your face."

Tears welled in Faith's eyes. "That's from you." Faith's hands flew over Sarah's chest searching for the source of the blood.

"I don't think so." Sarah moved her body and touched her

hand to the back of her head. "I hit my head on something, but I think I'm okay." The hot gun barrel had singed her hands, but she suspected her sweat had protected them from a bad burn.

Tears spilled over onto Faith's cheeks. Her voice sounded hoarse. "I don't see any broken skin or feel any broken bones, but you have a bad bruise on your breast."

"I'll explain that later."

"I thought you were d-dead." Faith removed her wet handkerchief from her pocket and wiped the blood from her own face.

"I almost was. I'll explain that later, too."

Sarah reached out her hand. "Help me get up, please." Faith stuck the bloody handkerchief back in her pocket. She rose and sniffled while she pulled Sarah into a sitting position then to her feet. Sarah cradled Faith's head against her neck. "Shhh. I'm all right." She raised her hand to wipe the tears from Faith's face but stopped when she saw her fingers were red with blood.

Sarah clutched the back of Faith's dress with one hand and tangled the other hand in her hair. She held her close and Faith returned her tight embrace.

For several moments, Sarah couldn't speak. She touched the side of her head to Faith's and whispered, "I thought I'd never see you again."

"Me, too," Faith whispered back.

Sarah suddenly turned away from Faith and kicked Litchfield in the side. "You bastard!" She stumbled for a moment and kicked him again. "You rotten bastard! I should kill you for even thinking about my woman." She drew her foot back a third time. and Faith grabbed her arm.

"Stop, please. He's as terrible as you think he is, but right now he's unconscious. It's not like you to attack a helpless man. He'll get what's coming to him"—she glanced at the copious amount of blood around him—"if he lives that long."

Sarah stopped kicking him, but her tension didn't subside. She took Faith's hand and moved away from Litchfield. "What...what happened with Mother?"

"She's alive but weak. It's too early to tell..." Faith couldn't finish the sentence. She closed her eyes and took some deep breaths. "Sarah, your mother saved my life."

"What? How?"

"The robbers were going to shove me out the door and shoot me. She talked them into taking her instead."

Sarah stared at Faith for a long time. At last she spoke. "That sounds like the mother I used to know."

"She must have done that for you, Sarah. I was astounded."

"I am, too. I can't wait to see her."

Faith's hand flew to her mouth. "Oh my God. Did you find Jessie? And did you see Benjamin?"

"Yes, and yes. They're both all right." Of course Faith didn't know, Sarah thought. The posse hadn't returned yet. They wouldn't have ridden pell-mell like she and Litchfield did. Besides, they would take the road to the center of town, not branch off on the trail leading here.

"Thank God," Faith said.

"You can be proud of your son—our son. Benjamin got to us in the nick of time and saved us both. He and Jessie are riding back with the posse. We'll tell you all about it later. Right now, I'm too exhausted to do much of anything."

Sarah kissed Faith's cheek. Faith turned her head and met Sarah's lips. The kiss deepened, and their tongues caressed each other.

When they finally separated, Sarah looked down at herself and the ground...and Litchfield. Blood covered her jacket and chest and some had pooled in the dirt. Litchfield's torso was soaked in red. Even Faith had blood on her dress. "That blood must be Litchfield's."

Sarah realized her wounded arm needed attention. She twisted it a bit. Damn, it hurt. She felt blood dripping from her hand. She pointed to the blood drops and said, "I guess some of that blood over there is mine."

"Did Joel shoot you in the arm?"

"No, that's from earlier."

Faith's voice rose an octave. "What happened earlier?"

"I'll explain it all later. Check your boyfriend."

Faith stamped her foot. "Don't even joke about that. He nearly killed you."

Litchfield's eyes were open. He glared at them. Turning his gaze to Sarah, he said,. "Did you shoot me, bitch?"

"No, you ass. You shot yourself."

"Thank God for small favors," he said very clearly. Then he closed his eyes and a breath puffed past his lips. His head shifted slightly to the side. Though he was lying flat in the dirt, something about the way he exhaled that last breath made Sarah think all the life had gone out of him. If he had a soul, maybe it had left him. Sarah didn't think he had much of a soul.

Faith circled around and cautiously approached him from near his head. She reached down and felt his neck for a pulse. She stood up straight. "He's gone."

"Thank God for big favors, too," Sarah said. She took a step and stumbled,. Faith grabbed her around the waist. She eased Sarah to the ground.

"Let me check your arm." Faith removed Sarah's jacket and saw the makeshift bandage. Blood was seeping right through the cloth. Faith untied it. "Something cut a furrow on your arm." She raised an eyebrow. "A bullet?"

Sarah nodded.

"You had a wounded arm, and you still had the strength to keep Joel from shooting you. That's amazing."

"I guess all that wood chopping finally paid off."

Faith chuckled and handed her the sodden binding. "Hold this against the wound to stem the bleeding. I'll put a new dressing on it in a moment, but first, you need some water in you." Faith went to Litchfield's horse and undid the canteen hooked to the saddle. She brought it back and held it for Sarah to drink from.

Sarah took a big swallow and choked.

Faith looked alarmed. She pounded Sarah's back. "Did I pour it too fast? Are you all right?"

When Sarah caught her breath, she laughed. "You can stop hitting me. It's whiskey. Not that I'm complaining, mind you, but I think I need water more." She whistled and Redfire came to her from where he had been standing during all the activity. "My canteen has water in it."

"Good. I can use the whiskey to wash your wound." Faith got the canteen of water for Sarah, and when she finished drinking, Faith poured some of the whiskey onto the bullet furrow.

Sarah hissed from the pain. "What a waste of good whiskey. Give me another swig of that."

Sarah grinned when Faith took a drink for herself before handing it back to her.

"Don't take too much. Alcohol dries you out." Faith tore some material from her petticoat and made another bandage for Sarah's arm. "There. That should stop the bleeding." She helped Sarah back into her jacket.

"I guess my arm started bleeding again when we struggled for the gun. Speaking of guns..." She limped to where Faith had tossed the pistol and picked it up. "This is mine. The bastard tried to kill me with my own gun." She put the ivory-handled pistol in her holster.

Her whole body suddenly felt extremely tired. "You know what, redhead?"

"What?"

"You've been kidnapped and put at risk. I've been chasing crooks, got captured, shot at twice, and banged my head on the ground. I sorely want to go home and relax. With you in my arms."

"That sounds like a perfect idea." Faith glanced toward Litchfield. "What about Joel's body?"

"We'll send someone, maybe Lindsay, to tell Herman we're safe and Litchfield's dead. We'll let him worry about the body."

"I don't understand why Joel did what he did. He had a good medical practice and a charming personality. Nearly everyone liked him. He could have made so much more of himself."

"He made the same mistake a lot of other people have made. He followed his baser instincts instead of his better ones."

"Let's hope we don't run into any other people like him."

"Amen to that."

Sarah grabbed Redfire's reins. "I think I'm going to need some help to get in the saddle. My leg's afire with pain."

"Why didn't you say so? You must be ready to drop. I'm going to ride behind you and hold you steady."

Sarah gave her a crooked grin. "That's the best offer I've had in days."

Chapter 26

Warm fingers brushed the hair away from Sarah's forehead, and she opened her eyes. She met Faith's loving gaze. "Good morning," Sarah said. She gave a slight groan as she stretched her body.

"More like good afternoon." The skin around Faith's eyes crinkled as she smiled.

Sarah frowned. "What day is it?"

"It's past noon on Tuesday. You slept a day and a half."

"Ugh. No wonder I'm stiff." Sarah sat up and swung her legs out of the bed. A cold nose against her leg made her jump. "Paddy! What are you doing in here?" She ruffled the dog's hair and patted him thoroughly.

Faith patted him, too. "He made such a fuss when we came home, I figured he earned a night or two in the house. He has barely left your side."

Sarah rubbed the base of his ears and kissed his head. "Good boy. I could have used you with me. No one could have sneaked up on me." She patted him again. "Go lay down now. We'll let you out in a few minutes." Paddy obediently lay on a comforter in the corner.

Sarah hesitated a moment. "What happened to Litchfield's body?" She closely watched Faith's expression but saw nothing to worry her.

"Benjamin turned it over to the sheriff. Then he told me what he knew of the story. He said he almost screamed when he thought you'd been gut shot."

"I bet. At first, I wasn't sure either. I had so much blood on me from the bullet hitting my arm." She held her hands out, looked at them, and dropped them to the bed to aid in pushing herself up. She stood and said, "No regrets about Litchfield?"

"Oh yes, I have regrets." Faith moved out of the way as Sarah went to the bureau for underclothes. "I regret that I ever met him. I regret that I hurt you by considering marriage to him. I regret that he was involved in all these events that hurt you so deeply. In fact..." Faith hesitated. "I—almost—regret that I didn't get to fire the shot that killed him."

Sarah had her underclothes and pants on and was choosing a shirt from the closet when those words stopped her in her tracks and turned her around. Faith, who was avowedly against violence, revealed the depth of her feelings by saying that. Sarah immediately embraced her. They clung to each other, not speaking. Nothing needed to be said.

Moments later, Faith murmured into Sarah's ear, "I better help you put your shirt on or we'll miss lunch."

They grinned and parted. Sarah said, "I want to see Mother after lunch. I'll need sustenance for that."

Faith gave her a sidelong glance. "And for tonight," Faith whispered.

Sarah suddenly felt warm and energized. She patted Faith's cheek. "Let's go find something to eat, redhead." She snapped her fingers at Paddy. "Come on, boy."

In the kitchen. Lindsay, Scott, and Jessie were already seated. Faith sent Paddy outside as Lindsay stood and threw herself into Sarah's open arms. Sarah felt a slight twinge of pain but managed not to show it. Lindsay said, "Thank God you're all right. We were so worried about you."

Scott rose and said, "My turn." When Lindsay let go of Sarah, Sarah lifted an eyebrow at Scott. He raised his arms toward her. "Please let me hug you, Sarah."

They embraced, and Scott said, "Having you back with us means the world to me. I apologize for the way I've acted. I'm sorry for everything I've done or said that hurt you...and Faith." He dropped his arms and stepped back. "You've both been extremely generous to us. And I'm more grateful to you than I can ever convey for you saving Jessie." He gazed toward Jessie, who was now standing next to Lindsay.

"Yes," Jessie said, "thank you, Aunt Sarah. For everything. And I mean that sincerely. Thank you for bearing me. Thank you for giving me to the best mother and father anyone could ever have. I'm sorry I was so mean to you. I wish I could take it all back."

Sarah gathered her into her arms. "I'm sorry, too, Jessie, for not getting to know you better sooner. For being standoffish and cold. And I'm sorry I came between you and Perry."

Jessie started to cry. "I see now that you couldn't help that. Life gets messed up sometimes. And thank you for saving me from those men. It helped me understand what you must have gone through years ago."

Sarah's eyes grew misty. "I was so afraid for you. And proud that you helped me." She held Jessie tighter, and they stood together in silence.

Lindsay cleared her throat. "Now that we've made our confessions and received absolution, suppose we settle down and eat lunch."

Sarah kissed Jessie's forehead and let her go. "Let's do that. I want to visit Mother afterwards."

Lindsay said, "All the more reason to get some food into you."

Sarah glanced quickly at Faith, and they both grinned.

* * *

Bonneforte's hospital had been growing in concert with the population. All available beds were in wards, with separate wards for surgical, pediatric, and general patients. Scott had persuaded hospital management—with a donation, no doubt—to place his mother in a corner of the surgical ward, curtain it off from the rest, and provide chairs for visitors.

A couple of nurses in long, dark dresses covered over with white aprons tended to patients in the open section of the department. One looked up and gave a short wave as Faith and Sarah passed through.

Faith said, "I've been here so often, some of them know me already."

When they entered the contrived "room," Cynthia seemed to be sleeping. Sarah stood back as Faith went to the bed and felt Cynthia's forehead. At the touch, Cynthia opened her eyes.

"Sorry to wake you," Faith said.

"I was resting, but I wasn't asleep," Cynthia said curtly. "And as you can tell, I have no fever."

Obviously, Sarah thought, her mother was her old self.

"Have you brought any news of Sarah?"

"I've done better than that." Faith gestured and Sarah approached the bed. She bent down to Cynthia, and they embraced. Sarah straightened back up and held her mother's hand.

"Oh, Sarah, I've been so worried about you. Faith told me...you found Jessie...and sent her home." Cynthia stopped, obviously tired from the effort of speaking.

"Mother." Sarah swallowed hard before she could continue. "Mother, Faith told me you took her place with the robbers. I'm extremely grateful to you for saving her. But I thought you were dead. You're tougher than you look."

Cynthia gave her a bitter-sweet smile. "Your father used to say that."

Sarah clasped Cynthia's hand between hers. "Thank goodness he was right. I had a difficult time thinking that I lost you. I went a little crazy." Faith gave her a questioning look, and Sarah knew she had some explaining to do. Later.

Cynthia lifted their hands to her lips and kissed Sarah's top hand. "You're here with us now, and we're all safe." She lowered her hands to the bed and kept hold of Sarah's. "I have some good news, too."

Emotional turmoil made it hard for Sarah to speak. Instead, Faith asked, "What good news is that?"

"Dr. Perlmann said I can go home tomorrow. All I need is rest...and a little nursing attention...so there's no reason for him to keep me here any longer."

"That's wonderful, Mother."

"He said Faith...talked him into it. She convinced him she was quite capable of...changing the dressings and seeing to my needs." She turned to Faith. "Thank you for that. Hospitals aren't my...first choice of accommodations."

"I figured as much. Besides, Benjamin is home to stay now. So you can have your own personal doctor."

Cynthia's face lit up. "I'm so happy to hear that. I like Benjamin."

"And he likes you." Faith's smile looked secretive. "Plus, I think he especially likes another member of your family."

Sarah had been looking back and forth between Faith and Cynthia during this exchange. Their rapport pleased and amazed her. A few days ago, Cynthia acted like she hated Faith. Now, wonder of wonders, they seemed almost friendly. As these thoughts rambled through her mind, Faith's last comment filtered through. Surely she wasn't talking about Sarah. Sarah puzzled about it for a few seconds. "You mean Jessie?"

Faith pointed at her. "You guessed right."

Sarah gave one of her big, full-faced smiles. "I hope you're right. But she still has to adjust to the situation between her and Perry."

"I didn't say the feeling was mutual. Not yet, anyway. But Benjamin seems interested. I think he's been interested for a long time now. We'll have to let nature take its course."

Sarah laughed. "If he takes after his mother, he won't wait for nature to catch up."

Faith elbowed her and Sarah grabbed her arm. "Come on," Sarah said, the laughter still bubbling, "let's get out of here and let Mother rest. Tomorrow will be a taxing day for her."

They said their goodbyes and headed home.

* * *

Everyone at home clamored for Sarah to tell them the full story of what happened.

Sarah said, "Let's wait for Mother to come home tomorrow. She'll want to hear it, too."

"No, no, no," Scott said. "You can tell it again to Mother. We're all too eager to hear the whole tale. You must tell us now."

So Sarah did. They all sat around the kitchen table while she spoke. Jessie filled in the parts that only she knew, and Benjamin added in his contribution to saving Sarah and Jessie. Then Faith spoke of being kidnapped, and she and Sarah told of the episode with Joel Litchfield.

"And that's the full account," Sarah said.

"Not quite," Lindsay added, drawing everyone's attention. "I went into town8 today, and Sheriff Schmidt told me Elias Kumber showed up to claim Dr. Litchfield's body."

"What?" Sarah nearly shouted her question.

"It seems they were cousins, or so Mr. Kumber said."

Sarah hit her fist into the palm of her hand. Then she grimaced from the pain in her arm. "I thought he looked familiar. Must have been a slight family resemblance there. I bet he was the one who was following Faith and me. I hope we've seen the last of that scum."

Lindsay laughed. "The sheriff must have felt the same way. He said he told Kumber he wasn't welcome in this town, that he should haul off Litchfield's body to some distant place and not show up here again."

"Good advice." Sarah stretched and yawned. "I should go to bed."

Faith, who had been seated next to Sarah, stood. "That's good advice, too."

"For all of us," Scott said. The whole family rose and went their separate ways.

As Sarah and Faith prepared for bed, Faith said, "Scott seems to have changed his ideas about us. Do you think he meant what he said?"

"I'm sure he did. Whether he will keep meaning it will hinge on how Mother reacts to us when she's back home."

"Is he that impressionable?"

"Unfortunately, yes. He's Mother's favorite. He knows it. She knows it. I know it. Whatever way Mother goes, he will go.

We'll have to wait and see." Sarah hopped into bed and pulled the covers over her. "Come on to bed, redhead. We have some catching up to do."

Faith climbed in and snuggled up to Sarah's side. She leaned her head on Sarah's shoulder. "Catching up? On what?"

Sarah wrapped a hand around Faith's breast and bent to kiss her lips. "You're pretty smart. I think you can figure that out."

* * *

The next afternoon, Cynthia came home in the wagon and Sarah carried her into the sitting room. The action caused some pain in Sarah's arm and leg, but this was her mother, dammit. She was worth a bit of pain.

Cynthia asked to stay for a while in the sitting room and hear everyone's story. So they recounted the adventure, and Sarah and Faith expressed how sorry they were that she got caught up in the turmoil meant for them. Sarah once again thanked Cynthia for saving Faith, and the others chimed in with their thanks, too.

"What prompted you to do that, Mother?" Sarah asked. "You wouldn't have anything to do with Faith before that."

Cynthia glanced down at her hands. She turned her wedding ring around and around and spoke slowly. "I suddenly remembered how lost I was when your father died. We loved each other so much." She looked up at Sarah. "Your father didn't approve of how I acted toward Faith. He said she was a fine woman. And he was right." She switched her gaze to Faith. "You treated us so generously, in spite of my misguided actions." She looked again toward Sarah. "And over the days I've been here, I saw that you and Faith loved each other the same way your father and I did. I couldn't bear to think of you suffering the loss I did, when I could stop it from happening."

"Thank you, Mother."

"Thank you, Mother Coulter," Faith said. "I'll be eternally grateful to you. You saved my life."

"And you saved mine." Cynthia took on her usual stern expression. "Please understand, both of you, I still don't approve of your relationship, but I'll make every effort to respect it as your choice."

"That's all we ask," Sarah said as Faith nodded.

"Now," Cynthia said, "if you'll help me to my bed, I believe I'd like to retire until dinnertime."

Sarah picked her up again and carried her to her bedroom.

Lindsay turned down the bed covers, Sarah placed her on the sheet, and Lindsay covered her.

Lindsay said, "I'll come back around dinnertime, Mother Coulter."

Sarah kissed her mother's cheek. "We'll see you then, Mother. Rest well."

Lindsay and Sarah returned to the sitting room. Only Faith was still there. "Everyone went their merry ways," she said. She put her arm in Sarah's. "Let's walk for a while."

They donned their coats and hats. When they stepped onto the porch, Paddy came over to be patted and hugged. He returned to lie in a corner, and they walked down off the porch and headed toward the sunset. Faith said, "Your mother is a tough old bird."

Sarah chuckled. "Yes, she is. I guess you noticed that she didn't ask us for forgiveness. That's not her way."

"I did notice. She and I resemble each other a little bit in that respect. I hate to ask for forgiveness."

"You've asked me for forgiveness before."

Faith waved a hand. "I mean with other people. I love you, and that makes it different."

"I accept that." Sarah smiled and reached for Faith's hand. "In the last few days, Mother and Scott and Jessie have all apologized to us in their own ways for their various actions."

"Yes, they have, and I'm very happy about that. The whole house should be more...peaceful. And, as a result, so can we be."

Sarah squeezed Faith's hand. "Yes. Peaceful." She took a deep breath and slowly let it out. "At last."

CPSIA information can be obtained
at www.ICGtesting.com
Printed in the USA
LVHW051604060421
683586LV00007B/591